THE LAST GUNFIGHTER:
SUDDEN FURY

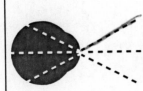

This Large Print Book carries the
Seal of Approval of N.A.V.H.

THE LAST GUNFIGHTER: SUDDEN FURY

WILLIAM W. JOHNSTONE
WITH J. A. JOHNSTONE

WHEELER PUBLISHING
A part of Gale, Cengage Learning

GALE
CENGAGE Learning·

Detroit • New York • San Francisco • New Haven, Conn • Waterville, Maine • London

GALE
CENGAGE Learning®

LIBRARY OF CONGRESS CATALOGING-IN-PUBLICATION DATA

Johnstone, William W.
    The last gunfighter : sudden fury / by William W. Johnstone with J.A. Johnstone. — Large Print edition.
        pages cm. — (Wheeler Publishing Large Print Western)
    ISBN 978-1-4104-5390-7 (hardcover) — ISBN 1-4104-5390-1 (hardcover) 1. Large type books. I. Johnstone, J. A. II. Title.
PS3560.O415L37 2013
813'.54—dc23   2012042062

Published in 2013 by arrangement with Pinnacle Books, an imprint of Kensington Publishing Corp.

THE LAST GUNFIGHTER: SUDDEN FURY

Chapter 1

Gunshots, then screams.

Both sounds were enough to make Frank Morgan rein in sharply as they came to his ears through the forest. Towering, thick-trunked redwoods surrounded him. The trees muffled sounds somewhat, but Frank heard the shots, followed by terrified shrieking, clearly enough so that he knew they were close by. He reached for the butt of the Winchester that jutted up from a sheath strapped to Stormy's saddle.

The rangy gray horse stood calmly as Frank pulled the rifle from the saddle boot. Stormy had been one of Frank Morgan's trail partners for a long time now, along with the big, wolflike cur known only as Dog. The horse was used to the sound of gunfire.

He would have to be, considering that Frank Morgan was the notorious gunfighter known as The Drifter.

Frank had drifted here to the redwood country of northern California from Los Angeles. A dustup down in those parts had left him hankering for some peace and quiet, so he had meandered northward along the coastline. In the back of his mind was a vague plan — the only kind he made these days — to visit Oregon, maybe even mosey on up to Washington. But he wasn't going to get in any hurry about it.

Judging by the violent sounds he heard, he was going to be delayed at least a little while. He wasn't the sort of man who could turn his back on trouble and just ride away. Never had been, never would be.

More shots banged, from both rifles and pistols. The yelling and screaming continued, too. Frank dug the heels of his boots into Stormy's flanks and sent the big horse trotting forward. Goldy, Frank's other horse, followed along behind, while Dog loped ahead, nose to the ground and growls coming from his thickly furred throat.

Frank couldn't ride too fast. He had to weave around the redwoods, most of which were at least fifteen feet wide at the base. Some of the giant trees were as much as twenty-five feet wide, or even larger in isolated cases. They were certainly the biggest trees Frank had ever seen in all his long

8

years of wandering.

Two more shots blasted, followed by another scream, and then an eerie silence fell over the forest. That quiet was more ominous than the noises had been. All the birds and small animals had fled as soon as the racket started.

They were probably the smart ones, Frank reflected with a wry smile.

He slowed Stormy to a walk. If whoever caused that ruckus was still up there ahead of him, there was no point in allowing galloping hoofbeats to announce his arrival.

He smelled smoke, and then something else — coffee, he realized after a second. Crews of loggers worked in this forest, felling and trimming the massive trees so that they could be hauled off to mills where they would be sawed into millions of board feet of lumber. That lumber was destined for the homes and businesses of the civilization that had spread pretty much from one end of the continent to the other, leaving only pockets of wilderness untouched. Maybe he was coming up on a logging camp, Frank thought.

Dog had gotten so far ahead by now that the big cur had vanished. Frank wasn't worried too much. Dog could take care of himself.

But whatever had prompted those men to scream like that had to be pretty bad. Maybe he was a little worried after all, Frank decided. He pushed Stormy to a faster pace.

A few minutes later, they broke out into a clearing. Huge stumps here and there told him where trees had been felled. Several large tents were set up around the clearing. Someone had dug a large fire pit in the center and ringed it with stones. Folks who lived in the woods had to be mighty careful with fire. A blaze that got out of hand in a forest like this could burn for days and consume hundreds of thousands of acres. There was already enough danger of fire from lightning strikes without adding to it with carelessness.

A small fire crackled in the pit. A coffeepot perched on a metal grate above the flames. To one side sat a large frying pan with some bacon and biscuits in it. The men who'd made this camp had been preparing a mid-day meal.

They'd never have to worry about that again. They were all dead, their bodies scattered around the clearing.

Frank's jaw tightened as he reined Stormy to a halt. His mouth was a grim line. He looked around the gore-splattered clearing and tried to figure out how many men had died here. He put the number at six, although it was hard to be sure because they appeared to have been torn limb from limb.

Frank had seen plenty of violent death in his life, but he wasn't sure he had ever come across anything like this before. He had heard stories about how grizzly bears could maul men until they barely looked human. As he gazed in horror around the clearing, his first thought was that a bear must have done this.

But it would take a grizzly to wreak such destruction, and he didn't think they lived in this part of the country. There were black bears in California, but he doubted if one of those smaller bears could have killed six men. A black bear might have mauled one or two men, but those gunshots Frank had heard would have brought it down.

"Dog, come away from there," he called as the big cur nosed around the torn-up bodies. Still holding the Winchester, he swung down from the saddle and studied Stormy and Goldy. The horses were a mite skittish, but that was probably from the coppery smell of freshly spilled blood that filled the air. They would be spooked even more if they were picking up bear scent, Frank thought. And Dog would be growling. Dog was curious about what had happened here, but the thick ruff of fur around his neck wasn't standing up as it would have been if he'd smelled a bear or some other immediate danger.

Because of that, Frank knew that whatever had done this was gone. He walked over to take a closer look at the bodies.

The men were still clad in blood-soaked clothing. Frank studied the boots that had metal calks on their soles, the thick canvas trousers, and the woolen shirts, and he knew he was looking at loggers. The saws and axes and other gear scattered around the camp testified to that fact as well. He saw several pistols and a couple of rifles lying on the ground where the men had dropped them. The guns hadn't saved them.

Dog lifted his head and growled. Somebody was coming. Frank swung around in time to see four men burst out of the woods, each of them carrying a long-handled, double-bitted ax.

They stopped short and stared in shock at the horrible scene laid out before them. They were dressed the same as the dead men, with the addition of caps or narrow-brimmed hats. A couple wore holstered guns strapped high on their waists. After a moment, all four men slowly came forward into the clearing, gazing around at the corpses as if they couldn't believe what they were seeing.

Finally, one of them lifted stunned eyes to Frank and demanded, "Mister, did you do this?"

Frank shook his head. "Do you really think one man could do this?" he asked. "I heard the shots and the screams and rode up to see what was going on. I imagine the same thing brought you fellas here. Did you know these men?"

"Yeah, we knew 'em," replied a broad-shouldered man with a bushy mustache that drooped over his mouth. "We were all part of the same crew."

"Then I'm sorry you lost your friends. Do you have any idea what might have happened?"

"The Terror," another man said.

"Yeah," a third man croaked. "The Terror of the Redwoods."

A frown creased Frank's forehead. "What's that?" he asked. "Some kind of animal?"

"It's not an animal, mister," the first man said with a shake of his head. In an awed voice, he went on. "It's a monster."

Frank's frown deepened. Stories about various monsters that were supposed to live

13

in the West, like the Sasquatch and the Wendigo, were common, but he had never really believed in them.

He was about to say as much when he heard hoofbeats approaching the clearing. Those gunshots had drawn a lot of attention. As Frank turned toward the sound of horses, three men rode into the clearing.

These newcomers were dressed very differently from the loggers. They wore range clothes and broad-brimmed Stetsons. They had gun belts strapped around their hips and thonged to their thighs, and they carried Winchesters as well. Frank recognized the sort of men they were: gun-throwers, hardcases . . . hombres much like himself.

Frank Morgan was middle-aged, a powerfully built man of medium height. The crisp dark hair under his high-crowned hat was shot through with silver threads. His face was too rugged to be called handsome, but it was the sort of face a lot of women looked at twice. He wore a butternut shirt, faded denim trousers, and boots aged to a comfortable fit. A Colt .45 Peacemaker rode in a plain brown holster on his right hip. A bowie knife with a staghorn handle rested in a fringed sheath on his left hip. The fringe was the only thing about Frank Morgan that could be considered even remotely gaudy.

He was a simple man with relatively simple needs.

The most overwhelming of which was to stay alive, because there were plenty of people west of the Mississippi who wanted the man called The Drifter dead.

Born and raised in Texas, Frank had returned to the Lone Star State after the Civil War as a young cowboy, figuring he would spend the rest of his life working on a ranch, only to discover that he possessed a natural talent for drawing a gun and firing it accurately faster than most men could blink. Even though he'd never intended to become a gunfighter, once his boots were set on that path, there was no getting off it. Lord knows he had tried from time to time.

But there were simply too many men, young and old, who wanted to match their speed and prowess with a gun against his. He had been forced to defend himself, and with each would-be conqueror who fell before his gun, the legend of The Drifter grew. Folks spoke his name in the same breath as Smoke Jensen, John Wesley Hardin, Ben Thompson, Falcon MacCallister, Matt Bodine, and all the other famous shootists. He couldn't shake the reputation that clung to him, and so he was forced to kill again and again.

The years had rolled by, turned into decades. He had married, tried to settle down. It hadn't worked. Violence had always reared its ugly head, often with tragic results. Now, thirty years after that young cowboy had returned to Texas from the war, he was alone, and he had vowed to himself that he would stay that way. Never again would he put anyone else's life at risk by becoming close to them. He had lost Vivian and Dixie, he had lost his friends in the town of Buckskin . . . From here on out, The Drifter would just . . . drift.

He faced the riders who had just entered the clearing. One of them gestured toward the bloody corpses and said, "By jingo! The Terror did this, didn't it?"

"That's right, mister," the man who seemed to be the spokesman for the loggers replied. "You fellas are huntin' the damned thing, aren't you?"

"Damned right we are. We're gonna collect that bounty."

The word "bounty" made Frank's jaw clench again. More than once, someone had placed a bounty on *his* head, most recently an old enemy from back East. He didn't like the idea of blood money, even when the fugitive in question deserved to face justice.

"Who's put out a bounty?" he asked.

All seven of the men looked at him as if the question surprised them. "Haven't you heard about it, mister?" one of the loggers asked.

Frank shook his head. "I just rode into these parts today."

"Well, the Terror's been around here for months now, scarin' folks. When it started killin' people, though, Mr. Chamberlain put out the word that there'd be a big reward for whoever kills it."

"Who's Chamberlain?" The name was vaguely familiar to Frank, but he couldn't place it.

That question made the men stare at him, too. Finally, one of the loggers said, "Rutherford Chamberlain, the timber baron. He owns the lease on these woods for miles around. It's his men who have been killed, so he said that he'd pay ten thousand dollars for the Terror's head."

Frank knew now why he had recognized Chamberlain's name. He had seen it on various documents his lawyers had shown him one time when he visited their offices in San Francisco. No one would think it to look at him, but Frank Morgan was one of the richest men in the country. He had inherited half of the far-flung business empire founded by his late wife, Vivian

17

Browning. The Browning holdings included some logging interests. Frank had never cared about business, and money mattered to him only as long as he had enough to keep him in supplies, so he trusted his attorneys to take care of everything for him. It was possible that he owned stock in Chamberlain's company. It was equally possible that he and Chamberlain were competitors. Frank didn't know and didn't care.

One of the gunmen who had ridden into the clearing had been staring at Frank with even more interest than the others, and now he said, "By jingo, I know who you are, fella! You're Frank Morgan!"

The man's habitual exclamation told Frank who he was, too. "And you're Jingo Reed," he said.

Reed's lips peeled back from prominent teeth in a grin. "You've heard of me, have you?"

"Wait a minute," one of the other hardcases said. "You mean that's the hombre they call The Drifter?"

"He sure is," Reed said. "I saw you gun down the McClatchey brothers in Flagstaff a few years ago, Morgan. You were mighty fast . . . but I reckon I'm faster."

Frank sighed. He figured he knew what was coming, but he hoped he was wrong.

"Hey, Jingo," one of Reed's companions said. "We need to get on the trail of that monster. I want that ten-grand reward."

"I do, too, but the varmint'll wait." Reed licked his lips. "I got somethin' just as big right here."

"Don't do it, Jingo," Frank warned. "I'm not looking for any trouble with you."

Reed grinned. "That's the way life is, Morgan . . . Trouble comes at you whether you're lookin' for it or not."

And with that, he clawed at the gun on his hip, his hand moving with blinding speed.

CHAPTER 2

Unfortunately for Jingo Reed, simply being fast didn't put him in the same league as Frank Morgan. Frank's Colt flickered out so fast, it was like the gun appeared in his hand by magic. Flame spouted from the muzzle as the Colt roared. Even starting his draw first, Jingo had barely cleared leather before Frank's bullet smacked into his chest and rocked him back in the saddle. Spooked by the shot, Reed's horse bucked and threw him off. He crashed down on the ground and lay in a limp sprawl, not moving.

"Damn it!" one of Reed's companions yelled. "He's done kilt Jingo!"

The man swung the barrel of his rifle toward Frank.

With more time now, Frank didn't have to shoot to kill again. He broke the man's shoulder with a bullet instead. The man dropped his rifle, swayed in the saddle, clutched at his wounded shoulder, and bawled in pain.

Frank shifted his aim toward the third hardcase, who quickly held up both hands in plain sight. "Don't shoot, Morgan," he said. "I don't want any part of this."

"That's a smart move," Frank told him. "You boys should have gone after the Terror while you had the chance. Now you've got to tend to your friend and take Jingo to the undertaker."

"All right to put my hands down?"

Frank nodded. "Just keep 'em away from your guns."

As the man dismounted and began helping his wounded companion climb out of the saddle, one of the loggers let out a whistle and said to Frank, "I never saw a draw that slick in all my life. Is it true, mister? Are you really Frank Morgan?"

Frank nodded. "That's my name."

"No offense, Mr. Morgan, but I figured you were dead by now. I've been hearin' stories about you since I was a kid. I've even read some of the dime novels about you."

Frank smiled. "Stories get exaggerated, and you've got to remember, dime novels are written by fellas who don't really know what they're talking about even when they're sober, which they usually aren't."

"Yeah, but you're still The Drifter."

Frank shrugged. "Reckon a couple of you boys could put Jingo on his horse?"

Two of the loggers picked up the gunman's corpse and draped it over the saddle. Reed's horse didn't care for having a dead body on its back, so another logger held the reins while the first two lashed the corpse into place. By now, the uninjured man had used his bandanna to tie up the wounded shoulder of his friend, who still whimpered in pain. The loggers had to help get him back on his horse.

The third hardcase mounted up again and said, "No hard feelings, Morgan. It sure as hell wasn't my idea for Jingo to slap leather like that. He's always wanted to make a big name for himself as a gunman, and I reckon he figured killin' you was the best way."

"No hard feelings," Frank agreed, "as long as you really let it go and don't try to bushwhack me later. I wouldn't take kindly to that."

"Don't worry." The man gave a harsh laugh. "I'm not that stupid. Anyway, I still want that ten-grand reward for the Terror, so I'm gonna be kind of busy hunting that monster. I don't have time to get myself killed throwing down on The Drifter."

Leading the other two horses, the man turned his mount and hitched it into motion. He rode off into the trees, and was soon out of sight among the thick, towering trunks.

The leader of the loggers stuck out his hand to Frank. "My name's Karl Wilcox. It's an honor to meet you, Mr. Morgan." He glanced around at the gory remains of his fellow loggers. "I just wish it was under better circumstances."

"So do I," Frank agreed.

Wilcox waved a hand at the other men. "This is Dave Neville, Asa Peterson, and Gus Trotter."

Frank nodded at them. "I imagine you fellas would like to gather up your friends' bodies. I'll give you a hand."

"Yeah, we've got a wagon back yonder in the woods. Gus, go get it." Wilcox grimaced. "The rest of us will start rolling up the bodies in blankets."

That was a particularly grim, grisly chore, since some of the bodies were in pieces. The loggers were able to tell which pieces went together, or least they claimed they could. Frank certainly wasn't going to argue with them. He hadn't known any of the dead men.

Gus Trotter came back with the wagon. Two mules were hitched to the vehicle, and numerous logging tools were heaped in the back of it. The loggers shoved those tools aside to make room for the corpses.

"What's the nearest town?" Frank asked.

"That'd be Eureka," Wilcox said. "That's where we'll take these poor fellas."

"I reckon that's where I'll find Rutherford Chamberlain, too?"

Frank wasn't sure why he wanted to talk to the timber baron. Maybe in the back of his mind, he was considering asking Chamberlain to call off the bounty hunting.

Wilcox shook his head. "Nope, Mr. Chamberlain doesn't go into town much. He conducts all his business from his house."

"Where's that?"

"About five miles north of here. You can't miss it. Biggest damn house I ever saw, and nearly all of it is made out of redwood."

"He lives in the forest?" Frank asked in surprise.

"That's right. He always says that since the woods made him his fortune, that's where he's gonna live. You plan to go see him, Mr. Morgan?"

"I might," Frank said.

"Be careful when you ride up. He's always got men on guard, and with everything that's going on in these parts, they're probably pretty nervous. They might get trigger-happy."

Frank nodded. "Much obliged for the warning. I'll keep it in mind."

The loggers made ready to leave for Eureka with their gruesome cargo, but they paused as Karl Wilcox said, "You know, Mr. Morgan, when we first got here, I thought for a second *you* had done that to our friends. Or rather, that dog of yours. I figured it was a wolf when I first saw it."

The other men nodded in agreement.

"I'm glad you stopped to find out what was really going on before jumping to conclusions," Frank said.

Wilcox nodded. "So are we. If we'd gone after you or the dog, I reckon you would've shot all four of us."

That wasn't likely, Frank thought, but he couldn't rule it out entirely. Anybody who came at him with an ax was asking for trouble, no doubt about that.

"Are you gonna look for the Terror?" Wilcox asked.

"I'm not in the business of hunting monsters," Frank said. Especially when he didn't really believe in them in the first place, he added to himself.

Of course, just because he didn't believe a monster had killed those men, that didn't mean he knew what *had* ripped them apart like that. That uncertainty was enough to make a trip through these shadow-haunted woods plenty nerve-racking, especially for a man traveling alone. It was a good thing the dangerous life he'd led had given him such icy nerves, he thought with a wry, inward grin.

The wagon rolled off toward Eureka, loaded down with six corpses and four live, scared men. Dave Neville handled the reins. Wilcox, Peterson, and Trotter gripped their axes tightly and swiveled their heads from side to side, constantly on the lookout for danger.

Before mounting up, Frank walked all the way around the clearing, studying the ground. A thick carpet of redwood needles covered it, built up from centuries of shedding by the huge trees. There were also a lot of brittle cones lying around. Frank had hoped that whatever killed those loggers might have left some tracks, but that wasn't the case. He didn't see any prints among the needles.

That left Dog's nose. "How about it, fella?" Frank asked the big cur. "You smell anything unusual?"

Dog trotted around the clearing. He paused in one spot, lifting his head and peering off into the woods.

"What is it, Dog?" Frank asked as he knelt

next to the wolflike beast. "You smell some sort of critter?"

Frank studied the ground at this spot. Something might have kicked through the needles, but he couldn't be sure about that. He whistled for Stormy and Goldy. The horses came over to him, and he swung up on Stormy.

"Trail, Dog!" Frank ordered.

Dog had a scent of some sort, all right, although he still wasn't reacting like he would if his quarry was a bear or some other sort of wild animal, Frank thought. Dog took off through the woods, nose close to the ground. Frank followed, riding Stormy and leading Goldy.

Dog didn't move so fast that he got out of Frank's sight. He weaved through the trees, heading first one direction, then another, as if whoever — or whatever — he was tracking didn't have any specific destination in mind but was just roaming aimlessly through the forest. That sounded like the behavior of an animal.

Maybe a grizzly bear had wandered over here into California from the Rockies, Frank thought. It wasn't impossible. That didn't explain why Dog hadn't growled when he picked up the scent, but there might be some reason for that. Or maybe the preda-

tor was some sort of freakishly large wolf —
but again, Dog would have reacted more
violently to wolf scent.

Frank had told Karl Wilcox that he wasn't
going monster hunting, but that was exactly
what he was doing, he realized. He didn't
believe the so-called Terror was something
supernatural, but he wanted to find out who
had killed those men anyway. Wholesale
slaughter like that rubbed Frank the wrong
way and always had.

Dog paused suddenly and lifted his head.
He sniffed the air, and now a growl came
from him. At the same time, Frank heard a
crackling in the brush off to his right. He
twisted in the saddle to gaze off into the
perpetual twilight under the giant trees, but
didn't see anything moving.

Then something crashed to his left. Dog
whirled in that direction and growled again.

Were there *two* of them, whatever they
were? That would help explain how six men
had died back there.

Frank felt his heart hammering in his
chest. He wasn't afraid; he had never run
into anything that a well-placed bullet
couldn't take down, and he didn't believe
he was going to here. But there was something about the gloom, and the trees towering over him like giants, and the memory of

blood and scattered body parts . . .

Somewhere not far away, a horse nickered, and another answered it. Frank took a deep breath. Riders in the woods were one thing; some bizarre, mysterious *something* that could rip six men limb from limb was another thing entirely.

But men could be mighty dangerous, too, he reminded himself. He had seen ample evidence of that in his life.

And as if to emphasize that, a gun suddenly cracked not far away on his right, and a bullet whined through the trees, much too close for comfort.

That wasn't enough trouble, though. More shots blasted from the left in return, and in the blink of an eye slugs were sizzling through the brush and smacking into tree trunks all around Frank.

"Son of a —" He threw himself off Stormy, grabbed the reins of both horses, and led them hurriedly toward a deadfall he had spotted up ahead. Rather than being felled by loggers, the massive redwood had toppled over due to some natural cause, probably years earlier. These trees took a long time to rot, though, so the log was still in fairly good shape. It stood fifteen feet tall, too, so it would offer some protection if Frank and the horses could get behind it.

He called, "Stay down, Dog!" to the big cur.

They reached the deadfall. That shielded them from the shots coming from one direction anyway. Frank heard a man shout, "Over here! I got it, I got it!"

The fool didn't have anything. Frank understood now what was going on. Two separate groups of hunters looking for the Terror of the Redwoods — and that ten-thousand-dollar bounty — had mistaken each other for their quarry and opened fire. They would be lucky if several of them didn't get killed.

That was one thing about offering a bounty like the one Rutherford Chamberlain had placed on the Terror — it brought out all the greedy, trigger-happy fools who would blaze away at anything in hopes of earning the money. Frank had tried to tell himself that what Chamberlain did was none of his business, but when folks started shooting at him, that *made* it his business.

He intended to have himself a talk with Rutherford Chamberlain. If he got out of these woods alive, that is.

The guns were still popping. Frank cupped his hands around his mouth and bellowed, "Hold your fire! Hold your fire!" He had to shout it twice more before the shooting began to die away.

"Hey," a man yelled into the lull, "who's that?"

"Hold your fire!" Frank shouted again. "You're just shooting at each other!"

Horses crashed through the brush. Somebody else yelled, "Don't shoot anymore!"

Frank breathed a little easier now. Both groups of hunters had ceased fire. Maybe they wouldn't start shooting indiscriminately again before they found out what was going on.

Three riders came into view, carrying their rifles at the ready. Frank stepped out from behind the huge log and raised a hand.

"Was that you we were shooting at, mister?" one of them asked.

"Yeah, but you were also shooting at another bunch over there," Frank replied, pointing with a thumb in the other direction.

That was where more shots abruptly sounded, and a man screamed at the top of his lungs in sheer terror.

CHAPTER 3

Frank wheeled in that direction. He had heard shrieks like that not long before, and six men had died. He jerked his Winchester from the saddle boot and broke into a run toward the sounds.

As thick as the woods were, he could move just as fast on foot as the other men could on horseback. He charged through the trees for several moments, then had to leap aside as a runaway horse suddenly loomed up right in front of him. The animal's eyes were wide and rolling with fright. Foam drooled from its mouth. It wasn't paying any attention to where it was going, and only Frank's superb reflexes kept the horse from trampling him.

He heard more crashing in the brush, as if other horses were bolting through the woods in panic-stricken flight. The gunfire had stopped, but the screaming continued. Frank couldn't be sure, but he thought it was a different voice now.

As if something had already stilled the first one.

Another shape appeared in the shadows before him, coming toward him at a fast rate of speed. Frank stopped and swung the rifle up, ready to fire if whatever it was attacked him. It wasn't a monster, though, or even some sort of wild animal. It was a man, running for his life like Satan himself was after him. A crimson smear of blood covered his face, and he kept looking behind him as he plunged heedlessly through the forest.

Frank lowered the Winchester and called, "Hey! Stop! You're all right!"

The man never slowed down. Frank stepped to the side so that the hombre wouldn't barrel right into him, leaned the rifle against a tree trunk, and then reached out to grab the man as he went by. Frank wrapped his arms around him, the muscles in his arms and shoulders bunching under the butternut shirt as he jerked the fleeing man to a halt.

The fellow wasn't going to settle down without a fight, though. He was too hysterical from fear to do that. He struggled frantically to get loose, twisting in Frank's grip and flailing at him. The fists thudded into Frank's shoulders and back and didn't really do any damage, but he got tired of it in a hurry anyway. He grabbed hold of the front of the man's shirt, shoved him back a step, and drove a short but powerful punch into the hombre's jaw.

The blow snapped the man's head to the side and made his eyes roll up in their sockets. Frank let go of him. The man's knees unhinged. He folded up and crumpled to the needle-covered ground at Frank's feet.

The riders had arrived while Frank was struggling with the stranger. They looked down at the stunned man, and one of them asked, "Who's that?"

"I think his name's Scott," another rider said. "I've seen him in Eureka."

"Man, looks like somethin' tore into him."

That was true. Most of the blood on the man's face came from a hideous gash that slanted across his forehead, but he had some smaller cuts and scratches on his cheeks, too. His shirt was torn and bloodstained, like something had tried to claw it off him.

Frank realized that the screaming had stopped. He picked up his rifle and said to the men on horseback, "A couple of you come with me. The other one stay here and keep an eye on this gent."

"Who are you to be givin' orders, mister?"

"The man who's giving the orders," Frank snapped. "Come on."

The tone of command didn't allow for any argument. One of the men shrugged and said, "I'll stay here with Scott. Just don't you fellas be gone too long. That critter's still roamin' around out here in these woods, unless I miss my guess."

Frank led the way, stalking forward with the Winchester at the ready. In a few minutes, he spotted what looked like two heaps of old clothing lying on the ground ahead of him. He had a bad feeling that there was more to the heaps than old clothes, though.

Unfortunately, he was right. He saw the torn and mangled bodies as he came closer. Blood formed reddish-black pools around both dead men. Not only had their flesh been shredded, but their throats were torn out as well. These injuries looked more like something an animal would inflict. Frank was getting back to the bear idea again. The killer hadn't taken the time to rip the bodies apart this time.

"Holy Mother o' God!" one of the riders who had trailed along behind Frank exclaimed when he saw the mutilated corpses. Frank heard retching behind him, but didn't look around.

"It was the Terror, that's what it was," the

35

other man said. "No doubt about it. The damn thing's gone on a real rampage this time."

Frank thought that eight dead men in less than an hour qualified as a rampage, all right. But he still wasn't convinced that some sort of monster had done this.

"There's nothing we can do for these fellas," he said. "Let's go back and see about that other one."

They returned to the spot where they had left Scott and the third rider. The injured man had regained his senses, at least to a certain extent. He sat with his back against the trunk of a redwood. He had his knees drawn up and his arms wrapped around them. He swayed back and forth and made soft moaning noises.

"I was gonna try to clean up those wounds a little," the third man said, "but he won't let me touch him. I figured if I tried too hard, I might spook him and make him run off again."

Frank nodded. "It was good thinking to leave him alone. I'll see what I can get out of him."

He went over to the man and hunkered on his heels, not getting too close to him. The man rolled his eyes in Frank's direction and cringed away.

"It's all right," Frank told him in a calm, steady voice, the sort of tone he would use on a frightened horse. "The thing that killed your friends and hurt you is gone. You're safe now."

The man's teeth chattered. "N-nobody's safe," he stammered. "Nobody's s-safe in the w-woods. The T-Terror's out there!"

"Did you see it?" Frank asked.

Scott jerked his head in a nod. "It . . . it came out from behind a tree . . . knocked Billy off his horse . . . I never saw anything move so f-fast."

"What did it look like?"

"Big! Hairy! Must've been . . . nine feet tall . . . and it had these . . . *claws* . . ." A shudder ran through the man's body. "It tore out Billy's throat . . . with one swipe . . . There was blood all over him . . . We tried to shoot it, but it was too fast . . . It went for Rance . . ." Scott sobbed. The tears left little trails in the gore smeared on his cheeks. "Rance's horse spooked, threw him. So did m-mine. The thing jumped on Rance . . . it was tearin' him up . . . slashin' at him with those claws like it was tryin' to . . . to dig his insides out . . . Then it . . . came for me . . . hit me once and knocked me clear across the open space between two trees."

Frank leaned closer. "How did you manage to get away?"

"Just luck. The thing started tearin' at me . . . like it had done to Rance . . . and then one of the horses stampeded right into it. Knocked it off of me. I got up and ran." Scott lifted horror-haunted eyes and gazed at Frank from them. "It could've come after me, could've caught me. I don't know why it didn't. Maybe the horse hurt it. Maybe it was just tired of . . . playin' with us."

One of the hunters said, "You hear that, boys? The thing's hurt! We can track it down for sure now."

Frank looked around at the men and told them, "You don't know that. Like this hombre said, maybe it had some other reason for leaving." He returned his attention to Scott. "You must have gotten a good look at it. Could it have been a bear? Maybe a grizzly that wandered over here from somewhere in the Rockies?"

Scott shook his head. That made the flap of skin that hung down from the gash on his forehead move. "It wasn't a bear," he said. "It was hairy all over like a bear, but . . . it wasn't a bear."

"How can you be sure of that?"

"It didn't have a snout like a bear. And it went on two legs."

"Bears can get around on two legs," Frank pointed out.

"Not like this."

"Some other sort of animal then?"

Stubbornly, Scott shook his head again. "No, it was more like . . . a man's face, but . . . bigger . . . hairier. It was the ugliest thing I've ever seen."

"Sounds like one of those Sasquatch critters they've got up north," one of the men said. All three of them had dismounted and stood around Frank and Scott now.

"Yeah," another man said. "I've heard 'em called Bigfoot, too. They're supposed to be nine feet tall and hairy, just like this hombre said."

Frank wasn't going to believe in such a thing, not unless and until he saw it with his own eyes. Even then, he'd be doubtful.

He came to his feet and said, "This fella needs medical attention. I want the three of you to take him to Eureka."

"Hell, no! There's ten grand on the hoof not far from here. We're gonna go find it."

The other two spoke up, voicing their agreement.

Scott clutched at the leg of one of them. "You can't!" he wailed. "It'll kill you, too, just like it did Billy and Rance!"

The man pulled his leg loose and said,

39

"We can handle some damned old Bigfoot."

"You don't know . . . It's worse than that . . . I can't even t-tell you how bad it really is." Scott closed his eyes and shuddered. "Like it's not even from this world."

"You saw what it did to those two men," Frank said. "Well, just a little while ago it killed six more the same way, only worse. Those hombres it tore apart. Flat out tore them apart."

One of the men rubbed at his angular jaw. "Maybe it would be better to come back later," he suggested. "Maybe get some more men first."

"That'll mean splittin' the bounty more ways."

"I'd rather have a little less to spend and still be alive to spend it."

"Well, I'm not goin'."

"Yes, you are," Frank said.

"Who the hell are you to be tellin' me what to do?" The man who had been arguing moved his hand toward the butt of his gun. "Folks say I'm pretty fast on the draw, and if you ain't careful, I might just show you."

"That wouldn't be a very good idea. My name's Frank Morgan."

The man's nostrils flared as he drew in a deep, startled breath. His face paled under its tan. "Morgan," he repeated. "The gun-fighter?"

"One and the same," Frank said.

"You'd best back off, Tom," one of the man's friends advised him. "Bein' fast for around here don't mean nothin' against a man like Frank Morgan."

"Yeah. All right." Tom nodded. "We'll do like you say, Morgan. We'll take this fella in and find a sawbones to patch him up. And I, uh, didn't mean any offense . . ."

"None taken," Frank assured him.

"What are you gonna do, if you don't mind my askin'?"

"Are you goin' after the monster?" one of the other men asked. "That'd be somethin', The Drifter takin' on the Terror."

"I thought I'd pay a visit to that fella Chamberlain," Frank said. "I don't believe it's a good idea to be throwing out a bounty like that. It can lead to more trouble than it's worth."

"It won't do you any good. From what I hear, Chamberlain's the big skookum he-wolf in these parts. He's used to doin' as he pleases."

"Maybe I can talk some sense into his head." Frank looked around. "If I can figure out which way's north. It's hard to tell in this blasted forest where you can't hardly

41

see the sky."

He had a keen sense of direction, though, so it only took him a few minutes to orient himself once he picked up his horses and Dog. As he rode off, he could hear the other riders moving through the trees toward the settlement of Eureka, to the east. Scott was riding double with one of them.

Frank kept his eyes and ears open. From the way Scott had talked, whatever had attacked them had struck with no warning, moving so fast that they couldn't even hit it with their shots. Frank didn't know if he would fare any better should the thing jump him, but he didn't intend to go down without a fight, even if he was facing some nine-foot-tall hairy critter with giant claws.

Nothing bothered him, though, and after a while he came to a fairly wide, hard-packed dirt road that led more directly northward. Frank had a hunch it led to Rutherford Chamberlain's house. He wondered how much it had cost to hack a good road like this out of the thickly timbered wilderness. It must have been a pretty penny.

But he supposed Chamberlain could afford it. A few minutes later, the road reached a huge clearing. The trees had been stripped from a small hill to form the estate, and at the top of the gentle slope stood a mansion the likes of which Frank hadn't ever seen anywhere except San Francisco, Denver, and Boston. As a matter of fact, he wasn't sure he had ever seen anything like it in those places.

He recognized the sort of men who came galloping around the house and charging toward him, though. They bristled with guns, and they were looking for trouble.

CHAPTER 4

Frank saw several rifles and shotguns among the men. He reined Stormy to a halt and said in a low voice, "Dog, sit. Stay." He didn't want the big cur to give the men any excuse for being trigger-happy.

For that same reason, he kept his hands in plain sight, well away from his guns. These men were Rutherford Chamberlain's bodyguards, he told himself, and they were just doing their job. With all the mysterious and deadly things going on in the forest these days, you couldn't blame them for being suspicious of strangers.

It went against the grain, though, for him to have guns pointed at him and not do something about it. That was just part of who he was.

"Take it easy, gents," Frank said in a loud, clear voice as the men on horseback surrounded him. "I'm plumb peaceable."

"Who are you?" one of the men demanded. "What are you doing here?"

Frank answered the second question. "I'm looking for Mr. Chamberlain. I just want to talk to him."

The spokesman, who had an ugly, raw-boned face and straw-colored hair under a black Stetson, sneered and said, "Well, he don't want to talk to you."

"Maybe you should ask him about that," Frank suggested.

The sneer didn't go away. It just got uglier. "Yeah, maybe you should just go to hell."

"I still haven't told you who I am."

"I've decided it don't matter. I can tell by lookin' at you that you're just some old saddle tramp, and Mr. Chamberlain ain't got time for trash like you." The man jerked a thumb toward the road. "Vamoose."

Frank knew that he ought to just tell this man who he was. Most likely, the name Frank Morgan would open the door of the mansion.

But he was just stubborn enough not to do that. This hombre's arrogance had gotten under his skin, and he knew it would be like a burr under a saddle if he didn't do something about it.

He pressed his heels against Stormy's flanks. The horse moved forward.

The leader of the guards jumped his mount ahead to block Frank's path. "Are you loco, mister?" he yelled. "You get outta here right now or you're gonna be sorry."

"I'm going to talk to Chamberlain, and you're not going to stop me," Frank said.

"There are eight of us —" the man began.

"No," Frank cut in, "I said *you're* not going to stop me."

The man's face flushed a dark, angry red. "Why, you son of a bitch!" he burst out. "You think I'm scared of you?"

One of the other men spoke up, saying, "Cobb, maybe you better be careful. I don't like the looks of this hombre."

"I don't either," Cobb snapped. "That's why I intend to change 'em a mite." He glared at Frank. "Get down off your horse, mister."

"Before I do, I want your word that this is between you and me," Frank said. "And I don't want any of your men bothering my dog or my horses either. If they try, they'll be sorry."

Cobb waved a hand impatiently. "Yeah, yeah. Whatever you say, mister."

"I have your word?"

"Hell, yeah!" Cobb looked around at the other guards. "You fellas stay out of it, hear?"

"I'll be glad to," said the man who had spoken earlier. He was looking intently at Frank, as if he recognized him. Frank thought that was possible. These guards all had the look of tough, hard-bitten hombres, the sort of men who traveled in the same circles he did.

Cobb swung down from his saddle, unbuckled his gun belt, and hung it on the saddle horn. He put his hat on top of it. He was a couple of inches taller than Frank, but probably packed about the same amount of weight on his rangy frame. He wore a white shirt, a black vest, and black leather wrist cuffs.

Frank dismounted as well and removed his gun and hat. Cobb gestured at the bowie knife on Frank's left hip and said, "Get rid of that pigsticker, too."

Frank slid the fringed sheath off his belt and tucked it and the knife in his saddlebags. "Just so we're clear," he said, "once I've gotten past you, your friends won't stop me from going on up to the house, right?"

"You won't get past me," Cobb said with a grin.

"But if I do —"

"Yeah, yeah. Let him talk to the boss, boys, if the boss is willin' to see him." Cobb looked at Frank. "I can't promise any more

47

than that."

"Fair enough," Frank said.

He hadn't gotten the words completely out of his mouth before Cobb let out a yell and charged him. The man was fast, but Frank was able to twist out of his way. As Cobb stumbled past, Frank hit him on the ear. It was only a glancing blow, but it must have stung. Cobb bellowed and swung around with a look of rage on his face. He threw a looping punch at Frank's head.

Frank blocked it, stepped in, and landed a hard right on Cobb's sternum. The blow rocked Cobb back a step and set him up for the left hook that Frank exploded on his jaw. Cobb went to one knee, a look of stunned surprise on his ugly face. Clearly, he hadn't expected Frank to land the first three punches.

With another angry roar, Cobb came up from the ground and launched himself into a diving tackle with his arms spread wide. Frank couldn't avoid the lunge. Cobb wrapped an arm around his thighs and drove him backward off his feet.

When Frank hit the ground, the impact knocked the air out of his lungs. He gasped for breath and rolled to the side to avoid Cobb's knee as Cobb tried to plant it in his groin. Frank brought his elbow back and clipped his opponent on the jaw with it.

Some of the other men yelled encouragement to Cobb, but most of them just sat silently on their horses, watching the fight. They made no move to interfere, though, and that was all Frank cared about where they were concerned. He twisted around, got his left hand on Cobb's throat, and bounced the man's head off the ground.

Cobb brought his left up and for the first time landed a punch cleanly. The knobby fist crashed into the side of Frank's head and sent him sprawling. That brought more shouts from Cobb's friends. Cobb dove after Frank, who rolled onto his back and managed to get his right leg up in time to drive the heel of his boot into Cobb's belly. Cobb's weight and momentum made the boot heel sink deeply into his midsection. He went "Oooff!" and doubled over.

Frank reached up, grabbed Cobb's vest, and hauled hard on it at the same time as he levered the man into the air on his leg. Cobb sailed through the air over Frank's head and crashed onto the ground. It was his turn to gasp for breath now. Frank had recovered his. He flipped over, landed on Cobb, and slugged him on the jaw again. Pinning his opponent to the ground with a knee in his belly, Frank hit Cobb twice

49

more, a left and then a piledriver right. Cobb's head lolled loosely on his neck as he lay there on his back with his arms and legs spraddled out.

"If you're thinking about hitting him again, Morgan, I wouldn't. He's out."

Frank looked up at the man who had tried to warn Cobb. Chest heaving a little from his exertions, he said, "You . . . recognized me."

"That's right. Cobb's damned lucky he just tried to thrash you. If he'd thrown down on you, you probably would've killed him. Better a beating than a bullet in the heart."

One of the other guards said, "Rockwell, who the hell is this jasper? You act like you know him."

The man called Rockwell shook his head. "No, we never met, but he was pointed out to me one night in a saloon in Fort Worth. His name's Frank Morgan."

"Morgan!" Several men muttered in surprise. The one who had exclaimed said, "You mean the gunfighter?"

"One and the same," Rockwell said.

Another man let out a whistle. "You're right. Cobb's lucky to be alive."

Frank went over to Stormy and got his hat from the saddle. He put it on and then buckled the gun belt around his hips. He paused to rub Dog's ears. The big cur had stayed right where Frank had told him to stay, even during the fight. He had probably growled a few times, though, frustrated that he couldn't tear into Cobb.

A couple of the guards had dismounted. They reached down, took hold of Cobb's arms, and lifted him to his feet. He sagged in their grip, and would have fallen if they hadn't been supporting him, but he was starting to come around now. He gave a groggy shake of his head and moaned.

"Come on," Rockwell said to Frank. "I'll take you up to the house. I think you knocked all the fight out of Cobb, but it'll be simpler if you're already inside when he wakes up good."

Frank nodded. He picked up the horses' reins and motioned for Dog to follow him.

Rockwell led the way along a path made of crushed rock that ran through a green lawn in front of the house. It widened out into an area where buggies could be parked. From there, the path ran on around the mansion toward a carriage house and several other outbuildings.

The house itself was one of the oddest, yet most impressive structures Frank had ever seen. It was a three-story Victorian topped by a square tower with a steep roof and a long metal spire that served as a lightning rod. There were more gables than Frank could count, each one topped by a lightning rod as well, and although he was no architect, they seemed to be placed rather haphazardly around the roof. A room jutted out from the front of the house, cutting off a porch that appeared to wrap the rest of the way around the house. The porch railings were wrought iron and decorated with elaborate curlicues and designs. Latticework framed the windows, and carvings were everywhere in the wood. Frank saw birds and animals, moons and stars, even human faces. The whole place had a reddish gleam in the sun, and he recalled that Karl Wilcox had said the mansion was made out of the redwood that had brought Rutherford Chamberlain his fortune.

Frank thought that if he had to live in a place like this, he would go plumb loco in a week.

Rockwell must have had an idea what he was thinking, because the man grinned over at him and said, "It's really something, isn't it?"

"It's something, all right," Frank said. "I'm just not sure what."

"The old man designed it himself. He says the woods made him a rich man, so it's only fitting that he lives here among the trees."

"I hear that he does all his business from here and doesn't go into town very often."

"Hardly ever," Rockwell said with a nod. "He used to get out more, but Mrs. Chamberlain passed away a few years ago, and now Mr. Chamberlain just stays in the house unless there's some sort of emergency."

"I guess he figures no one will bother him here," Frank mused. "It must have really shaken him up when this whole business with the Terror started."

"Ah, the Terror," Rockwell said. "I sort of figured you were here about that. Going after the money, are you?"

"I want to talk to Mr. Chamberlain about the bounty," Frank said, not answering the question directly. Let Rockwell draw whatever conclusions he wanted to. As they came up to the porch, Frank went on. "What do you think about the Terror? Ever seen it?"

"No, and I don't want to." Rockwell stopped and looked over at Frank. "Call me hardheaded, but I'm not sure the damned thing really exists. The evil that men do is bad enough without there being monsters in the world."

Frank started to say that he felt the same way, but he surprised himself by not doing it. After the things he had seen this afternoon, he wasn't certain what he believed anymore. The only things he knew for sure were that something was killing men in the forest and that it needed to be stopped. But he didn't think that posting a bounty was the best way to go about it. That might just get some innocent men killed.

Frank tied Stormy and Goldy to a fancy hitching post in front of the house and told Dog to stay. Then the two men walked up onto the porch. The front door was a massive slab of varnished red-wood with a bronze lion's-head knocker so big that for a second Frank thought Chamberlain must have gotten it from a real lion. Rockwell grasped the knocker and rapped it sharply against the door.

"They probably heard the commotion inside," he said, "so they'll know that something was going on —"

As if to support his words, the door opened almost right away. A tall, cadaverous man with white hair and a white mustache stood there. He wore a black suit. Frank had seen enough butlers in his life to recognize the breed. He halfway expected the gent to talk with a British accent, but the butler sounded American as he asked, "What is it, Rockwell? Who is this man?"

"He's here to see Mr. Chamberlain," Rockwell said. "His name is Frank Morgan."

If the name meant anything to the butler, for once Frank couldn't see it in the man's eyes. The butler turned to him and asked, "What's the nature of your business? I'll have to explain to Mr. Chamberlain why you wish to see him."

"It's about the bounty," Frank said. "The bounty on that thing the loggers call the Terror."

The butler's eyes widened slightly, but only for a second before he controlled the reaction. He said, "Have you come to collect? Do you have the creature's head with you?"

"No, and no," Frank said. "I don't much believe in bounties, and I sure don't believe in hacking off somebody's head just to collect one."

"I don't understand. Why do you wish to see Mr. Chamberlain if you don't intend to collect the reward?"

"That's between him and me."

The butler looked at Rockwell. "I fail to see why you brought this man to the house. I don't think he has any need to see Mr. Chamberlain —"

"I do," Rockwell said. "Like I told you,

he's Frank Morgan."

The butler shook his head. "Is that name supposed to mean something to me?"

"He's The Drifter, for God's sake! He's a gunfighter. Some say the last real gunfighter, since Smoke Jensen and Matt Bodine hung up their guns and Wes Hardin's dead. If he's got something to say, I reckon the boss would be well-advised to listen."

"Very well," the butler said with a sigh. "Please, come in, Mr. Morgan. I'll see if Mr. Chamberlain is willing to speak with you."

Frank took off his hat as he stepped into the house. "Much obliged, Mister . . . ?"

"Dennis, sir. Just Dennis. No mister required."

"See you later, Morgan," Rockwell said as he stepped back from the door. He lifted a hand in farewell, a gesture that Frank returned. He didn't particularly like Rockwell, but the man didn't seem like a bad sort.

"You can wait in the library," Dennis said. The redwood floor in the foyer had been polished to a high sheen. The hallway down which the butler led Frank was the same way. Portraits of stern-looking men and impassive women hung on the walls.

Dennis ushered Frank through a pair of

double doors into a large, rather dark room. Bookshelves lined all four walls from floor to ceiling. The furnishings consisted of a writing desk and several comfortable-looking armchairs. Thick drapes hung over the room's single window. They were pulled back part of the way to let in some light.

"I'll advise Mr. Chamberlain that you're here, sir," Dennis said.

"No hurry," Frank told him, and meant it. The sight of all these books intrigued him. Like a lot of men who spent most of their time alone, he was an avid reader and nearly always had a book or two, sometimes more, stuffed in his saddlebags. He wouldn't mind taking a look at the volumes Rutherford Chamberlain had collected.

Dennis left the room, closing the doors behind him. Frank set his Stetson on one of the chairs and walked over to the nearest bookshelf. Most of the books were bound in expensive leather. He always read cheap editions, because they took quite a beating from being toted around in his saddlebags. He spotted a novel he had read before and enjoyed, Jules Verne's *Twenty Thousand Leagues Under the Sea*. This was a different edition, though, so he was about to take it down and flip through it when he heard the library doors open behind him. He turned, expecting to see either Rutherford Chamberlain or the butler Dennis, explaining that Chamberlain had refused to see him.

Instead, a blond, very attractive young woman had stopped just inside the library, and she seemed to be as surprised to see Frank as he was to see her.

CHAPTER 5

"I'm sorry, I was looking for my father," she said. "Were you waiting to speak to him?"

So she was Chamberlain's daughter, Frank thought. She was probably used to seeing men with pomaded hair, wearing expensive suits, waiting in here for her father — not hombres in dusty old range clothes.

And not hombres who were packing iron either, he thought as he saw her startled gaze go to the Colt on his hip.

"That's right, Miss Chamberlain," he said. "My name is Frank Morgan."

She didn't seem to recognize the name any more than Dennis had. "Father knows you're here?"

"I suppose he does. That fella Dennis went to tell him."

"I see. Do you mind if *I* ask what your business is with my father?"

She came closer as she asked the question. Frank saw intelligence in her brown eyes. He saw something else, too. Worry at the very least. Maybe even fear.

He was too polite to refuse to answer. Anyway, he was curious about her interest. He said, "I want to speak to Mr. Chamberlain about the bounty he's placed on that thing they call the Terror."

The young woman wore a dark blue dress with long sleeves and a high neckline. Despite its demure cut, the dress was snug enough to reveal an excellent figure. Her breasts lifted as she inhaled sharply, and the look in her eyes definitely became one of fear.

"Are you here to collect?" she said. That was the same question Dennis had asked, Frank noted, but there was a lot more urgency in this young woman's voice. "Have . . . have you killed . . . it?"

Frank shook his head. "No, ma'am, I haven't. I haven't even seen it."

She sighed in relief.

"But I've seen its handiwork," Frank went on. "It killed eight men this afternoon."

The blonde shrank back a step as if he had lifted a fist and threatened to hit her. "No!" she said, the exclamation coming from her in a strained half whisper. "That can't be true!"

He knew she wasn't actually calling him a liar. She just didn't want to believe what he had told her. Nodding solemnly, he said, "I'm afraid it is. I saw the bodies myself. They've been taken into Eureka."

"Do you . . . do you know who they were?"

"Six of them were loggers from a crew working about five miles south of here," Frank said. "The other two men were hunters who were after the bounty on the Terror. It got them instead of the other way around."

"How . . . how terrible."

He had a feeling that she had to force herself to say it, as though she was glad it hadn't been the other way around.

"Are you going after the Terror, Mr. Morgan?" she continued.

"I'm not a bounty hunter, of men or monsters," he said. That didn't mean he wasn't going after the Terror — he hadn't decided about that yet — but if she got that impression from his words, fine. He went on. "What do you know about it? Have you ever seen it?"

She didn't answer him. Instead she looked around, then said, "I have to go." Before Frank could say anything else, she turned and disappeared through the double doors. He heard the quick patter of her feet on the hardwood floor of the corridor.

A second later, more footsteps approached the library. These were heavier, a hard, determined stride that had to belong to Rutherford Chamberlain. The young woman must have heard them coming. Frank thought that must be why she had rushed out of the library. For some reason, she didn't want her father to know that she had been in here talking to the visitor.

The woman had left the doors open. A moment later, a man in a brown tweed suit appeared in them. He was about the same height as Frank, and his broad shoulders indicated that he had been a powerful man at one time. Age had drained him of some of his vitality, though. Age and perhaps grief, Frank thought as he recalled Rockwell's comment about how Chamberlain's wife had died several years earlier. Chamberlain's hair and mustache were iron gray. Deep-set eyes looked out from a face that tended toward gauntness. The collar of his shirt was a little too big for his turkey neck.

Despite his appearance, there was nothing the least bit frail about his voice. It was deep and commanding. "You're Morgan?" he asked as he came into the library.

"That's right."

"I'm told that you're a . . . gunfighter.

What's your business with me, sir?"

Right to the point. That was fine with Frank. "It's about the bounty on the Terror."

Chamberlain gave an impatient wave of his hand. "You're free to go after it just like anyone else. You don't have to make any special arrangements in advance."

"I don't want the bounty," Frank said. "I think you should call it off."

"Call it off?" A snort of disbelief came from the timber baron. "That creature has killed almost half a dozen men. If the bounty helps rid the forest of it, the money will be well worth it, sir."

"It's killed more than half a dozen men now. Eight more died this afternoon."

Chamberlain's eyes widened in a look of shock. "Eight men?" he repeated, his voice going hoarse. "But who . . . how . . ."

Quickly, Frank explained about the deaths of the loggers and the two bounty hunters. As he spoke, the hollows in Rutherford Chamberlain's cheeks became even more pronounced. "Dear Lord," he whispered when Frank was finished. "Dear Lord." Chamberlain's back stiffened. "Perhaps I should invoke the Devil's name instead, since that creature must come from the foulest, deepest pits of Hell!"

"I wouldn't know about that," Frank said. "All I know is that you're going to have more men dying in those woods if you leave that bounty in force. They'll be killing each other by accident, rather than running into the Terror. It almost happened this afternoon."

He told Chamberlain what had happened when the two groups of bounty hunters opened fire on each other. Chamberlain's impatience grew visibly as he listened.

"It's not my fault if those men are careless," he snapped. "I fail to see where it's my responsibility."

"Your bounty is the reason they're out there in the first place, running around the woods and shooting at everything that moves," Frank argued. "You can put a stop to it by spreading the word that there's not going to be any bounty."

Chamberlain shook his head stubbornly. "I won't do it. I want that thing dead, no matter what it takes."

"What about when your own loggers start getting shot by men who are hunting the Terror? That won't be very good for morale among your crews. They're liable to walk off the job."

Chamberlain frowned for a moment as if that possibility hadn't occurred to him, but then a sneer replaced the frown. "There are always more men looking for jobs," he declared. "If anyone is afraid to work in the woods, let him quit and I'll simply hire someone to replace him. Anyway," Chamberlain went on, "don't you think I've already had men quit because they're afraid of the Terror?"

Frank supposed Chamberlain had a point there. "All I'm saying is that the woods aren't going to be safe for anybody as long as a bunch of trigger-happy fools are roaming around with visions of ten thousand dollars in their heads."

Chamberlain looked at him intently for a moment, then said, "Ah, now I see where this is going. You want me to rescind the bounty and then hire *you* to hunt down and kill the monster. And I suppose the fee you'll suggest will be the same amount as the bounty, only you won't have to deal with any competition."

The accusation took Frank by surprise. He shook his head and said, "You've got it all wrong, Chamberlain. I didn't come here to get the job for myself."

"Why not?" Chamberlain hooked his thumbs in his vest and glared at Frank. "You're a gunfighter. You admitted as much. That means you sell your skills as a killer to the highest bidder, doesn't it?"

"I'm not a hired gun," Frank snapped. "Never have been. Any time I've fought, it was to save my life or the life of someone else, or because I believed in a cause."

"If you kill the Terror, you'll be saving the lives of all the men who might die because of it in the future." Chamberlain nodded emphatically. "Now that I think about it, this is an excellent idea. Set one cold-blooded killer to catch another. I like it."

Anger welled up inside Frank. "I reckon we're done here," he said as he picked up his hat and took a step toward the library doors.

"Wait a moment, Mr. Morgan," Chamberlain said. "I'll do what you want. I'll rescind the bounty on the Terror . . . but only if you agree to hunt down and kill the creature yourself."

Frank shook his head. "Forget it."

"Of course, since you've seen what the monster can do, I can understand if you're afraid to go after it by yourself."

Frank had to laugh, a reaction that startled Chamberlain. "I've had plenty of damned fools try to prod me into gunfights by calling me a coward," he said. "It didn't work then, and it's not going to work now. You can say whatever you want. I'm not taking the job."

"Then I suppose we *are* done, just as you say," Chamberlain responded coldly.

Frank clapped his hat on his head, gave the timber baron a curt nod, and started toward the door.

"But you realize, of course," Chamberlain added to his back, "this means the ten-thousand-dollar bounty is still in effect."

"Folks do foolish things all the time," Frank said without turning around. "I can't talk sense into all of them."

He stalked out of the library and headed toward the front of the house. The butler, Dennis, wasn't around, but Frank didn't need any help finding his way out.

Just before he reached the front door, though, a voice spoke from a door to the side of the foyer. "Mr. Morgan, please wait."

Frank stopped and frowned. He turned and saw Chamberlain's daughter standing there just inside the open doorway, which led into what appeared to be a small sitting room.

"I need to talk to you," she went on.

"I don't want to be rude, Miss Chamberlain," he said, "but your father and I have finished our business."

"I know. I hope you'll forgive me, but . . . I was listening just outside the library door.

I knew you were talking about . . . the Terror . . . and I wanted to hear what you said."

Frank remembered her earlier reaction. He might be wrong, but he thought the idea that the Terror had been killed had frightened her. He didn't have any idea why that would be true, but the possibility intrigued him enough that he wanted to find out if his hunch was right.

"Your father's liable to try to have me thrown out if he realizes I'm still here, but I reckon I can spare you a minute or two."

"Thank you," she said, obviously relieved. "Please, come in here, where we won't be disturbed."

She moved back. Frank stepped into the sitting room, which was furnished with a pair of armchairs and a small table with a lamp on it. The blonde eased the door closed, then turned to face Frank, whose natural courtesy where women-folks was concerned had prompted him to remove his hat again. Holding the Stetson in front of him, he asked, "What can I do for you?"

"We haven't been formally introduced," she said. "My name is Nancy Chamberlain."

Frank nodded. "It's a pleasure to meet you, miss. Wish it had been under better circumstances."

"So do I. I heard my father offer you the job of tracking down and killing the Terror."

"Yes, ma'am. I turned him down, though."

"He said he'd take back that damned bounty if you did."

The vehemence in her voice surprised him. So did the way she clasped her hands together in front of her, so tightly that she squeezed the blood out of her fingers and made them turn pale.

"That's right," Frank said. "I don't think the bounty's a good idea, but I still don't want the job."

"I wish you'd take it," she said. "You look like the sort of man who . . . who can handle a difficult job."

"You want me to find the Terror and kill it?"

Nancy Chamberlain shook her head. She took a deep breath and said, "No, Mr. Morgan, I want you to find the Terror . . . and bring him home."

"Him?" Frank repeated with a surprised frown.

"That's right. You see, Mr. Morgan, the Terror is my brother."

CHAPTER 6

Frank couldn't help but stare at her. He wasn't sure what he'd been expecting from her, but the news that the Terror was not only human, but her brother as well, sure wasn't it.

That would help explain, though, why she had seemed to be more worried about the Terror than about the men who had died that afternoon.

"I'm afraid you're going to have to explain that, ma'am," Frank said slowly.

Nancy's fingers knotted together even tighter. "What people have started calling the Terror . . . he's my brother, Benjamin. He's not a monster, not at all."

"Miss Chamberlain, less than two hours ago I talked to a man who had just seen the Terror. He said the thing was nine feet tall, covered with hair, and had claws so big and sharp that it could, well, tear men apart with them."

Nancy grimaced and shook her head. "You know how people exaggerate when they're scared. Ben *is* big . . . well over six feet, in fact . . . and I suppose since he's been living in the woods, his hair and beard have gotten a little long and shaggy. As for the claws, I just don't believe it."

"I saw what they did with my own eyes," Frank said as gently as he could. "It was bad, ma'am, mighty bad."

"I don't care!" Nancy burst out. "Ben couldn't hurt anyone! He's too gentle! And if he did, it . . . it's not his fault. . . . There's something wrong in his head . . ."

She raised her hands, covered her face with them, and began to sob.

Despite his age and experience and almost supernatural skill with a gun, Frank was like most men in one respect: He didn't have any idea what to do when confronted by a crying woman. He shifted his feet awkwardly, thought about patting Nancy on the shoulder and saying, "There, there," then decided that would probably be the wrong thing to do. So he just waited quietly instead.

After a couple of minutes, Nancy's sobs died away to sniffles. She lowered her hands from her red-eyed face and looked at Frank. "You don't believe me, do you?"

"It's not that I don't believe you, ma'am," he said. "But like I told you, I *saw* those men who'd been killed. It's hard to believe that whatever did it could even be human."

"He is, I tell you, and . . . and no matter how much I don't want to admit it, I know he probably *did* kill those men. But it's not his fault. He's not right . . . in his thinking."

"You mean he's a lunatic?"

She grimaced again. "That's such an ugly word. It makes you think of people locked away in some horrible, squalid place where all they do is rave all day . . . Ben's not like that. He never was. He was always sweet and gentle and kind. He was almost like a little child." Nancy shook her head. "Please don't misunderstand, Mr. Morgan. Ben's not one of those people who can't learn. He doesn't have the mind of a child in the body of a grown man or anything like that. He's actually very bright. But he . . . he lives in a world of his own, I suppose you could say. It got worse after Mother passed away. Ben didn't want to be around other people, even me, and we had always been close. He just wanted to be alone. That . . . that's why he ran away."

This sounded to Frank almost like a story from a fairy-tale book. But he couldn't think of any reason why Nancy Chamberlain would lie to him about it. She was telling the truth, he sensed, or at least she *thought* she was.

"So your brother left home and went off to live in the woods," he said.

"Yes. Like Thoreau. Although I don't suppose you know who that is."

Frank didn't take offense. He didn't think she was actually trying to insult him. It was just a little casual condescension.

"Begging your pardon, ma'am, but I don't reckon anything like what's been going on in these woods ever happened around Walden Pond."

"Oh! I'm sorry —"

Frank stopped her with a motion of his hand. He had indulged his curiosity this far, he thought. He might as well go the rest of the way.

"Tell me more about your brother," he urged.

"Well, like I said, Ben lives in a world of his own. But it was always a peaceful place. He never hurt anyone, never got in any sort of trouble. I never even heard him raise his voice in anger, except . . ."

"Except what?" Frank said.

"When he and Father argued." Nancy sighed. "They were just too different to ever get along very well. Father thought that

73

someday Ben would take over the business."

Frank nodded. "A lot of fathers expect that out of their sons."

It was a good thing *he* hadn't expected his son to follow in his footsteps, he thought. He hadn't even been aware that he had a son with Vivian until Conrad Browning was a grown man. Conrad had inherited the other half of the Browning business empire, and he had done a good job of running it. But he was an Easterner, the farthest thing from a drifting gunfighter like his pa.

Although, Frank reminded himself, Conrad and his wife, Rebel, now lived in Virginia City, Nevada, and on the few occasions when Conrad had found himself drawn into dangerous situations with Frank, he had given a pretty good account of himself. He could handle a gun when he had to, and throw a decent punch.

"Ben had no interest whatever in the timber business, or any other business," Nancy went on. "He never did. Father tried to force him to work in the company office in Eureka. It didn't go well. They argued again and again. Ben just wasn't the sort of son that Father could be proud of."

Frank was no expert on such things, but he knew it was a mistake to try to force a youngster's feet onto a path he didn't want to follow. He was proud of Conrad, no matter how different the two of them were. It had taken Conrad a while to do some growing up and see that, but Frank was glad they had finally come to an understanding.

"Finally, after Mother passed on, Ben said that he wasn't going in to the office anymore. Father insisted that he was. They wound up shouting at each other, and . . . and Father told him to get out. He said he wouldn't have a son who was so shiftless and lacking in ambition. He . . . he said that Ben was no longer his son."

Frank shook his head. "That had to hurt."

"Yes, of course it did. I tried to tell Ben that Father didn't mean it, but we both knew that he did. I told Ben he didn't have to leave, but he insisted. He said he didn't want to have anything to do with the world of men anymore. He was going to go off into the woods and live by himself, surrounded by nature."

"Like Thoreau," Frank said.

Nancy smiled. "Yes. Like Thoreau."

"How long ago was this?"

"Two years."

"But the Terror's only been causing trouble for a few months," Frank pointed out. "How do you know what's been happening has anything to do with your brother?" He didn't want to mention another possibility that had occurred to him, but he felt like he had to. "Ben might not even be alive anymore."

"He's alive!" she said. Then she looked down at the expensive rug on the floor of the sitting room. "At least, he was just before all this started."

"How do you know?"

"Because I . . . I saw him in the woods."

Frank had to frown again. "You go out in those woods by yourself?"

"You have to understand, Mr. Morgan. Ben and I grew up around these giant redwoods. They're not frightening to us. The forest has always been our home. You're not scared of the place you grew up, are you?"

Frank thought back to the rolling, wooded hills of the Cross Timbers in north central Texas. With a faint smile, he said, "We don't have two-hundred-foot-tall trees where I'm from that grow so thick you can hardly see the sun. Anyway, there are wild animals in the forest, bears and wolves and things like that."

"We know how to avoid the dangers. I've never been afraid to go in the woods. I was out there that day when I ran into him. Right after he left, I used to meet him and try to talk some sense into him, but gradu-

76

ally I came to see that it wasn't going to do any good. I hadn't seen him for months before that day." She sighed. "I was surprised. He . . . he had stopped taking care of himself. When he first went out there, he built a cabin and lived in it, but he told me that day that he didn't go to the cabin anymore. He wouldn't say why, but I got the impression he thought it was a bad place for some reason. He had let his hair and his beard grow, and he would barely talk to me. He seemed frightened of everything. You see, Mr. Morgan, that's how I know he couldn't be guilty of the things everyone is saying he is. He's too scared to hurt anyone."

Frank knew she wanted to believe it, but he also knew that folks who are scared sometimes lash out at other people. If Ben Chamberlain really was the Terror of the Redwoods, maybe he was hurting people because he was afraid that *they* were going to hurt *him*. So he went after them first.

"But it wasn't long after that," Nancy went on, "when some of the loggers started talking about seeing a monster in the woods. I know it must be Ben. Before that, he had always been careful to avoid people. Something must have happened to change him . . . maybe whatever it was that made him afraid to go back to his cabin . . ."

"Maybe it changed him so that he's not as gentle and peaceful as you remember him," Frank suggested.

"No! I know my brother, Mr. Morgan. He's not capable of such violence."

For everybody who had ever gone loco and started killing, there was somebody who claimed it wasn't possible, Frank thought. Nancy might not want to believe it, but that didn't mean it wasn't true.

Still, maybe she was right, Frank thought. What if she was? If some of those bounty hunters came across a big, hairy fella in the woods who ran off when they spotted him, they would go after him and do their best to kill him. Frank had no doubt of that. If Ben Chamberlain was innocent, he didn't deserve that fate. Even if he was guilty, the idea of him being gunned down like a rabid animal didn't sit well with Frank.

And he sure didn't like the thought that somebody might chop the head off Ben's corpse, bring it back here to collect that ten grand in blood money, and haul it out of a sack right in front of Nancy.

But did he want to get more involved in this than he already was, when he'd just been passing through the area? Oregon was still waiting for him.

Oregon wasn't going anywhere, he reminded himself. It was just possible that Ben Chamberlain was innocent of the killings. In that case, somebody needed to find him and get him back safely to his father's house before the bounty hunters started taking potshots at him.

There was still one question he wanted an answer to before he agreed to help Nancy. "If you're so sure your brother is what they're calling the Terror," he said, "why haven't you told your father about it?"

"I have," she replied with a bitter twist of her mouth. "I told him about seeing Ben in the woods. He didn't believe me. You see, when Ben left, he didn't tell Father where he was going. Father thinks that Ben ran off to San Francisco or somewhere like that. He said that's probably where Ben is now, drinking and . . . and associating with loose women."

"No offense, Miss Chamberlain, but your father strikes me as a stubborn man."

She laughed, but there was no humor in the sound. "That's certainly true, Mr. Morgan." She looked intently at him. "But I think you can match him . . . if you want to. Will you do it? Will you find Ben and bring him back here, so I can keep him safe?"

79

"How do you know he won't just run off again?"

He could tell she hadn't thought about that. She was so worried that all she wanted was to have her brother back with her.

"I'll figure out something," she said. "I'll just have to find a way to make him listen to reason."

That might be easier said than done, Frank thought. But that part of it was her problem, not his.

"If it turns out he killed those men, he'll have to face justice for it," Frank warned her.

"I'll deal with that when the time comes, too," she said. What seemed to be her natural spirit was returning. She lifted her chin with a touch of defiance. "At least if he's here, or even in jail, he won't be shot down like an animal."

Frank didn't have any other questions to ask or arguments to make. He had to come to a decision, and as usual, he didn't brood over it. He knew instinctively what he had to do. With a nod, he said, "All right, Miss Chamberlain. I'll do my best to find your brother and bring him back here to you."

She reached out and put a hand on his arm. "Thank you so much, Mr. Morgan."

"Don't thank me yet. I haven't done anything."

"No, but if you tell my father that you'll take the job after all, he'll stop offering that bounty."

"I'll have to tell him that I'm going to kill the Terror to get him to do that."

Nancy smiled. "He doesn't have to know the truth, though. He'll see that I was right, once you bring Ben back here."

Frank hoped he got a chance to do that. With every hour that went by while the woods were full of bounty hunters, the odds against Ben Chamberlain's survival went up.

"I'll talk to your father, and I won't mention anything you told me," Frank said as he put his hat on. He didn't feel completely comfortable about deceiving Rutherford Chamberlain, but the man had already made up his mind about his son. Chamberlain wouldn't believe that Ben was the so-called Terror until he saw it with his own eyes.

"Thank you so much!" Impulsively, Nancy threw her arms around Frank and hugged him. He gave her an awkward pat on the back, well aware he was old enough to be her father. In fact, he was pretty sure that Conrad was several years older than Nancy.

His saddle might even be older than she was! He was glad when she stepped back and smiled up at him.

"There's one more thing," he said. "If I locate your brother, he's not going to know me, and he probably won't listen to me, even if I tell him that you sent me to find him. Is there anything he'd know, something I could tell him or some object he'd recognize, so he'd be more likely to believe me?"

Nancy frowned in thought for a moment, then reached behind her neck. Frank realized after a second that she was unfastening the clasp of a necklace. She took it off, pulling a small locket out from under her dress. As she pressed the necklace and locket into his palm, he felt the warmth that the metal had taken on from being nestled next to her skin.

"Ben gave me that," she said. "His picture is in it. If . . . if there's anything left of the person he used to be, he'll recognize it."

Frank nodded as he tucked the chain and locket into his shirt pocket. "That sounds like just what I need."

He opened the door of the sitting room and looked out into the foyer. It was empty at the moment. As he started toward the library, the butler stepped into the hall at the far end. Dennis raised white eyebrows in surprise.

"I came back to talk to Mr. Chamberlain," Frank said. He glanced toward the sitting room door, which was still open a crack. Nancy smiled gratefully at him through the gap.

"I'll see if he's willing to speak to you again, sir," Dennis said. He knocked quietly on one of the library doors, then went in. A moment later, he reappeared. "Please come in, Mr. Morgan."

Frank was glad that Chamberlain had agreed to see him again. They hadn't left things on a very cordial basis.

Chamberlain was behind the big desk in the library. "What is it, Morgan?" he snapped.

Frank didn't beat around the bush. "I've changed my mind," he said. "I'll take the job."

Chamberlain's rather bushy eyebrows lowered in a frown. "You'll find the Terror and kill it?"

Frank didn't like to lie, but he had made a promise to Nancy Chamberlain. He thought about the lines of worry he had seen etched on her pretty face, then said, "That's right."

Chamberlain leaned back in his chair. "May I ask what prompted this reversal?"

"I decided it was more important that you lift the bounty and get all those trigger-happy fools out of the woods."

"And I suppose the ten thousand dollars had nothing to do with it?"

Frank shrugged. Let the old buzzard think whatever he wanted to.

Chamberlain stood up and came around the desk. "I'm surprised by this, Morgan, and I don't mind admitting it. I thought you were too stiff-necked to admit that you were wrong. But I'm glad you changed your mind. I'll put out the word about the bounty being lifted immediately, but it may take some time for it to reach everyone who's looking for the Terror."

"Make it as fast as you can," Frank said.

"Of course." Chamberlain stuck out his hand. "We have a deal."

Frank shook with the timber baron and said, "We have a deal."

He hoped it was one that would bring an end to the bloodshed in the redwoods.

CHAPTER 7

Chamberlain offered him a drink to seal the bargain, but Frank refused as politely as possible. He wasn't much of a drinker to start with, preferring a good cup of coffee instead, and he wanted to get started on this job as soon as possible.

"Send a man into Eureka to spread the word about lifting the bounty," Frank suggested. "If you've put up reward posters, have him take them down."

Chamberlain frowned, clearly not liking it that Frank was giving him orders. But he said, "Very well. I'll take care of it this afternoon."

Frank nodded and turned toward the door.

Behind him, Chamberlain said, "Bring me his head, Morgan. Bring me the damn creature's head."

Frank didn't say anything, didn't turn. He just stood there for a second, jaw clenched, before he went out and closed the library door behind him.

Chamberlain didn't know what he was asking for. All he knew was that something was killing his men and threatening his business. At least, that was all he would admit, even to himself. No wonder he felt the way he did.

Dennis was waiting in the corridor. He followed Frank all the way to the front door of the bizarre redwood mansion this time. The two horses and Dog were right where Frank had left them. Dog probably hadn't moved since he sat down. His tail thumped against the ground, though, when Frank stepped out of the house and started down the steps from the porch.

The gunman called Rockwell lounged nearby on a wrought-iron bench that didn't look the least bit comfortable. A quirly dangled from his lips. He took it out, stood up, and sauntered over while Frank was untying his horses' reins.

"You were in there quite a while," he commented. "Strike a deal with the old man?"

"As a matter of fact, I did. I'm going to hunt down the Terror, and Chamberlain's going to call off the bounty."

Rockwell's eyebrows rose in surprise. "You got him to back down? I didn't think that

86

was possible."

"I offered him an arrangement he liked better, that's all."

Rockwell took another drag on the smoke. "I can tell you who's *not* going to like it. All those hombres who've started wandering around in the woods looking for monsters. They all think they're going to be the one to kill the Terror and collect that ten grand."

"Chamberlain's going to send someone to town to spread the word." Frank swung up in the saddle. "And I'd appreciate it if you'd pass it along, too, Rockwell."

The gunman shrugged his narrow shoulders. "Sure. Some of the boys have been going out into the woods to do some hunting during their spare time. I'll tell them not to bother anymore."

Frank rested his hands on the saddle horn and looked down at Rockwell. "Something else I'm wondering about . . . why does Chamberlain need to hire so many bodyguards?"

"He's a rich man. Rich men have enemies. Chamberlain does especially. You ever hear of Emmett Bosworth?"

Frank pondered the question and then shook his head. "Can't say as I have."

"He's the boss's biggest competitor. He's got the second biggest logging operation in northern California . . . and he'd like to have the biggest. Bosworth's managed to get some leases that Chamberlain wanted to get his hands on. Those two gents don't cotton to each other."

Frank wasn't surprised. No matter what a man's business, he always had competitors. And if he was ruthless enough to be successful, which Rutherford Chamberlain obviously was, those competitors often became sworn enemies. Frank had seen it in mining, ranching, and every other business there was.

Including the business of being a fast gun.

"So Chamberlain's worried that this fella Bosworth might try to move in on him?"

"Yeah. There have already been some squabbles between logging crews over lease boundaries. That's when Chamberlain brought in me and Cobb and the other boys. All that's sort of faded out over the past six months —"

"Since the Terror showed up," Frank said.

"Yeah. The loggers are all more worried about the monster than they are about Bosworth. But Chamberlain kept us on anyway, since he figures he'll have more trouble with Bosworth sooner or later."

Frank nodded. Chamberlain was probably right about that. Greed, ambition, call it whatever you wanted to, it was a powerful force that was seldom denied for long.

But Frank had a more pressing problem, finding and capturing the Terror, and once that was done and he'd kept his promise to Nancy Chamberlain, The Drifter would be riding on. He wasn't going to get involved in any timber war.

Frank turned Stormy's head and lifted a hand in farewell to Rockwell as he rode away. He wasn't exactly sure where he was going, but he knew he wouldn't be able to catch the Terror here on Chamberlain's estate. If Nancy was right and the creature really was her brother, Ben would probably avoid his father's house. And if Nancy was wrong, if the Terror was some sort of mindless, animalistic monster, instinct would keep it from coming too close to the haunts of man. The trouble had started when the logging crews began to make their way deeper into the woods.

Frank knew where the Terror had been earlier in the day. He had seen the grisly evidence with his own eyes, heard the screams of the men being torn apart. He turned Stormy toward the south and rode slowly back the way he had come. Picking up the trail of the creature would be a long shot, but Frank was willing to give it a try.

Considering everything he had seen earlier in the day, he wouldn't have been surprised if he'd found more mutilated bodies, but the forest seemed to be quiet and peaceful again. He heard an odd sound in the distance, but after a few minutes he figured out that it was the *chunk! chunk!* of ax blades biting deep into tree trunks. A logging crew was at work somewhere within hearing distance, but in this dense redwood jungle, it was impossible to tell how far away or even exactly which direction the sounds came from.

After a while, Frank found the camp where he had first encountered the creature's bloody handiwork. After loading up the bodies to take them to Eureka, Karl Wilcox and the other loggers hadn't returned, so the place looked almost like it had when Frank left it. The campfire in its ring of stones had burned down and gone out, but not before boiling the coffee dry and scorching the bottom of the pot.

The frying pan was the big difference, though. The bacon and biscuits that had been in it earlier were gone. Somebody had come along and helped himself — or itself — to the food.

Frank dismounted and hunkered next to the ashes. He called Dog over and said,

"Take a whiff, boy. See what you smell around here."

Dog circled the dead fire with his nose to the ground, pausing halfway around the ring of stones to lift his head and gaze off to the west. Frank knew that the Pacific Ocean lay only a few miles in that direction, the endless waves washing in over jagged rocks that lay at the bottom of steep cliffs. Between here and the sea, though, lay thousands of acres of thickly timbered woodland where the Terror could be hiding.

Frank stood up and grasped Stormy's reins again. "All right, big fella," he told Dog. "Trail!"

Dog set off through the trees while Frank mounted up. He followed the big cur, leading Goldy. Dog didn't range too far ahead, but even so, there were times when Frank couldn't see him. He followed the crackling sounds of Dog's passage through the undergrowth.

As the brush thickened, the going became even slower and more difficult. Frank would have thought that the lack of direct sunlight under the towering redwoods would have kept other vegetation from growing so well, but obviously, these hardy plants had adapted.

After half an hour or so, Frank and Dog

and the horses emerged from the woods, coming out into an open, parklike area about fifty yards wide. Beyond it, a rocky ridge jutted up about a hundred feet. Part of it formed a sheer cliff. Redwoods lined the top of the cliff, growing right to the edge. At the base of it lay a tumbled mass of broken trunks and branches.

It took Frank a moment to figure out what had happened. Over the centuries, erosion had eaten away at the cliff face, so that some of the trees on top of it had lost their anchorage and fallen. Lightning strikes or windstorms might have toppled some of the other redwoods. The debris formed by those natural occurrences had scattered along the base of the cliff to form a maze of sorts, as if giant fingers had flung down a handful of matches and let them fall where they might. In places the trees had stacked like make-shift walls.

Dog turned and started northward, still following the scent that had brought them this far, and Frank was about to follow him when something about the jumbled tree trunks along the cliff caught his attention.

"Wait a minute, Dog," he said. "I want to take a look over there."

Dog looked in the direction he'd been going and whined, then turned and came back, as if he were humoring Frank. That brought a grin to The Drifter's face. Dog was a stubborn old cuss, sort of like Frank himself. Maybe that was one reason they got along so well.

When Frank reached the edge of the tumbled-down tree trunks, he reined in and dismounted. Leaving Stormy's reins dangling because he knew the rangy gray stallion wouldn't wander off, he started into the tangle of logs on foot.

He hadn't gone very far before he realized what had caught his attention over here. Somebody had stacked up broken branches, some of which were as big around as the trunk of a regular tree, as well as the upper sections of the redwoods, which were much narrower than the bases, and made walls out of them. Those walls formed a crude cabin built up against the cliff face. From a distance, it looked natural and blended in with the rest of the jumbled logs.

Densely intertwined branches formed the roof. Whoever had built this dwelling had left an open space for the door. An old blanket hung over it.

Frank slid his Colt from its holster. Nancy Chamberlain had mentioned that her brother Ben had built a cabin for himself when he left home and moved to the woods.

Was this it?

And more importantly, was this the lair of the Terror?

Frank moved closer, the heavy revolver gripped tightly in his hand. When he was about ten feet from the blanket-covered doorway, he called, "Hello, the cabin! Anybody home?"

There was no response from inside. Frank said, "Ben! Ben Chamberlain!"

Still nothing.

Dog had come up behind him. The big cur pressed against Frank's leg. Frank felt Dog's muscles trembling, and knew it wasn't from fear, but rather from the desire to explore inside that cave-like structure.

"All right, Dog," Frank said quietly. "Check it out."

Dog bounded forward and pushed past the blanket to disappear into the cabin. Frank stalked closer, ready to go in with his gun blazing if he heard any commotion.

Instead, a few moments later Dog reappeared. A few cobwebs clung to his wolf-like face, as if he had pushed his nose into some dusty, empty hole.

"Nothing, huh?"

Frank pushed the blanket aside with his left hand, thrust the gun in front of him with his right. Although the afternoon was well

94

advanced now and the sun would soon be dipping toward the horizon, enough light still spilled through the doorway for Frank to be able to see as he looked around the inside of the cabin.

There was only one room. Whoever had built the place had dug a fire pit in the ground in the center and left some openings above it in the thatched roof for the smoke to drift out. On one side of the room was a crude bed, little more than some blankets piled up on some branches. Had to be uncomfortable as hell, Frank thought as he looked at it.

On the other side of the room was the only real sign that a civilized person had ever lived here. An old wooden trunk with a curved lid sat there. Leather straps ran around it, but the leather was rotting now. It had brass corners and a brass latch, all of which were tarnished and dull. Frank went over to it and lifted the lid. He had no idea what he would find inside.

A frown creased his forehead as he saw that the trunk was empty except for a few books. The scent of mildew drifted up to his nose. The books had gotten wet at some point in the past, and they were moldering away now. He holstered his gun and knelt in front of the trunk, reached inside to pick up one of the leather-bound volumes.

The smell was even stronger as he opened the book. He saw words written on the flyleaf. Moisture had caused the ink to run, but the writing was still legible.

Property of Benjamin Andrew Chamberlain.

That pretty well answered his question about whether or not this was Ben's cabin, thought Frank. Out of curiosity, he turned the pages to the title page. *Five Weeks in a Balloon*, by Jules Verne. Frank smiled. He had read this one, too, and he was willing to bet that this particular copy had come from the library in Rutherford Chamberlain's mansion. Maybe that edition of *Twenty Thousand Leagues Under the Sea* had belonged to Ben, too.

Frank put the book back and stood up, carefully closing the trunk's lid. Maybe the trunk and the books inside it were rotting away, but they belonged to Ben Chamberlain and Frank made it a habit to respect other folks' property. He could come back for them, though, and take them to the Chamberlain mansion once he had returned Ben himself to that redwood edifice.

He took a quick look around the rest of the cabin. His boot prints and Dog's tracks were the only marks that disturbed the hard-packed dirt floor. No one had been here recently. That agreed with what Nancy had told him about her brother avoiding the cabin that had once been his home in the woods.

Ben had hacked several cubbyholes into the cliff face, probably using a hammer and chisel and enlarging openings that were already there. Frank could see the marks of the tools on the rock. The young man must have used them for storage of some sort, but they were empty now except for cobwebs. That explained how Dog had gotten the silky strands stuck on his muzzle. He might have smelled the last vestiges of food scent in some of them and stuck his nose in to see what was there.

Satisfied that he had seen everything there was to see, Frank turned toward the doorway. He stopped when he spotted something else from the corner of his eye, a flash of white from the corner where the crude bunk was. Something was wedged up between the branches and the cabin wall. He went over and knelt to reach in and pull it out. The shadows were starting to grow thick in here now, so he couldn't see very well. He thought maybe what he'd seen was a piece of paper.

Instead, what his fingers encountered was a smooth cylinder of some sort, maybe an inch or a little more in diameter. It had a slight curve to it, he realized as he closed his hand around it and started working it past the branches.

His jaw tightened and his breath hissed between his teeth when he pulled the thing out and saw that it was a bone. He was no expert on anatomy, but he was pretty sure it was an arm bone from a human being.

A sudden sick feeling made Frank's stomach clench. Still holding the bone, he stood up and moved closer to the doorway so the light would be better. He studied the thing closely, hardly wanting to admit, even to himself, that he was looking for teeth marks.

A feeling of relief went through him as he realized the bone was still smooth. The flesh and sinew were gone, but they had been stripped away by insects rather than *gnawed* off. That made him feel a little better.

Still, he couldn't help but wnder how a man's arm bone had come to be here in this cabin that had belonged to Ben Chamberlain. Was it Ben's bone? Was Nancy's brother dead after all, as Frank had warned her that he might be? Or had the bone come from somebody else?

He had no way of answering those questions right now, and the fading light reminded him that night would be falling soon. He wasn't a superstitious man, but clearly there was *something* in these woods that was dangerous, and he didn't particularly want to spend the night out here. He had a pretty good idea which way Eureka was from here. He would head for town, find a hotel room, and ride out here to take up the search for the Terror again the next morning.

Frank went over to the trunk, opened it again, and put the bone inside with the books. He would figure out what to do with it later, when he had a better idea who it belonged to.

"Come on, Dog," he said to the big cur. "I don't want to spend the night out here, and I don't reckon you do either."

Frank pushed the blanket aside and stepped out of the cabin. As he did so, Dog growled. That warning was enough to make Frank lift his head and look around, and as he did so, he caught a glimpse of orange flame in the shadows under the trees on the other side of the clearing. At the same time, the wicked crack of a rifle shattered the peace of the late afternoon.

CHAPTER 8

Frank heard the bullet's whine as it went past his ear. The slug smacked into the cabin wall behind him and chewed splinters from it, showering them in the air.

Frank could have retreated into the cabin, but then he would have been pinned down there. Instead, he threw himself to the left, into the jumble of fallen trees. He crouched behind one of the massive redwood trunks, safe for the moment from the hidden rifleman's fire. Bullets wouldn't ricochet among these trees, as they might have if he had taken shelter in a cluster of boulders.

Dog was right next to him, having followed his lead. Stormy and Goldy were still out in the open, though, and Frank worried that the bushwhacker might turn his gun on the horses next.

"Hyyaahh!" he shouted at them. "Get out of here, you jugheads!"

The horses turned and dashed away. They

were accustomed to gunshots, but they knew how to get out of the line of fire, too.

Of course, that left Frank on foot for the moment, but that couldn't be helped.

Staying low, he worked his way through the fallen trees, putting some distance between himself and the last place the bushwhacker had seen him, right in front of Ben Chamberlain's cabin. The hidden gunman hadn't fired since that first shot, but Frank's instincts told him the man was still out there, just waiting for another crack at him.

He took his hat off so that its white crown wouldn't give away his position, and slowly raised his head until he could peer through an open space among the tree trunks. Fifty yards was mighty long range for a handgun, but he thought that with luck and good aim, he could reach the trees on the other side of the clearing where the bushwhacker was hidden. He needed to get a little better idea of where the man was, though.

Still holding his hat in his left hand, Frank slowly raised it and moved it in a slightly jerky, up-and-down motion from right to left, as if it were on his head while he was creeping along behind the trees. It was an old trick, but the reason it had been around for so long was that it usually worked.

Another shot blasted from across the clearing. Frank flung the hat away from him like it had been hit, even though the bullet had missed. He had spotted the muzzle flash from the bushwhacker's rifle. Of course, the man might not stay in the same place. But that was all Frank had to go by, so he lined up his shot, figuring windage and elevation and distance with the instinctive skill of a man who had been using his guns for decades and was still alive.

He squeezed the trigger.

The Colt roared and bucked in his hand. He couldn't see where the shot landed, but the rifle across the clearing suddenly started barking rapidly, the bushwhacker triggering rounds as fast as he could work the weapon's lever. Frank ducked lower as splinters rained around him. A grim smile tugged at his mouth. He had come close enough to shake the son of a buck up anyway.

After a couple of minutes, the rifle fell silent. Frank crawled about ten yards to his left and found another gap in the trees big enough for him to peer through. He saw a flicker of movement under the trees opposite him, and a moment later, he heard the swift rataplan of hoofbeats. The sound faded quickly into the distance.

A trick of some sort, or had the bushwhacker really lit a shuck out of there? Once Frank had forted up in the fallen trees, the man might have decided that killing him was going to be more trouble than it was worth, and riskier, too. Frank retrieved his hat and then waited where he was. Patience had kept him alive more than once during the long, rugged years.

The sun set during the next fifteen minutes. By then, the light was bad enough that Frank risked moving out from his cover behind the trees. He whistled, and Stormy and Goldy came trotting up a moment later. He grabbed Stormy's reins and swung into the saddle.

"Let's get out of here," he said to his trail partners. "It'll be dark by the time we make it to Eureka."

Actually, it was dark well before that. Frank, Dog, and the two horses were still deep in the woods when the last of the light faded away, to be replaced by thick, shrouding shadows. Frank had been underground once in a cave where there was no light at all. It wasn't quite that utterly dark under the trees, because a faint glow from the stars filtered down through the leafy canopy. But it was dark enough he couldn't see his hand in front of his face, and that was the truth.

He couldn't hear anything except the

hoofbeats of his horses either, as they picked their way along. He had to trust Stormy's instincts and let the stallion find his own path, because he couldn't see well enough to guide the horse. Luckily, the redwood branches didn't start growing out from the trunks below a height of eighty or ninety feet, so he didn't have to worry about an unseen branch knocking him out of the saddle.

After a while, Stormy started moving a little faster. The gray light from the stars increased, too, and when Frank tilted his head back and looked up, he could actually see some of the little glowing pinpricks in the heavens above him. The tree canopy had thinned. There was a good reason for that. Frank realized that they were on a road now, more than likely one of the logging trails that Chamberlain's crews had cut into the forest. From what he could see of the stars, he thought he was headed northeast, which would take him toward Eureka.

Suddenly, he reined in sharply as a sound came from somewhere behind him in the towering trees where he had been until a short time earlier. It was like the howl of an animal, but he had never heard a wolf or anything else that sounded exactly like the guttural scream that floated through the forest. It went on for a long moment, finally trailing off into a series of fading, yelping cries. It wasn't a howl of pain or anger or anything else that Frank could pin down.

All he knew was that it was one of the loneliest sounds he had ever heard.

And that he was damned glad he wasn't back there in the woods with whatever had made it.

"Come on, horse," he said as he heeled Stormy into motion. "Let's get on to town."

Eureka was a large enough settlement so that Frank saw the lights of the place well before he reached it. Located on Humboldt Bay, Eureka was the center of the logging industry in this part of northern California. Frank could tell it was a prosperous town by the number of two- and three-story brick buildings he saw as he rode down the main street. The street was paved with cobblestones. It had to be. Otherwise in this rainy climate, it would be a morass of mud most of the time.

Frank saw an impressive sign that read CHAMBERLAIN LOGGING COMPANY on an even more impressive brick building. Given the house where Rutherford Chamberlain lived, Frank was a little surprised the company headquarters wasn't built out of redwood, too.

He could also tell that Eureka was where the loggers came when they wanted to blow off some of the steam that built up because of their grueling, perilous profession. He passed the Bull o' the Woods Saloon, the Redwood Saloon, and the High Climber's Saloon. A place that discreetly called itself the Woodsman's Retreat had a red light burning in the window, so it was pretty obvious why the woodsmen retreated there. Like any boomtown, no matter whether the cause for the boom was gold, oil, or timber, Eureka was a mixture of high finance and low vice.

Frank was hungry, but he wanted to find a place for his horses and a hotel room for himself before he went looking for a café. He stopped at the first stable he came to, Patterson's Livery and Wagon Yard. The proprietor, a stocky man with a short, reddish-brown beard, came out of the barn wiping his hands on a rag and greeted Frank with a friendly nod.

"Those are some mighty fine-lookin' horses, mister," he said. "You lookin' for a place to keep 'em for the night?"

"That's right. You have room?"

"Sure do. You'll be gettin' the last two empty stalls, though."

Frank dismounted. "My dog's used to staying with the horses. Is that all right?"

The liveryman's eyes narrowed a little. "Is that a dog or a wolf?"

"He's a dog," Frank said with a chuckle. "In fact, his name is Dog."

"Reckon I'll take your word for it. As long as he's tame and don't bother the other horses, he can stay here."

Frank nodded. "He won't cause any trouble."

The man reached for Stormy's reins. "I can unsaddle for you."

"Better let me," Frank said with a shake of his head. "This old hellion's been known to take a bite out of a man's hide when he wasn't looking. He sometimes takes a notion to kick, too."

"One-man horse, eh? Well, you go right ahead. Plenty of grain in the bin. We didn't talk about the price."

"No need. I'm sure it'll be fine. You don't strike me as a man who's in the habit of overcharging anybody."

Frank led the horses along the barn's center aisle to the two empty stalls. He unsaddled and rubbed down Stormy, then made sure that both horses had plenty of water and grain. The liveryman watched Frank tending to the animals and commented, "You take good care of those crit-ters, mister. Treat 'em like friends."

"They *are* my friends," Frank said. "I tend to travel around a lot. Spend more time with them than anybody else."

"I live out back. Got a soup bone in the kitchen that dog of yours can have, if that's all right."

Frank nodded. "We'd be obliged. And if you can point me to the best place in town to stay, and to get a good meal, I'd be obliged for that, too."

"Sure. The Eureka House is the nicest hotel, or so I've heard. They're supposed to have a good dining room, too, or you can go across the street to Harrigan's Restau-rant. Or if you don't care about fancy and just want some good food, there's a hash house down by the Bull o' the Woods Saloon that's run by a Chinaman who's a mighty good cook. You won't go hungry in Eureka, that's for sure."

"Good to know," Frank said with a grin. "I've kind of gotten in the habit of eating."

He got directions to the Eureka House, then left the stable and set off up the street carrying his saddlebags slung over his shoulder and his Winchester in his left hand. He saw a large number of wagons parked in front of various buildings, but not too many saddle horses tied up at the hitch racks. Nor did he pass many people dressed like he was. Most of the pedestrians were either townsmen or loggers. This wasn't ranching country.

The looks that he got from the people in the lobby of the Eureka House reminded him of that as he walked toward the desk with his spurs jingling. The men wore expensive suits and had pomaded hair. The women wore gowns with bustles and had their hair piled high on their heads in elaborate arrangements of curls.

Frank didn't care. He got the same sort of reaction every time he walked into a hotel in Denver or San Francisco, and those towns were a lot bigger than Eureka.

Still, if he told the truth, he'd have to admit that he got a little satisfaction out of the expression on the face of the clerk when he set the Winchester on the desk in front of him and said, "I'd like a room, please."

The clerk swallowed. "Do you intend to keep that weapon in the hotel?"

"That's right," Frank said. "A room for me *and* my Winchester."

The man turned to glance behind him. "I'm not sure if we have anything available . . ."

Frank saw several keys hanging on their

pegs. "I'll bet you do," he said. He took a fifty-dollar gold piece out of his pocket and slapped it on the desk. "Why don't you check and see?"

The man's eyes widened at the sight of the coin. He pretended to turn and look again, then said, "Why, ah, I believe we *do* have a room available, sir."

"I thought you might," Frank said dryly.

The clerk turned the register around. Frank signed his name, and in the space for where he was from, he wrote *San Francisco*. That wasn't exactly true — he wasn't really from anywhere anymore, since he was always on the drift — but some of his lawyers had offices in San Francisco, so that was as good a place to put down as any.

"Will you be staying with us long, Mister . . ." The clerk checked the register. "Morgan?"

"That depends. Keep that fifty and let me know if it runs out."

"Of course. Do you have a preference as far as rooms go? We have one overlooking the street . . ."

So now the hombre was asking his preferences. The sight of a gold coin usually made quite a difference.

"If you have anything on the back, I'd rather be there. Quieter, you know."

"Yes, sir, certainly. Room Twelve should do you nicely." The clerk took the key and handed it to Frank. "Do you need any help with your, ah, belongings?"

"No, thanks." Frank picked up the Winchester. "I reckon I can manage."

"All right then. Take the stairs to the balcony and go along it to a hallway. You'll find Room Twelve down that corridor."

"Much obliged."

"We have an excellent dining room, if you haven't eaten."

Frank nodded. "I've heard about that. But I was thinking maybe I'd try the Chinaman's hash house instead."

He ought to be ashamed of himself, he thought as he turned toward the stairs, hoorawing the poor, pasty-faced gent like that.

He had just started up the stairs when the clerk stopped him by calling, "Mr. Morgan?"

Frank turned. "Yeah?"

"Frank Morgan?" From the sound of it, the man hadn't really paid much attention to his name until now.

"That's right."

The man reached down to a shelf under the desk. Frank tensed. His right hand never strayed far from the butt of his Colt. Now he was ready to hook and draw if the clerk

111

brought a gun out from under the desk.

Instead of a gun, the man waved a small, thin book with a gaudy yellow cover in the air. "*This* Frank Morgan?"

"Oh, Lord," Frank muttered. "Are they still putting those things out?"

"Yes, sir. This is the new one. *The Drifter and the Battle of Tonto Basin* —"

"Those stories are all made up," Frank broke in. "I've been to the Tonto Basin, but I don't recall any battle while I was there."

That wasn't strictly true, but he was sure whoever had written that dime novel had done a heap of exaggerating and embellishing.

"But you *are* Frank Morgan, the famous gunfighter. I knew you were in the area. I heard some men talking about you earlier this evening." The clerk could barely contain his excitement now. "You've come to hunt down and kill the Terror of the Redwoods!"

He had told Rutherford Chamberlain to spread the word, Frank thought wryly. Obviously, the timber magnate had done so. Maybe that would put a stop to a bunch of trigger-happy monster hunters blundering around the woods, shooting at each other and anything else that moved.

"I'm here on business," he said to the clerk. "My business. Understand?"

112

"Yes, sir!"

Frank just shook his head and went on up the stairs. He had been dealing with fame — or rather, notoriety — for a long time now, and he didn't like it any better than he had when he first started getting a reputation as a fast gun.

He found his room, which appeared to be very comfortably furnished with a four-poster bed, dressing table, mahogany wardrobe, and a couple of armchairs. After washing up with the water in the basin on the dressing table, he left his saddlebags and rifle in the wardrobe and started back downstairs. He didn't think he would need the Winchester just to eat at the Chinaman's place.

When he reached the lobby, the clerk he had talked to only a few minutes earlier wasn't there anymore. He'd been replaced by an older man with thinning black hair and a mustache. Frank didn't ask where the other clerk had gone. The fella was probably out telling anybody who would listen to him how the infamous Frank Morgan was staying at the hotel.

Frank stepped out onto the porch and turned toward the Bull o' the Woods Saloon, the location of which he had noted earlier as he rode in. The proprietor over at the livery stable had said that the hash house was next to the saloon. Frank hadn't gone very far, though, when a man who'd been crossing the street stepped in front of him, blocking his path.

"Hold it right there, Morgan," the man snapped as his hand hovered over the butt of his gun. "You and me got some business to take care of."

CHAPTER 9

The man's aggressive stance made Frank instinctively want to reach for his own revolver, but the sight of the badge pinned to the stranger's vest prompted him to control the impulse. Despite what many star packers thought of him because of his reputation, he went out of his way to avoid trouble with the law.

"Marshal," Frank said with a nod. "What can I do for you?"

The lawman frowned. He was middle-aged, with a rugged face, slicked-back gray hair under his hat, and the beginnings of a gut under his vest and brown tweed suit.

"You know who I am?"

"I can read," Frank said. "Your badge says *Marshal*. U.S. or town?"

"Town," the man replied curtly. "Name's Gene Price. I'm the law here in Eureka."

"Pleased to meet you, Marshal. I reckon I don't have to introduce myself."

Price snorted. "You sure as hell don't. It's all over town how the famous gunslinger Frank Morgan's come here to hunt down that critter folks say is out in the woods."

"You don't believe in the Terror?" Frank asked, hearing the skepticism in Price's voice.

"I believe somebody has killed over a dozen men lately. I saw the bodies with my own eyes, down at the undertaker's. That's all I know for a fact. That, and it happened outside of my jurisdiction."

"So what do you want with me?" Frank was hungry, and he was starting to get a little impatient. "There's no law against getting some supper, is there? Because that's what I was on my way to do."

Price shook his head. "No, and I don't care what you do out in the woods. But I don't want you starting any gunfights here in my town, Morgan."

"Marshal . . . I never *start* gunfights."

Price's face flushed angrily, evidence that he understood the implication in Frank's words. "You know what I mean. You got a heap of blood on your hands. I don't want you getting any more on them while you're in Eureka."

"I never go looking for trouble. You have my word on that."

Price gave Frank a grudging nod. "We understand each other then." He started to turn away.

Frank stopped him. "Marshal, what can you tell me about Rutherford Chamberlain?"

A frown creased the lawman's forehead. "What do you want to know? He's the biggest businessman in these parts. I'm not saying that Eureka would dry up and blow away if it weren't for his logging operation, but I reckon he's mighty important around here."

"And Emmett Bosworth?"

Price looked even more suspicious. "Bosworth would like to be where Chamberlain is now. He's made a good start on it, too."

"Any trouble between their crews while they were here in town?"

"Some," Price admitted. "Not lately, though."

"Since the Terror showed up."

It wasn't a question, but Price treated it like one anyway. "That's right. Everybody who works in the woods is so nervous about whatever it is, they don't have the time or energy to squabble with each other."

That was interesting, thought Frank, and it agreed with what Rockwell had told him. But it didn't have any connection with the task he had taken on, at least as far as he could see. He had asked the question out of sheer curiosity. The next one was more pertinent.

"Do you know Ben Chamberlain?"

"Ben?" The lawman appeared to be more puzzled than ever. "Sure, I know Ben. Used to see him here in town every now and then, but he was never much of one for socializing. Kept to himself mostly. And I haven't seen him at all in . . . oh, hell, a couple of years now, I reckon. I've heard that he had some sort of falling-out with his pa and went off to live in San Francisco. That's just gossip, though. I can't say how true it is."

Frank suspected it wasn't true at all, but he didn't say that to Price. It might be better if folks around here continued thinking that Ben Chamberlain had gone to San Francisco after the argument with his father.

Price went on. "You're asking a lot of questions, mister, considering that you're working for Rutherford Chamberlain."

"I just like to know what I'm getting into, that's all."

"Whatever you get into, do it somewhere else besides here."

This time, Frank let the marshal stalk away without stopping him.

As he walked on down the street toward

118

the hash house, Frank thought about all the marshals and sheriffs over the years who had warned him not to start any trouble in their towns. They knew his reputation, and they weren't really interested in anything he had to say. He had never really understood that attitude until he had worn a badge himself. The time he had spent being responsible for the safety of his friends in Buckskin had taught him to be a little more tolerant of suspicious lawmen.

He spotted the eatery next to the boisterous Bull o' the Woods Saloon, which took up most of a block and had its entrance on a corner. A number of men in the calked boots, overalls, and flannel shirts of loggers stood on the boardwalk in front of the saloon's big windows. They wore solemn expressions as they talked among themselves, and several of them cast glances toward Frank as he approached. Elbows nudged into sides, and one by one the rest of the men turned their attention toward him, too.

Frank paused outside the door of the hash house and gave them a friendly nod. "Evening," he said.

None of the men responded. They just kept looking at him with blank or unfriendly stares.

Frank didn't know what that was about, but he was too hungry to worry about it. He went on into the hash house.

The place was long and narrow, with a counter on the right and a row of tables along the left-hand wall. Most of the tables were occupied, as were the stools in front of the counter. A swinging door at the end of it probably led into the kitchen.

A man with a round, friendly face worked be hind the counter. He was dark-haired, about thirty years old, and wore a white apron. Except for the slight slant of his eyes, he didn't really look Chinese. He smiled at Frank and waved him onto one of the empty stools.

"What can I do for you, mister?"

Frank glanced at the specials chalked onto a board on the wall behind the counter and said, "I'll have a bowl of stew and plenty of corn bread. Coffee hot?"

"You can bet that hat of yours that it is," the man assured him.

"Then fill a cup and keep it coming."

"Sure thing."

The man's voice didn't have a hint of an accent, but when he turned to a small open window behind the counter and called through it, he spoke in what sounded to Frank's ears like fluent Mandarin. Not that

Frank was an expert in Chinese dialects, but nearly thirty years earlier, he had spent some time in the Sierra Nevadas while hundreds of laborers from China had been building the Central Pacific Railroad through the mountains, and he had picked up a smattering of the lingo, just like he could speak a little of the tongues of several different Indian tribes, as well as a little German and French. Having grown up in Texas, though, he was better with Spanish than any other foreign language.

When the proprietor brought over a cup and saucer and the coffeepot, Frank said, "I'm Frank Morgan."

The man's eyebrows rose, but he didn't spill a drop as he poured the hot, black brew. "I've heard of you, Mr. Morgan," he said. "I suspect nearly everyone in Eureka has by this time. My name is Peter Lee."

Frank put out a hand. "Pleased to meet you, Peter. You sound like you've been in this country for a while."

"As far back as I can remember," Lee said as he shook hands. "Although I was born in China. I was two years old when my parents came here to work on the Central Pacific."

Frank nodded. "You grew up speaking English?"

"I did. You see, one of the supervisors took

me in when my father was killed in an accident only a couple of months after we got here. My mother . . ." Lee shrugged. "Well, I don't know what happened to her. She was gone by the time I was old enough to remember anything."

Frank took a sip of the coffee. "Some fellas might be a little bitter about that."

Lee shrugged and said, "I never knew any difference. The people who raised me were good folks. Taught me how to work hard and take care of myself."

"Looks like you're doing a fine job of it," Frank said with a meaningful nod at their surroundings.

"I do all right." The door at the end of the counter swung open, and a very attractive young Chinese woman came through it carrying a bowl of stew, which she placed in front of Frank. Peter Lee said, "My wife and our children help me run the place."

Frank nodded politely to the woman and tugged on the brim of his Stetson. "Mrs. Lee," he said. "It's a pleasure to meet you, ma'am."

She smiled and didn't say anything, just retreated back through the door into the kitchen.

Frank picked up the spoon Lee placed on the counter beside the bowl and dug in. The stew smelled good and tasted better. It was full of big chunks of beef, potatoes, carrots, wild onions, and spices. Lee brought over a plate with a big hunk of corn bread on it, and when Frank sampled that, it was equally as good.

"What brings you to Eureka, Mr. Morgan?" Lee asked as he leaned on the counter. "As if I didn't know."

"You've heard about it, eh?"

"You're the talk of the town tonight. Some people are glad that a man with your reputation is going after the Terror, while others are upset that Mr. Chamberlain isn't offering that ten-thousand-dollar bounty anymore. And some of the loggers think that it would be better to have a lot of people hunting the monster, instead of just one man."

"What do you think, Mr. Lee?"

The man shrugged. "Until that so-called Terror comes in here and sits down at my counter, it's not really any of my business, is it?"

"It can't be good for your trade if it starts to cut into the logging that's going on around here."

"That hasn't happened . . . yet."

But it would eventually, Frank thought, if the men who worked in the woods kept dying. That was something to ponder.

He wasn't in much of a mood for pondering at the moment, though. He'd been shot at several times today, as well as having that ruckus with Cobb at Chamberlain's redwood mansion. All he wanted to do right now was sit here and eat some of Mrs. Lee's excellent beef stew and corn bread.

Lee moved off along the counter to refill other coffee cups, leaving Frank alone with his meal. For the next few minutes, he ate with great enjoyment.

He should have known the peaceful respite wouldn't last. It had been his experience that they never did. Because of that, he wasn't really surprised when the door of the hash house opened and several men clumped into the long, narrow room. Frank glanced at them, saw that three of the newcomers were dressed in range clothes, while the other three were loggers.

"Morgan," said one of the men in range garb, "I want to talk to you."

This hombre didn't have a badge like Marshal Price, so Frank didn't see any good reason to talk to him. He spooned more stew into his mouth, took a bite of the corn bread.

The man who had spoken took a step closer. "Damn it, I'm talkin' to you, Morgan. You deaf?"

Without looking at the man, Frank said, "I just want to enjoy my supper, friend, and having to kill you would put a serious crimp in those plans."

"Why, you —"

Even though Frank seemed casual, didn't even appear to be paying any attention to the man, the slightest move toward a gun would have sent him into a blur of deadly motion. Instead, one of the other men stepped forward and brushed the belligerent one back.

"Take it easy, Dawson. I'll handle this."

He was the biggest of the bunch, even bigger than the burly loggers. Long, dark red hair fell from under a high-crowned brown Stetson, and he sported a beard of the same hue.

"Listen, Morgan," he said. "My name's Erickson. Maybe you've heard of me."

Frank took a sip of coffee. "Can't say as I have."

That nonchalant comment made Erickson's jaw clench for a second, but he controlled his obvious anger.

"The talk's all around town about how you're gonna hunt down the Terror. Because of you, Rutherford Chamberlain took back that bounty he put on the monster. We don't like that. My friends and I planned on finding that critter ourselves."

"That's too bad," Frank said, not meaning it at all. "But you probably just would've gotten yourselves killed by other fellas who were out there hunting for the Terror."

"That's our lookout, not yours," Erickson snapped. "Not only that, but you killed Jingo Reed and busted Matt Sewell's shoulder so that he'll never be the same again. Jingo and Matt were good men. Friends of mine."

Frank didn't really believe that. Hardcases like Erickson appeared to be didn't have many real friends. Erickson was just using what had happened to them as an excuse to pick a fight with Frank.

"You ride out in the morning and keep going," Erickson went on. "Leave this part of California. Leave the Terror to us. You do that, and we'll let what happened to Jingo and Matt slide . . . this time."

"And if I'm not interested in doing that?"

Erickson grinned. "You'll be sorry."

Peter Lee had come back to stand on the other side of the counter from Frank. He leaned forward and said in a low voice, "Please, Mr. Morgan. If there's a gunfight in here, innocent people might be hurt. That wall between us and my family isn't thick enough to stop a bullet."

126

Frank glanced around. All the other customers in the place looked as nervous as its proprietor. Some of them probably would have made a break for the door by now if the six big men hadn't been blocking it.

"There's not going to be a gunfight," Frank told Lee with a shake of his head.

Erickson heard what he said. "You're gonna get out of town?"

"Nope. But you're not going to make me draw on you either." A faint smile touched Frank's lips. "I promised the marshal I wouldn't kill anybody in his town if I could help it."

"You son of a bitch." Erickson strode forward. "So you're not going to draw on me, are you?"

"No. I'm not."

Erickson reached over and picked up the coffee cup that Frank had set down on the counter. The cup was still about half full. Erickson tilted it as if he were about to pour the coffee on Frank's head.

The Drifter's hand shot up and clamped around Erickson's wrist, the fingers closing like iron bands. Erickson's eyes widened with surprise at the strength of Frank's grip. A man as big as he was probably hadn't run into too many hombres brave enough to take him on in a hand-to-hand battle.

127

But he had never run into Frank Morgan before.

"I said I wasn't going to get in a gunfight with you," Frank told him. "I never said anything about not beating the hell out of you if you want to push it that far."

Erickson's lips drew back from his teeth in a furious grimace. He let go of the cup. It fell toward the counter. Peter Lee made a grab for it, caught it so that while most of the coffee splashed out, the cup didn't shatter.

At the same time, Erickson threw a piledriver punch with his other hand. It might have connected, if not for the fact that Frank squeezed the other wrist with such force that the bones ground together. Erickson flinched and leaned in the direction of the agonizing pain, and that threw his aim off. Frank ducked the punch, hammered a blow of his own into Erickson's midsection. The air gusted out of Erickson's lungs and his normally florid face turned gray. He stumbled back a step as Frank let go of his wrist. That put him in position for the sharp, crossing left that Frank slammed into his jaw. Still seated on the stool in front of the counter, Frank brought his right leg up, planted his booted foot in Erickson's belly, and shoved him hard. Erickson flew backward to crash down in a heap at the feet of the men who had come into the hash house with him.

Those men were staring in shock, because the whole altercation had happened so fast that it was hard for their eyes to follow it. They knew that Erickson had landed on the floor, though, something that never happened in a fracas.

Erickson looked up, hate burning in his eyes as he glared at Frank. "Get the bastard!" he rasped.

The other men surged forward, and the battle was on.

CHAPTER 10

The loudmouth called Dawson led the charge. He came at Frank swinging wild punches. Frank stood up and grabbed the stool he'd been sitting on, raising it sharply with the legs pointed at Dawson so that the man's momentum carried him right into them. Dawson said, *"Ooof!"* and doubled over as the stool legs jabbed into his belly.

Frank dropped the stool and clouted Dawson on the jaw with a hard, looping right. The punch drove Dawson to the floor, where the next man to attack, one of the loggers, tripped over him and fell forward. Frank was ready for him, meeting him with a left jab that made blood spurt from the man's nose as it pulped under Frank's fist. The logger howled in pain and fell to his knees.

The space between the counter and the tables was narrow enough so that all of Frank's opponents couldn't charge him at the same time. That went a long way toward evening up the odds.

The men who'd been eating supper in the hash house scrambled to get out of the way as the last man in range clothes and one of the other two loggers bulled their way around their fallen comrade, knocking over one of the tables as they did so. Food flew in the air. The man in range clothes grabbed a chair and lifted it over his head as he rushed in. Frank snatched the stool from the floor again and used it to block the chair as it descended. That bone-jarring impact snapped the legs off the chair.

"Stop it!" Peter Lee cried. "Please don't bust up my place!"

Frank felt bad about what was happening, but these men had sought him out and started the trouble. He was defending himself. And he would see to it that Lee got paid for the damages, one way or another.

The man who had wound up holding two broken chair legs came at Frank, slashing back and forth with the makeshift clubs. Frank had to give ground as he tried to fend off the blows with the stool he still held. Recklessly, his opponent came too close, so when Frank saw his opportunity, he lifted his leg and kicked the man in the groin. Better a pair of sore balls than a bullet.

The man screeched in pain and dropped the broken chair legs as he clutched at himself. He toppled to the floor and curled up in agony.

That still left three men on their feet, though, because Erickson had managed to get up again. With his jutting red beard and the long hair streaming around his face because his hat had fallen off, he looked like a berserk Viking as he came at Frank with an incoherent cry of rage. Frank dropped the stool again and bent over to let Erickson's wild, flailing punches sail harmlessly over his head. He drove forward, burying a shoulder in Erickson's midsection. As the big gunman's momentum carried him forward over Frank's back, Frank grabbed him around the thighs and lifted.

It was quite a feat of strength, demonstrating just how much power there really was in Frank's muscular body. Erickson came completely off the floor and turned a flip as Frank heaved the man over his back. Erickson came down with a crash that seemed to shake the whole building.

That left two of the loggers facing Frank, and they hesitated now as Erickson rolled onto his side, tried to push himself up, and failed. With a sigh, Erickson slumped back down and lay still.

One of the loggers held his hands palms out toward Frank. "That's enough, mister," he said. The man looked at the bodies scattered along the counter in various stages of pain and semiconsciousness. "By God, that's enough."

Frank's chest rose and fell quickly from the exertion of the past few minutes, but his voice was steady as he said, "You boys called the tune. If you don't want to dance to it, that's your business."

The other logger said, "Forget it, Morgan. I don't want to tangle with you."

Frank nodded and bent down to check Erickson's pockets. He found a double eagle and flipped it to Peter Lee. "That ought to pay for the broken chair and anything else that got busted, as well as the food that was ruined. Fair enough, Peter?"

Lee bit the coin and satisfied himself that it was real. "Fair enough," he told Frank. "Erickson may not feel that way when he gets his senses back, though."

"Then he should have thought twice before he came in here to make trouble." Frank turned back to the two loggers. "What did you do, go in the Bull o' the Woods and get Erickson and his friends all stirred up?"

"Don't blame us, Morgan," one of the

men said. "Erickson was already hot under the collar. A lot of men in Eureka feel the same way tonight. They don't like you comin' in here and takin' over the hunt for the Terror like you done. Hell, you're just one man. You can't stop that monster."

"You'd rather have a hundred trigger-happy fools blundering around in the woods shooting at anything that moves . . . including *you*?"

The loggers just frowned. They didn't have any answer for that.

Frank shook his head in disgust. Sometimes, trying to help folks brought an hombre nothing but grief. Unfortunately, though, he wasn't the sort of man who could turn his back on trouble.

He picked up his hat, which had gotten knocked off during the brief brawl, and waved it at the men on the floor. "Get them out of here. They're cluttering up Mr. Lee's place."

Dawson was able to stand up and stumble out of the hash house under his own power. So was the man with the broken nose, which was still leaking crimson. The loggers helped the other two out, including a groggy Erickson, who kept shaking his head and muttering incoherently.

Frank called after them, "If any of you

fellas have a problem with what happened, you can take it up with me. If I hear about anybody bothering Mr. Lee or his family, just because this little fracas happened in his place, I won't take it kindly. And I'll be looking for whoever's responsible."

The threat in his voice was clear. Every now and then, it came in handy to have most people think of him as a cold-blooded, gunslinging bastard.

Peter Lee and his pretty wife and their two little kids, a boy and a girl about five and six years old, came out from behind the counter to clean up the mess left by the fight. Frank pitched in to help, and so did some of the customers who hadn't fled as soon as they had the chance.

"I'm sorry about this, Peter," Frank said.

"It wasn't your fault."

Frank shook his head. "Maybe I could've tried a little harder to head it off before anybody started throwing punches. Seems the Good Lord didn't put much backup in me when He made me, though."

"I got that impression," Lee said dryly. "You want some more stew and corn bread?"

Frank smiled. "I *did* sort of work up an appetite again."

Lee laughed as if he couldn't help it. "I'll

see what's left out in the kitchen."

While Frank waited for Lee to come back, he became aware that the proprietor's two children were staring at him. He smiled at them, which caused them to scurry off behind their mother's skirts and then peep out at him timidly. Mrs. Lee just gave Frank a tired smile and herded the youngsters back into the kitchen. The customers who were left returned to their meals.

A few minutes later, Lee brought Frank a fresh bowl of stew and another piece of corn bread, as well as refilling his coffee cup. Frank dug in, and was enjoying the food when he heard the hash house's front door open again. Footsteps clumped toward him, and when he glanced over, he saw Marshal Gene Price approaching him. The lawman wore a scowl on his rugged face.

"I thought I told you not to start any trouble in my town, Morgan," Price said.

Frank shook his head. "I didn't start it."

"That's not how I heard it. I heard you were in here brawling with half a dozen men."

"Well, that's almost true. But there were actually only four of them who got into the fight. The other two decided they didn't want any part of it."

"And you didn't start it?"

"One against six? Do I look like a fool to you, Marshal?"

Price just grunted and didn't answer the question. "You've got enemies here," he said. "It'd be better all the way around if you rode out and didn't come back."

Frank shook his head. "Not until I finish the job I said I'd do."

"I could just throw you in jail, you know." Price's voice held a worried edge. He was digging himself a hole, and he seemed to know it. He might have to try to arrest the notorious gunfighter Frank Morgan, and chances are, that wouldn't end well. But his pride wouldn't allow him to back down.

"On what charge?" Frank asked.

"Assault. Disturbing the peace."

Peter Lee surprised Frank a little by speaking up. "That's not how it happened, Marshal," he said. "Those men came in here looking for Mr. Morgan, intending to cause trouble. They attacked him. He was just defending himself."

Price glared at the hash house proprietor. "You sure about that?"

Lee nodded toward the men at the tables. "Ask any of my customers. They were all here when it happened."

The lawman turned to look at the men, several of whom nodded in agreement with what Lee had said. The gestures seemed rather reluctant, as if they didn't want to get involved in this possible trouble, but their honest natures forced them not to lie.

"All right then," Price finally said with ill-concealed disgust. "But I'll be keeping my eye on you, Morgan. You break the law, and you'll wind up behind bars before you know what happened."

That was an empty threat, and probably everyone in the place knew it. But Frank just nodded and said, "I always try to be a law-abiding man, Marshal."

Price snorted and turned to stalk out of the hash house. Frank watched him go, then said quietly to Lee, "You may have made yourself an enemy there, Peter."

Lee shook his head. "Marshal Price is a windbag. I'm not worried about him. I don't think Erickson and his cronies will bother us either. You made it pretty clear what would happen if they did."

Remembering how he'd been bushwhacked at Ben Chamberlain's old cabin that afternoon, Frank said, "I couldn't do much about it if I was dead."

Peter Lee smiled. "Don't get yourself killed then."

Frank laughed and reached for his coffee cup. "Words to live by," he said.

The logger with the broken nose was named Roylston. He sat at a big table in the back of the Bull o' the Woods Saloon holding a bloody rag to his nose and cursing in a low, monotonous voice.

The other men at the table ignored him. The one who'd been kicked in the groin sat gray-faced and hunched over. Every now and then he grimaced and took a nip from the bottle in front of him. His name was Treadwell, and at this moment, he wanted to kill Frank Morgan more than he had ever wanted anything else in his life.

Big, red-bearded Erickson wanted to kill Morgan, too, but even more than that, he wanted to collect the ten-thousand-dollar bounty on the head of the Terror. With Morgan around, the chances of doing that were slim.

But if Morgan was dead, Erickson thought . . .

Across the table, Dawson said, "It don't matter. Let Morgan go after that damn monster. It'll tear him into little bloody pieces, the same way it's done with everybody else unlucky enough to run into it."

Dawson's voice was thick because his jaw

was swollen where Morgan had hit him. Anger burned in his eyes, too, the same way it burned in the eyes of the other men.

Erickson, Dawson, and Treadwell weren't really friends. They hadn't even known each other before they came to this area of northern California, drawn by reports of the Terror and the ten-grand bounty. Each of them fancied himself a gunman. They were tough and weren't above skirting the law when it was advantageous — or profitable — to do so. They had met here in the Bull o' the Woods, recognized each other as kindred spirits, and formed a rough partnership of sorts . . . although it wouldn't have taken much to tempt each of them to double-cross the others. Still, they were as close to being friends as men like them could be.

Erickson had a bottle of his own, like Treadwell, and the other men were sharing a third bottle. Erickson had worried that a couple of his ribs were busted, but the pain that shot through him every time he took a breath had eased a little, dulled by the whiskey he was pouring down his throat more than likely. The whiskey didn't do anything to ease the anger inside him, though.

"I wouldn't count on that," he said in

reply to Dawson's comment about the Terror getting rid of Frank Morgan. "Morgan's not like most men. He wouldn't have lived as long as he has, with the rep he's got, if he wasn't plenty tough."

"Those fellas who ran into the Terror were tough, too," one of the loggers said. "Damn thing tore 'em apart like a wolf with a rabbit. That's why there needs to be more than one man goin' after it. It may take an army to get it."

Erickson shook his head. "Not an army. Just a handful of men . . . if they're the *right* men. Like us."

Roylston had his head tipped back, trying to stop the trickle of blood that still came from his nose. Now he straightened his head and said, "I'm not goin' back out there. Not to cut trees for Chamberlain. He's not payin' me enough to risk my life with nothin' but an ax and maybe a six-gun to defend myself."

"Then come in with us," Erickson said. He nodded toward the other two loggers. "You and Jenkins and Sutherland. The six of us, we'll find the Terror and kill it."

"What's the point in that?" Roylston asked. "The old man lifted the bounty. He won't pay ten grand for the monster's head anymore, not unless Morgan brings it in."

"He'd put the bounty on it again quick enough if Morgan was dead," Erickson said, putting into words what he'd been thinking.

The other five men stared at Erickson for a long moment without saying anything. Then Treadwell rasped, "Are you sayin' what I think you're sayin'?"

"Once Morgan's out of the way, there'll be no body stoppin' us from going after the Terror. And Chamberlain's bound to pay off once we get it."

The logger named Jenkins shook his head. "For get it. They say Morgan's as fast as Smoke Jensen or Matt Bodine. What you're talking about is a good way to get *us* killed."

"Six against one," Erickson said. "Those are mighty good odds."

"Yeah. You would have thought so."

Erickson's face flushed angrily. "That was different. He had the edge because we couldn't all rush him at once."

"And what you're talking about now is murder."

Erickson leaned forward and glared at Jenkins. "What I'm talking about is ten thousand dollars, you damned fool. Even split six ways, that's more money than you can make in three or four years."

Jenkins thought it over and finally shrugged. "Well . . . you're right about that."

"Of course I'm right."

"But we'll be risking our lives going up against Morgan."

"You're not already risking your lives by going into the woods where that monster is?"

Roylston took the bloody rag away from his swollen nose and looked at it. "You're right about that. Count me in."

"Me, too," Sutherland said.

Erickson looked at Jenkins. "How about it?" he demanded.

Jenkins sighed. "All right. I'll throw in with you, too, Erickson. I don't much like it, but . . . ten thousand is a hell of a lot of money."

"It sure is." Erickson reached over to Roylston. "Let me give you a hand with that," he said as he took hold of Roylston's nose and gave it a quick, hard squeeze before Roylston realized what he was about to do.

Roylston howled in pain, making the other men in the saloon look around. They went back to their drinking right away, though, when they saw there wasn't going to be a fight. Roylston sat there with both hands cupped over his nose, shocked by what Erickson had just done.

"What the hell did you do that for?"

"You don't want that nose to be all crooked when it heals up, do you?" Erickson asked. "I just straightened it back up. Now you'll be handsome for the ladies, once you've got all that money in your pocket."

Dawson grunted. "A man with enough money in his pocket is already handsome to the ladies."

Still muttering curses, Roylston shoved his chair back and stood up. "We'll have to go out to the camp and get our gear. Then we'll come back into town. I don't cotton to the idea of spending another night in those woods."

"And then tomorrow we'll start trying to figure out a way to get rid of Morgan," Erickson said. "Right?"

Roylston nodded. "We're with you."

The three loggers left the saloon. Dawson watched them go, then commented, "I liked a three-way split of that reward money better than divvying it up six ways."

Erickson took a slug from the whiskey bottle. "It'll still be a three-way split," he said with a leer. "Those dumb woodsmen will come in handy while we're getting rid of Morgan and then when we go after the Terror . . . but once we've got the monster's head, we won't need them any more, now will we?"

Dawson thought about it for a second, then began to smile. Even Treadwell didn't look quite as pained as he had earlier.

"Yeah, I think the Terror of the Redwoods is gonna claim at least three more victims," Erickson said, "before we collect that ten-grand reward."

CHAPTER 11

After the long, eventful day, Frank slept well that night. He had the veteran frontiersman's natural ability to take advantage of any opportunity for some good sleep, and the bed in the hotel room was mighty comfortable. After breakfast the next morning in the hotel dining room — where the food was all right, but not as good as that served up by Peter Lee and his family — Frank headed for Patterson's Livery and Wagon Yard.

The proprietor was working on a wagon's broken axle as Frank came up. He gave Frank a friendly nod and said, "Mornin', Mr. Morgan. I hear you got mixed up in a little excitement last night."

"You could call it that," Frank acknowledged with a grin. "I'm getting a mite old for so much excitement, though. I'm a little stiff and sore this morning."

Dog must have heard Frank's voice. He

came bounding out of the livery barn, tail wagging.

Frank grabbed the big cur by his shaggy ruff as Dog stood up and put his front feet on Frank's shoulders. He scratched Dog's ears as he asked, "This old boy give you any trouble last night?"

"Nope," Patterson said. "Not a bit. Tell you the truth, I slept a little better than usual, knowin' that he was in the barn. Anybody who'd tried to sneak in and steal anything would've been in for a surprise."

"That's the truth," Frank agreed. "I'll be leaving Stormy here today — that's the gray I was riding yesterday — and taking Goldy out instead."

"Goin' monster huntin', are you?"

"Word does get around in a hurry, doesn't it?"

"All over town," the liveryman said with a nod. "A lot of people aren't too happy about it either. They don't like it that Mr. Chamberlain took back that bounty, and they think more than one man ought to be goin' after the Terror."

"What do you think?"

Patterson shrugged. "I'd say it depends on who that one man is."

Frank saddled Goldy and then, with a wave of farewell to Patterson, rode out of

Eureka with Dog loping along at his side. He headed southwest, where the thickly wooded land bulged out past Humboldt Bay. That took him in the direction of the crude cabin he had discovered the day before. He hadn't forgotten that Dog had been following a trail of some sort when they came across the cabin. It hadn't rained during the night, so Frank thought there was a good chance Dog could pick up the scent again.

As he rode, Frank pondered the events of the day before. They were all pretty straightforward . . . except for one. That ambush attempt while he was at the cabin puzzled him. He had just ridden into this part of the country. Why would anyone have a reason to bushwhack him?

Of course, he had plenty of old enemies. As many men as he had killed in gunfights, there were a lot of hombres — brothers, fathers, sons of men who had gone down with his lead in them — nursing grudges against him. One of them could have trailed him here and seized the opportunity to take a few potshots at him.

Frank wished he had gotten a look at the bushwhacker, even though he might not have recognized whoever it was.

Dog ran ahead as usual. It was a nice

morning, with thick, white clouds filling about half the blue sky and a crisp breeze. Frank couldn't feel the breeze any longer, though, as soon as he rode into the forest, and he saw the sky only in occasional patches. He was back in the green twilight world under the towering redwoods, surrounded by their trunks like the legs of giants.

It took all of Frank's instinctive skill to guide him back to the spot where Dog had first picked up the trail the previous day. When they found the place where men had died at the hands — or whatever — of the Terror, Dog cast around until he caught the scent again. At Frank's order, he took off through the trees, with Frank following on Goldy.

By mid-morning, they reached the open area and the cliff with the tumbled tree trunks piled at its base. Frank reined in at the edge of the trees and dismounted. He looked across the clearing at the cabin, which showed no signs of any other visitors since the day before. Letting Goldy's reins dangle, Frank explored the edge of the trees on foot, looking for anything that might tell him who had hidden here and taken those shots at him.

The only thing he found was the stub of a

quirly, which meant absolutely nothing because there were hundreds, if not thousands, of men in the area who rolled smokes just like this. Frank could tell that this one had been pinched out before the man who'd been smoking it threw it down. That told Frank the man knew at least a little something about how to act in the woods. Discarding a still-lit quirly could start a forest fire that might burn thousands of acres.

With no other clues to tell him who ambushed him, Frank turned his attention back to the cabin. He took hold of Goldy's reins and led the horse across the clearing, then left him outside the jumble of fallen trees while he and Dog checked out the primitive dwelling that Ben Chamberlain had made for himself. Everything still looked the same inside. Frank lifted the lid of the trunk and saw the books and the long, slender bone he had put there. Giving in to an impulse, he took the bone from the trunk and carried it outside, where he rolled it up in the slicker that was tied on behind his saddle. He had in mind taking it back to Eureka with him later on, finding one of the local doctors, and asking the man to confirm his opinion that the bone was human.

With that done, Frank swung up into the saddle. "All right, Dog," he said to the big cur. "If you can still follow that scent, let's see where it leads. Trail!"

Dog still had the scent. He took off, heading north. Frank followed. Their course paralleled the ridge, which gradually tapered down until it was gone and the trees closed in around them again. Dog turned west then, toward the Pacific.

Frank knew they couldn't go very far in that direction before they would come to the ocean. After a few minutes, he heard the ringing of axes. The sound told him that a logging crew was working somewhere nearby. The recent deaths had everybody worried, but work had to go on.

He came to a road that had been cut through the forest. Deep ruts told him that wagons traveled it regularly. He suddenly heard a chuffing noise, and after a moment recognized it as the sound of a donkey engine. Those steam engines had a number of uses in a logging operation, Frank knew, so the presence of one meant that he must be close to one of Chamberlain's work camps.

Dog was still following the scent he'd first picked up the day before. It led toward the camp, Frank realized. A frown creased his forehead. Would the Terror, whatever it was, attack a whole camp full of loggers? It had done exactly that the day before, Frank reminded himself, although to be fair, that camp was only a small one. That crew hadn't had a donkey engine with them. This camp would be a larger one, with more men on hand in case of trouble.

A sudden burst of gunfire punctuated the stuttering roar of the engine. Frank stiffened in the saddle for a second as he heard pistols popping and the sharper crack of rifles, even the dull boom of a shotgun. There was a battle going on up there.

The question was, was it a battle between men . . . or between men and a monster?

Dog heard the shots, too, and recognized them as the sound of trouble. He raced ahead. Frank urged Goldy to a faster pace along the rough road.

The flurry of gunfire began to die away. A few more shots blasted out; then an eerie silence fell over the forest, broken only by the donkey engine's racket. There were no animal sounds. The rumble of the engine would have scared away most of the creatures who lived in these woods. The explosions of guns would have sent the rest fleeing. The carpet of needles on the ground even muffled Goldy's hoofbeats.

Dog ran around a bend in the road and out of sight. A second later, Frank heard the big cur growling and snarling. He pulled his Winchester from the saddle sheath and had it ready in his hands as he used his knees to guide Goldy around the curve.

He came in sight of a large clearing, dotted with the stumps of the trees that used to be there. Tents were set up among the stumps. A couple of wagons were parked to one side of the clearing, and the mule teams that had brought them here were penned up in a pole corral nearby.

The donkey engine still chuffed and rumbled. Steam rose from the funnel-shaped stack on top of the large, cylindrical boiler, and the gears it drove still turned, winding a thick metal cable around a drum. That cable snaked off into the woods. Frank knew the other end would be wrapped around a log that was being dragged out of the forest. This was a collection point. A number of felled redwoods were lined up end to end in the clearing, ready to be hooked together and dragged along the road by a team of oxen or possibly by a larger donkey engine that could be brought out when the crew was ready to transport these logs to the sawmill.

Frank had worked for a time as a logger during his wandering years, when he was trying to put his reputation as a gunman behind him, so he knew a little about how such operations worked. But not much anymore, because things had changed quite a bit since then. They hadn't used donkey engines in those days, only mules and oxen and the muscle and sweat of the loggers themselves.

Those thoughts went through his head for a second when he saw the steam engine mounted on its low, wheeled platform and lashed in place with thick ropes between several stumps. The other things he saw around the clearing drove everything else out of his mind.

Bile rose in Frank's throat at the sight of the bloody heaps that had been men. It looked like the Terror had gone on another killing spree. Frank counted the corpses, feeling sicker with each one. There were eleven dead men in this camp.

Dog stood stiff-legged a short distance from the carnage, still growling. The coppery reek of fresh blood probably bothered him as it mixed with the sharp tang of powder smoke lingering from the shooting. The smell bothered Frank, that was for sure.

Sitting still in the saddle, Frank gazed around the clearing. The Winchester was in his hands. He was ready to snap the rifle to his shoulder and open fire instantly if he caught sight of the thing that had done this.

Then he remembered his promise to Nancy Chamberlain. He had told her that he would do his best to bring her brother home safely. He couldn't just gun down Ben Chamberlain.

Yet, how could he try to capture a thing that could do . . . *this?*

Nothing moved in the woods. After several minutes had gone by, Frank was convinced that whatever had carried out this mass murder was gone. Even so, he kept the rifle in one hand as he dismounted.

He stepped over a man's arm that had been sheared off cleanly at the shoulder and flung across the camp. A few feet away lay a man who still had both arms, but no head, only a stump of a neck like the tree stumps that dotted the clearing. Frank moved on past several more bodies, all of them awash in gore from the deep wounds that covered their bodies. He had never seen anything like it in his life.

And as he looked closer, he realized that was true. He *hadn't* seen anything exactly like this before, not even the previous day when he had stumbled across those victims of the Terror. With a puzzled frown on his face, he turned and went back to the first body he had looked at, the one without a head. After studying it for a moment, he forced himself to ignore the revulsion he felt and picked up the severed arm nearby so that he could take a closer look at it.

"Well, what do you know about that?" he said softly.

Carefully, he bent over and placed the arm back on the ground where he had found it. The authorities would need to take a look at this scene of death and destruction, and it might be a good idea to leave it as much like he'd found it as possible.

There was nothing he could do for these men except try to find whoever was responsible for their grisly deaths. He mounted up again, called Dog, and then rode into the woods. Dog whined in complaint. He wanted to pick up the trail he had been following earlier. But Frank had something else in mind. He started making a circle around the clearing where the logging camp was located, trying to stay about fifty yards out from it. If he hadn't found what he was looking for by the time he rode all the way around the camp, he would move out a little farther and try again.

It took him about half an hour of careful searching before he found a spot where a number of horses had stood not long before. He couldn't see their hoofprints on the thick carpet of fallen needles, but to his experienced eye, the fresh droppings told the story as plainly as if it had been written out with pen and ink or printed in a book.

A number of riders had made their way through the forest to this point, then stopped their horses and left the mounts standing here for a while. Probably one member of the party had been given the chore of holding the reins. The others had crept forward, using the trees for cover, until they reached the edge of the camp where the loggers were working.

Then they had opened fire with rifles, taking the woodsmen by surprise and probably killing several of them with the first volley. The loggers who hadn't been killed outright had put up a fight — Frank had heard the evidence of that with his own ears — but they hadn't been able to mount enough of a defense to keep the bushwhackers from cutting them down one by one. Finally, all of Chamberlain's men were dead.

Then, the riflemen had come out of hiding to take care of the second part of their job. With axes that they had either brought with them or found in the camp, they had walked among their victims, swinging the keen-edged weapons again and again as they chopped their victims to pieces.

Frank had noticed that something was different about the severed arm he'd found, but it had taken him a few minutes to realize what it was. The day before, he had seen what the Terror of the Redwoods left behind after an attack. The wounds were ragged, not clean. Flesh that had been torn and shredded looked different from flesh that had been cut.

Men had committed murder here, not a monster.

But would anyone else have noticed that? Frank wondered. Or would they have seen just more evidence of the Terror's blood-thirsty rage? Would they have been blinded by blood and revulsion and failed to see the truth?

Frank thought there was a pretty good chance that was exactly what would have happened.

"Come on, Dog," he said. "Let's see what else we can find."

CHAPTER 12

The men kept a sharp eye out as they rode through the giant redwoods. Even though none of them had ever actually seen the Terror, they had heard plenty about it. Everybody had, in this neck of the woods. The Terror was the talk of every saloon and whorehouse and logging camp.

After what had happened today, that would be even more true. The news of the Terror's latest massacre would spread like wildfire.

That was exactly what their boss wanted.

One of the men, named Radburn, spoke up. "Hey, Grimshaw, when do we get our money?"

Jack Grimshaw, who was ramrodding this gang of killers, leaned over in the saddle and spat. "You anxious to get paid, Radburn?"

"Damn right I am. You know doin' this didn't sit well with me."

One of the men, a lunger everybody called Hooley, gave a mean-sounding laugh. "Why, I thought you'd killed men before, Radburn," he said. "I didn't realize you was a blushin' little flower."

Radburn was a chunky man with a squarish red face that got even redder when he was angry, like now. "I've killed my share, and you know it," he snapped. "That don't trouble me. I'm talkin' about what happened afterward."

"Without that, folks wouldn't think the Terror was to blame," Grimshaw explained patiently. He was a gaunt-faced, middle-aged hombre with iron-gray hair under a black Stetson. "You know as well as I do why it was necessary."

Hooley cackled, then coughed. "Because the boss paid us to do it that way," he said in a voice wet with sickness.

"That's right," Grimshaw nodded. "If that bothers you too much, Radburn, I don't reckon you have to take his money."

Radburn muttered for a couple of seconds under his breath, then replied, "I never said anything about not takin' the money."

"I didn't think so."

They rode on, fifteen hard-faced men, all of them with plenty of blood on their hands even before today.

But there was more blood staining them now, a lot more, Grimshaw reflected. He had seen a lot of ugly things in his life, but right offhand, he couldn't think of anything uglier than taking axes and chopping a bunch of dead men into pieces.

Would it fool people when they found the bodies? Grimshaw thought it would, since everybody in these parts was so worked up to start with about the monster in the woods. But the important thing, as far as his boss was concerned, was that more damage had been done to Rutherford Chamberlain's logging operation. Whatever had been killing men out here in the woods was doing Grimshaw's employer, Emmett Bosworth, a favor, but Bosworth wasn't a patient man. He had decided to push things along a little faster, and for that reason, he had recruited Grimshaw and the other gunmen.

Grimshaw, Radburn, Hooley, and the others had all been involved in range wars in the past. A timber war was really no different. Rutherford Chamberlain had the trees, and Emmett Bosworth wanted them. Simple as that. Grimshaw had assumed at first that he and his fellow gunmen would be carrying out the same sort of campaign they had waged on behalf of various cattle barons —

161

ambushing Chamberlain's men, sabotaging his equipment, generally making life hell for anybody who worked for Chamberlain.

Bosworth had come up with another idea, though. He wanted to take advantage of the fear that was spreading through the forest. The so-called Terror already had men plenty spooked. If the Terror seemed to be going on an even worse killing spree, Chamberlain's men might finally start refusing to venture into the woods and do their work.

A man couldn't cut logs without loggers. That was Bosworth's idea, and it was a good one, as far as Grimshaw was concerned. When Chamberlain had to give up his lease on this prime area of timber, Bosworth would move in, and then Grimshaw and the other men would have a new job.

They would go into the woods, hunt down the Terror, whatever it was, and kill it.

"Son of a bitch."

The disgusted words came from one of the men toward the rear of the group. Grimshaw reined in, hipped around in his saddle, and asked, "What is it, Nichols?"

The man's horse had slowed almost to a stop, taking each step gingerly.

"Damn horse has gone lame. I'm gonna have to get off and walk for a spell, see if he can shake it off." Nichols looked around.

"Unless I can ride double with one of you fellas."

"I don't think so," Grimshaw said.

Nichols's lean, beard-stubbled face got a worried frown on it. "You're gonna get ahead of me, though."

"Afraid of the Terror, Nichols?" Hooley asked.

Nichols flushed. "Well, wouldn't you be?"

Hooley hunched over in his saddle as a fresh fit of coughing struck him. When it was over, he straightened and shook his head.

"I ain't afraid of anything. No reason to be."

The rest of them knew what he meant. Hooley coughed up blood a dozen times a day. He wouldn't last another six months, no matter what. Probably not another three. When a man spent all his waking hours staring down that particular barrel, he really didn't have any reason to be scared of anything else.

"Well, then, why don't you stay with me, so I won't have to ride on in to Eureka by myself?" Nichols suggested.

"You think I won't?"

"I'm hopin' you will." Nichols looked around. "I don't much cotton to the idea of bein' out here in the woods by myself."

Hooley thought it over for a second, then shrugged. "Sure. Why the hell not? The rest of you fellas go on. Me and Nichols will be there later." He frowned at Grimshaw. "You better not spend our part of the money on hooch and whores before we get there, though."

"Don't worry, you'll get your *dinero*," Grimshaw assured the lunger. "Come on, boys."

Nichols dismounted as the others rode on, with the exception of Hooley, who sat there with his hands crossed and resting on the saddle horn. While Hooley waited, Nichols examined the horse's front legs and hooves.

"I was hopin' maybe he'd just picked up a rock or somethin' in his shoe," Nichols said. "Looks like he's gone lame, though." He sighed. "It's gonna be a long walk back to town."

"We might as well get started." The other gunmen had already gone out of sight. Hooley licked his lips. "I'd just as soon not stay out here any longer than we have to."

Nichols picked up his horse's reins and started leading the animal as Hooley turned his mount to follow the others. Grinning, Nichols said, "Thought you wasn't scared."

"I ain't. I just don't care much for the woods, that's all. I'd rather be in town where I can get a drink and rest my eyes on a nice-lookin' woman if I want to."

The two men made their way through the towering trees, moving slowly because of Nichols's horse. They had gone maybe half a mile when both animals began to act a little strange. Hooley's horse lifted its head and pricked up its ears, then gave a violent shake of its head. Nichols's mount started pulling back on the reins, as if it didn't want to go forward anymore.

"What's got into these damn jugheads?" Nichols asked.

"They act like they smell somethin' they don't like." Hooley sniffed the air. "Can't say as I smell anything, though."

"A horse's nose is more sensitive than yours." Nichols dropped his hand to the butt of his gun. "I don't like this, Hooley."

"Don't go scarin' yourself. You know how horses can get all spooky for no good reason. One of 'em starts to act up, and then the other one has to do the same thing. There's nothin' to worry about."

"You don't know that," Nichols insisted. "There's so many damn trees, you can't see fifty yards. You don't know what's out there."

"Neither do you."

Nichols tugged on the reins. "Come on,

damn it," he snapped at his horse. "You want the Terror to get you?"

"We don't know there's any such thing as a Terror," Hooley pointed out.

"Oh, yeah? Well, *somethin'* killed all those other men. We didn't take cards in the game until today, remember?"

"Probably a bear, or maybe a mountain lion."

"I don't think they have mountain lions around here, or bears big enough to —"

Nichols's horse suddenly reared up on its hind legs, jerking the reins out of his hands. The horse whinnied in fear as it pawed at the air with its forehooves.

From the corner of his eye, Hooley caught sight of something moving in the trees to his left . . . something big, and fast. He exclaimed, "Son of a bitch!" and jerked his horse around. His gun seemed to leap into his hand. He might be sick, but his illness hadn't affected his speed with a Colt. His head snapped from side to side as he looked for the thing, whatever it was. He wanted something to shoot at. Hooley had never run into anything he couldn't kill, except for the thing that was eating him up from the inside out.

Nichols was yelling curses at his horse as he tried to grab the reins and bring the animal back under control. Despite being lame, fear gave the horse some unexpected agility. It twisted away from Nichols and bolted, running around one of the giant redwoods that was close to twenty feet in diameter.

The horse didn't come out from the other side. Instead, it screamed in pain.

"It got my horse!" Nichols babbled. "Son of a bitch, son of a bitch! My rifle's still on my saddle!" He turned and lunged toward Hooley. "Pull me up behind you! Let's get the hell out of here!"

Hooley was having trouble keeping his own mount under some semblance of control. The horse danced back and forth skittishly as the screams continued to come from behind the big tree. Nichols clawed at Hooley's leg and tried to climb up behind him.

"Get off!" Hooley cried. He slashed at Nichols with the six-gun, raking the barrel across the other man's face. Nichols fell back with a cry of pain as blood flew from the gash on his forehead opened up by the gunsight.

"Hooley!" he yelled. "Hooley, you gotta help me!"

"I'm not ridin' double," Hooley said. "That damn thing's too fast." He hauled his horse's head around and jammed his boot heels into the animal's flanks. The horse broke into a frantic run.

"Hooley!" Nichols shrieked behind him. "Hooley, don't leave me out here! Don't let it —"

The desperate plea was cut off abruptly by a gurgling cry. Hooley leaned forward in the saddle and didn't look back as he sent his horse racing around and between the giant tree trunks. He didn't want to see what was happening back there. All he wanted was to get out of here before whatever that thing was caught him, too.

Funny, he thought as his heart pounded heavily in his chest, maybe the time he had left to him, however long it might be, was still precious to him after all.

Frank heard yelling in the distance. In this thick forest, it was hard to judge how far away such sounds were. Couldn't be too far, though, he told himself, because the thick vegetation tended to muffle noises and keep them from carrying as well.

"Stay with me, Dog!" he called as the big cur tried to bound ahead out of sight. Frank didn't know what they were heading toward, but it couldn't be anything good.

There were no shots. Frank didn't know

what that meant. He had a feeling it wasn't a good sign. It was like the man who had gotten into trouble hadn't even had time to pull his gun, only to scream in fear and pain.

Dog had been tracking the bushwhackers who had attacked that logging camp, and Frank had been following. He estimated their numbers at more than a dozen, so he didn't plan on jumping them. He had more in mind following them, finding out who they were and, more importantly, who they worked for. He thought he had a pretty good idea, but he needed confirmation of that.

The sounds had died away quickly. Without them to guide him, Frank wasn't sure if he was headed in the right direction or not. But then Dog dashed ahead, as if he had caught a familiar scent again, and Frank pushed Goldy hard to keep up.

A minute later, Dog stopped short, planting his feet and stiffening his legs as he growled. Frank reined to a halt behind him and pulled the Winchester from its sheath. Up ahead, lying next to the base of a tree, was a horse. The animal lay still. Blood still welled from a gaping wound in its neck.

"Back, Dog," Frank said quietly. The big cur obeyed, backing up until he was next to Frank and Goldy. Frank sent the horse forward at a slow walk.

He circled to the left, around the tree and the body of the horse. The horse wore a saddle, so Frank had a feeling that its former rider was around here somewhere. A moment later, he saw he was right. A man lay on the ground on the far side of the tree, face down. He was as motionless as the horse. The back of his shirt was shredded and soaked with blood.

The man had lost so much blood, it had formed a pool around him on the ground. Frank knew he couldn't still be alive. So for the next couple of minutes, instead of dismounting, Frank sat there, looking and listening intently, taking in everything that was going on in the woods around him.

That wasn't much of anything. The forest was quiet and seemingly peaceful again. Frank knew better, though. He knew the fear and death that lurked in these trees. He had seen it with his own eyes. How many men had died in the past two days? Close to two dozen? He couldn't even keep track anymore. The deaths blended into a succession of grisly images.

Finally, satisfied that whatever had done this was no longer nearby, Frank swung down from the saddle and hunkered on his heels next to the body. He held the rifle in one hand, took hold of the dead man's shoulder with the other, and rolled the corpse onto its back. The man's face was smeared with blood, but not a lot of it. The blood looked like it had come from a gash in the man's forehead. Other than that, his face was unmarked.

It was a horrifying sight anyway, because it was frozen and twisted in lines of such fear that the man must have died feeling sheer terror all the way down to his soul. Frank's jaw tightened as he studied the man's face. He tried to put aside for the moment the fear and the blood and concentrate on what the man must have looked like in life.

After a moment, he came to the conclusion that he had never seen the dead man before.

He had seen the type plenty of times, though. The narrow, unshaven face, the weak mouth and chin, the small, deep-set eyes . . . This man had been a hired killer. Frank was sure of it. And it didn't take much to figure out from there that he'd been a member of the gang of gun-wolves that had massacred the men back there at Chamberlain's logging camp and then mutilated their bodies.

He wondered if Marshal Gene Price

would recognize the gunman. Still hunkered beside the body, he began looking around for some broken branches he could use to fashion a travois using one of his blankets. He wasn't going to load the gruesome corpse onto Goldy's back, but would drag it back to Eureka on a makeshift sled instead. The blanket he used would be ruined, but Frank could afford to buy another.

Spotting some branches that might work, he straightened to his feet.

And just as he did, a rifle cracked. Frank heard the high-pitched whine of a bullet whistling past his ear.

CHAPTER 13

Instantly, more shots rang out. Slugs smacked into the tree, spraying bark and splinters into the air.

Frank was already moving, though, his superbly honed reflexes taking over at the first sign of danger. He called, "Dog! Cover!" and threw himself into a dive that carried him behind the tree. He heard bullets thudding into the redwood, but they had no chance of penetrating all the way through the massive trunk.

He glanced over and saw that Dog had darted behind another tree. It was smaller than the one where Frank had taken shelter, but big enough to shield the shaggy, wolflike creature from any harm. And Goldy, he was glad to see, had dashed off out of sight among the trees. The horse was smart, and a quick learner. He hadn't traveled with Frank Morgan for very long without realizing what those loud, unpleasant noises meant and what he should do to avoid them.

Frank was surprised that neither Dog nor Goldy had scented the bushwhackers creeping up on them. He supposed that the smell of freshly spilled blood — and the stench of whatever had done this — might have masked any other scents, at least enough to keep the animals from noticing anything else unusual. As Frank lay there on the carpet of needles, he wondered who was shooting at him.

Of course, it was possible the riflemen were the same ones who had attacked the logging camp. But they had been headed the other direction, toward Eureka. They might have gotten behind him, but Frank considered it unlikely.

The only other explanation, though, was that there were *two* gangs of killers out here, as well as something that could claw a man to death or rip him apart with apparently equal ease.

The woods were getting a mite crowded, Frank thought with a grim smile as he cradled the Winchester's smooth stock against his cheek and crawled to one side so that he could risk a glance around the trunk.

The sound of the shots told him that this was indeed a different group, or at least a smaller one. He estimated that five or six men had opened fire on him. The larger gang could have split up, but again, he couldn't see any reason why they would have done that and why some of them would have circled around to get behind him. Checking their back trail maybe? He couldn't rule it out.

The bushwhackers stopped firing. They must have realized that they could throw lead at that tree all day without doing any real damage. Frank looked over at Dog. The big cur was trained to respond to hand signals, too, as well as Frank's voice. Frank made one of those signals now, a gesture that meant *Hunt!*

Staying on his belly, Dog crawled out from behind the tree where he had taken cover. Either the bushwhackers didn't see him, or they didn't care that he was on the move.

If it was the latter, they might have reason to regret their carelessness in a few minutes, Frank thought.

Dog disappeared into the brush. Frank waited. He knew how to be patient. The ability to remain still and silent had saved his life on numerous occasions.

He heard the crackle of broken branches, and knew that at least some of the bush-whackers were on the move. Dog wouldn't make that much racket while he was hunting, not on his worst day.

The sounds continued, moving to Frank's left now. He twisted in that direction and snugged the Winchester's butt against his shoulder. His eyes narrowed as he searched for any sign of movement that would give him a target. Some of the brush swayed a little, and then he caught a glimpse of a rifle barrel.

Frank opened fire, cranking off three rounds as fast as he could work the rifle's lever. The bullets lashed through the brush. A man cried out in pain, and then someone returned the fire. They hurried their shots, though, and the slugs just hit the tree several feet above Frank's head as he crawled backward, out of the line of fire.

At the same time, a man yelled in surprise and pain, and Frank figured that Dog had found his quarry. He knew it a second later when he heard snarling and snapping. Somebody shouted, "Son of a bitch!" and another man added, "Let's get out of here!"

Frank stood up and pressed his back against the tree trunk. When he heard hoofbeats, he stepped out and triggered several more rounds in that direction. He couldn't see the fleeing bushwhackers, so he didn't have any real hope of hitting them, but at least he could hurry them on their way. No shots came back toward him, so he was convinced that whoever the ambushers were, they had given up on killing him.

At least for the moment.

"Dog!" Frank called.

A minute later, the big cur came bounding out of the brush. The flecks of blood on his muzzle testified that he had sunk his teeth into at least one of the gunmen. Frank roughed up the fur on his head and said, "Good boy!"

He whistled for Goldy, who promptly answered the summons just as Dog had. Frank took down his bedroll, removed one of the blankets from it, and used the blanket and those broken branches he had decided on earlier to make a travois. Once he had the corpse loaded onto it, he replaced the rest of the bedroll, taking care that the bone he had found in the primitive cabin was still wrapped up securely.

The morning's developments meant that he needed to return to Eureka now, instead of continuing his search for the Terror. For one thing, it was clear now that more danger lurked in the woods than just the supposed monster. Frank wanted to get a lead on the man whose body he had found, if possible.

He planned to keep his theories about Emmett Bosworth to himself for the time being, though. He would just tell the marshal that he had found the dead man in the woods, and wouldn't say anything about the massacre at the logging camp. Somebody else would come across that soon enough, Frank figured. More of Chamberlain's men were bound to show up there and make the grisly discovery.

Dragging the travois with its gruesome burden behind his horse, Frank rode toward Eureka. He kept the Winchester across the saddle in front of him, just in case he ran into any more trouble — human . . . or otherwise.

Treadwell's face was gray with pain as he hunched forward in his saddle. "Bad enough that bastard Morgan kicked me in the balls last night," he grated. "Now he had to go and shoot me, too."

"You'll live," Erickson told him. "Morgan's bullet just knocked a chunk of meat out of your arm." The big, red-bearded man laughed curtly. "At least you can sit your saddle without hurtin' too bad. That wolf-dog of Morgan's practically tore poor Sutherland's ass off."

"It ain't funny," Sutherland said as he leaned far forward in the saddle, trying to ease the injured area. "That critter was vicious."

Dawson urged his horse up alongside Erickson's. "Who do you think that other hombre was, the one Morgan found?"

"I don't know," Erickson said with a shake of his head. "I didn't get a good look at him. All I know is that he was dead. Nobody could lose that much blood and still be alive."

Jenkins said, "The Terror got him. That must be what happened."

"We'll get the Terror," Erickson said. "But we need to get Morgan first."

"Don't you reckon Old Man Chamberlain would pay us the bounty anyway if we showed up at his house with the thing's head?"

Erickson frowned in thought. "I don't know. He might not. He might say it didn't count anymore. You fellas who worked for him know him better than I do. Is he a tight-fisted old son of a bitch?"

"He pays fair wages," Jenkins said. "He don't go out of his way to give anybody anything extra, though."

Erickson nodded. "There you go. Chances are, he'd use any excuse not to have to pay the bounty. So it'll be better if we kill Morgan first, *then* the monster."

"Easier said than done," Treadwell complained. He nodded toward the bloody rag tied around his arm. "We didn't do a very good job of it today."

"This was just our first try," Erickson said. "We'll stick like burrs to Morgan, and the next time . . . we'll fill his hide with lead."

Hooley caught up with the rest of Bosworth's hired gunmen before they reached Eureka. When Jack Grimshaw heard the horse coming up fast behind them, he reined in and motioned for the others to do likewise. Hooley galloped up and joined them, bringing his mount to a sliding stop on the logging road they were following now.

Grimshaw saw the wild look in Hooley's pale, watery eyes and guessed that something had happened. "Where's Nichols?" he asked.

Hooley shook his head. "I don't know. I had to leave him back there."

"You were supposed to stay with him," Grimshaw said.

"Yeah, well, that was before somethin' spooked his horse and made it run away. Damn horse ran right into whatever it was that scared it, though. I never heard an animal scream like that in my life."

"So you ran off and left Nichols there on

180

foot with that thing in the woods?"

"It already had him," Hooley snapped. "What was I supposed to do, stay there and get torn up, too?"

One of the other men asked, "Did you see the thing?"

Hooley shook his head. "Not really. Just caught a glimpse of it through the trees. It was mighty big and fast. Shaggy, too, like a critter. But it's a critter the likes of which ain't never been seen around here before. Or anywhere else either."

"Maybe so," Grimshaw said, "but I don't like the fact that you just left him there. We're supposed to all be working together."

"Easy for you to say. You weren't there."

Hooley's tense, angry attitude as he spoke and the way he moved his hand just slightly toward the butt of his gun made Grimshaw stiffen in the saddle. He was ready to slap leather, too, if Hooley wanted to push the matter.

Radburn moved his horse up and said, "Damn it, we already lost one man today. We don't need the two of you gunnin' for each other, too."

Grimshaw kept his cold, level stare locked on Hooley for a couple of seconds longer, then nodded. "Radburn's right. What's done is done. We'll let it go."

"Just don't be callin' me a coward," Hooley warned.

"I never said that." Grimshaw's lip curled. "I can't help what you think of yourself, though."

That comment was almost enough to set Hooley off again, but Radburn pushed his horse up alongside Hooley's and caught hold of the lunger's arm. "Come on," he urged. "Let's get on to town and collect our pay."

"Now you're talkin'," one of the other men said. "Maybe the boss'll have another job for us, too."

The group of riders got moving again. Grimshaw said, "I wouldn't count on anything else right away. Bosworth'll want to let what happened today soak in on everybody for a while."

The atmosphere among the hired killers eased as they approached the settlement. Most of them were thinking now of the money they had coming to them, and how they would spend it. The saloons and whorehouses in Eureka would do a booming business tonight.

While they were still outside of town, Grimshaw reined in and said, "We'll split up here. The rest of you drift into the Bull o' the Woods one or two at a time as usual.

I'll see the boss and meet you there in a little while."

"Don't lose any of that money along the way," Radburn cautioned.

Grimshaw snorted. "I know you fellas. I'm not enough of a damn fool to try something like that."

"Damn right," Hooley said, still a little proddy from the earlier confrontation. "We'd hunt you down and take it outta your hide."

Radburn used his horse to crowd Hooley's mount toward the saloon. "That's enough. Let's go get a drink." He licked his lips. "Killin' is thirsty work."

Grimshaw left the others at the saloon and headed on up the street toward the Eureka House. It was midday, and the town was busy, the streets full of pedestrians and buggies and wagons, and a few men, like Grimshaw, on horseback.

He drew up in front of the hotel and dismounted. After tying his horse at the hitch rail, he went inside, striding through the lobby without stopping at the desk. He knew where he was going.

His destination was a suite of rooms on the front of the hotel, overlooking the street. Grimshaw raised his hand to knock, but someone inside jerked the door open before he could rap on the panel. Emmett Bosworth stood there in his shirt sleeves, his collar undone. He must have been looking out the window and seen Grimshaw approaching the hotel. He glared at the gunman.

"Is it done?"

Grimshaw nodded and opened his mouth to speak, but Bosworth held up a hand and stopped him. The timber magnate opened the door a little wider and inclined his head toward the divan, where an attractive, nearly nude woman lay curled up with her eyes closed and a satisfied smile on her face.

"Give me a few minutes," Bosworth ordered under his breath.

Grimshaw nodded and stepped back as Bosworth closed the door. He understood now why Bosworth hadn't wanted him to say anything. He didn't want the woman to overhear any details of the job that might come back later and implicate him in mass murder.

Grimshaw strolled down to the end of the corridor and waited, looking out a window at the alley that ran alongside the hotel. He didn't see anything more interesting than a big yellow cat rummaging through some garbage. He heard the door of Bosworth's suite open again, heard some quiet words exchanged between Bosworth and the woman as she left, but didn't turn around. She hadn't gotten a look at his face, and he figured Bosworth would want to keep it that way.

A moment later, he heard a heavy footstep behind him and turned. Bosworth gestured curtly.

"Come on."

Bosworth had fastened his collar, put on a tie and his coat. He looked like the successful businessman he was. As he led Grimshaw into the sitting room of the suite, he went on. "Can I get you a drink?"

"You damn sure can," Grimshaw said, recalling what Radburn had said a few minutes earlier about killing being thirsty work. That was sure true. He had been craving a shot of whiskey ever since they'd finished chopping those poor devils into little, bloody pieces.

Bosworth picked up a cut-crystal decanter of bourbon from a fancy sideboard and splashed the fiery liquor into a couple of glasses. He handed one to Grimshaw and said, "To the success of your mission."

"Yeah," Grimshaw said. He clicked his glass against Bosworth's and then threw back the booze. It burned quite satisfactorily in his gullet.

Some men were content to guzzle any sort of rotgut or panther piss. Grimshaw liked the finer stuff in life, including liquor, which was why he had attached himself to Emmett Bosworth a year earlier, when the timberman had first approached him about ramrodding a crew of troubleshooters, as Bosworth called them, while he expanded his operation into the area of northern California now controlled by Rutherford Chamberlain.

Grimshaw had known right away what Bosworth was getting at. Any time one strong man tried to take something away from another strong man, there was bound to be trouble. In most cases, gun trouble. Grimshaw had been in that position many times in the past and knew what went with the job. He'd helped Bosworth recruit other men, some of them known personally to Grimshaw, like Radburn. Others, like Hooley, he had only heard of from mutual acquaintances.

There had been problems along the way. Grimshaw had lost a man early on, when he was just getting started putting the bunch together. But now the group was at full strength, and Bosworth was ready to make his move. The attack on Chamberlain's camp this morning was just the opening salvo.

Bosworth sipped his bourbon. "You did it like we discussed?"

Grimshaw nodded as he helped himself to another drink, feeling confident enough in his relationship with Bosworth to do so. "Yeah," he said. "It went just like you wanted it. Better get ready for a real uproar. I expect the news will be all over town before the day's over."

"I hope it is. Once the rest of Chamberlain's men hear about it, they'll be quitting him in droves."

"Maybe," Grimshaw said. "The Terror's been around for a while, though, and not many of them have quit so far."

Bosworth shook his head. "The Terror has never gone on a rampage like this before. And in a few days, the monster will strike again." He sipped his drink again. "I was thinking that perhaps next time, the Terror will burn down Chamberlain's sawmill."

"You sure that's a good idea?" Grimshaw asked with a frown. "That seems like something a mite too intelligent for that varmint to do."

"You'll make it look like an accident," Bosworth assured him. "The fire will start while the Terror is ripping apart some of Chamberlain's men."

Grimshaw considered the idea for a moment, then slowly nodded. "Might work," he conceded. "Let me mull it over some more."

"Take your time . . . just not *too* much time. We don't want Chamberlain's men to start believing they're safe again."

Grimshaw downed the rest of his second drink and set the empty glass on the sideboard. "The fellas will want their money."

"Of course. Wait here."

Bosworth left the room, going through a door into the adjacent bedroom. He closed the door behind him. Clearly, he didn't want Grimshaw to see where his cash was hidden.

That was all right with the gunman. He had no interest in robbing Emmett Bosworth. He would make a lot more *dinero* in the long run by carrying out the ruthless timber baron's orders.

Bosworth came back with a handful of greenbacks. "Four thousand dollars, as we agreed. I won't ask you how you plan to split it with the others."

"And I won't tell you," Grimshaw replied with a faint smile as he took the money. He would keep twelve hundred for himself, since he was the ramrod of this bunch, and give two hundred apiece to the rest of the men.

Wait a minute, he thought. Nichols was dead. That left an extra two hundred.

Well, the others could divvy that up however they wanted, he decided. They'd feel good about getting a little extra.

While he was waiting for Bosworth to come back with the money, he had smelled a faint, sweet fragrance in the room. He knew it had been left behind by the woman who'd been here. The scent had a subtle quality that wasn't like the flowery lilac water whores tended to splash on in abundance. It was a lot more ladylike than that.

Now, against his better judgment, he gave in to his curiosity and asked, "Who was the gal?"

Instantly, Bosworth's rugged face hardened. Grimshaw knew he had pushed the man too far. Bosworth was tall and broad-shouldered, and his frame still retained some of the muscular power that swinging an ax as a young man had given him. Grimshaw hoped that Bosworth wouldn't lose his temper and throw a punch at him. He'd hate to have to shoot the man.

"Never you mind about who the lady was," Bosworth snapped. "Suffice it to say, she has a husband who wouldn't be happy if he knew what had happened here this morning."

Grimshaw shrugged. "Sure, Boss. Sorry I brought it up."

He wasn't surprised by Bosworth's answer. He knew what effect wealth and power in a man had on some women. He held up the roll of bills. "I'll go give the boys their share. Much obliged."

"Just keep doing your job," Bosworth said. "There'll be a lot more where that come from."

That was exactly what Grimshaw was counting on.

He tucked the roll away inside his shirt as he left the suite. He wasn't going to walk through a hotel lobby, even a hotel as high-class as the Eureka House, carrying that much money in the open.

When he reached the porch, he paused and looked both ways along the street. A man on horseback caught his attention. The hombre was riding a big, gold-colored horse and had a shaggy dog that looked more like a wolf padding along beside him. The man had rigged a crude travois, and he was dragging it along behind the horse with something loaded on it . . .

Grimshaw stiffened as he looked closer at the thing on the travois. Then he nodded

slowly as if realizing that what he was looking at was inevitable. He had known this
man was in Eureka. He had heard the talk.
And sooner or later, they were bound to
run into each other.

Grimshaw gave his hat brim a tug, stepped
down off the porch, and walked out in the
street to intercept the man. As the fella
reined in, Grimshaw lifted his left hand in
greeting, smiled, and said, "Howdy, Frank.
Long time no see."

CHAPTER 14

Frank didn't recognize the man who had hailed him right away, although he knew he should remember the hombre. The stranger was almost as old as Frank, and while Frank couldn't put a name with the face right offhand, he recognized the casual stance, the alertness in the eyes, the way the man's right hand never strayed far from the butt of his gun. He was ready to hook and draw in case this fella had an old grudge against him that needed settling.

Then the stranger said, "Remember that time we decided to go fishin' in the Brazos River while it was flooding? Like to washed us both away."

"Jack!" Frank exclaimed as the name came back to him. "Jack Grimshaw!"

"That's right." Grimshaw stepped closer and reached up, extending his hand. "How are you, Frank?"

Frank clasped the man's hand. "I'm all

right. A little stiffer than I used to be when I get up in the morning."

Grimshaw chuckled. "Ain't we all?" He let go of Frank's hand and gestured toward the body on the travois. "Somebody run into some trouble?"

"Bad trouble," Frank agreed. He frowned slightly. "You wouldn't happen to know him, would you?"

"Let me take a look."

Grimshaw moved closer to the corpse and studied its face. Frank swung down from the saddle and stood beside him, holding Goldy's reins.

"What do you think?"

Grimshaw shook his head. "Sorry. Don't think I've ever seen him before. I don't see any wounds either. What did he die of? Looks like it was pretty bad, judging by the expression on his face."

"You don't see any wounds because he's lying on his back. The Terror got him. Clawed him wide open."

"The Terror?" Grimshaw sounded surprised. "You mean that monster folks say is out in the woods? You really believe in a thing like that, Frank?"

Grimshaw's tone implied that he might think a little less of his old friend if Frank replied in the affirmative.

193

"I wasn't sure at first," Frank said, "but I've seen its handiwork now, several times. It's real, all right. I just don't know exactly what it is."

That was true. He knew that Nancy Chamberlain was sincere in her belief that her brother Ben was the Terror, and while Frank hadn't found any real evidence supporting that theory, he hadn't come across anything to invalidate it either. The jury was still out as far as he was concerned.

"Well, whatever got him, I'm sorry this hombre had to die the way he did," Grimshaw commented. "Looks like it was a bad way to go."

"Yeah."

"Where are you takin' him? The undertaker's parlor?"

Frank shook his head. "I thought I'd stop at the marshal's office first, see if maybe he recognized the gent."

Grimshaw chuckled and nodded down the street. "I don't think you'll have to go all the way to the marshal's office. Judgin' by the badge on that hombre's vest, the law's comin' to you."

It was true. The body on the travois had drawn quite a bit of attention as Frank rode into town. One of the townies must have run down to Marshal Gene Price's office to tell him about it.

Grimshaw reached up and ticked the tip of his index finger against the brim of his Stetson. "I'll be moseyin' on, Frank. Mighty good to see you again. Maybe we can get together later and have a drink, catch up on old times."

"Still don't care much for badge toters, eh?"

Grimshaw shook his head. "They make me antsy, even when I ain't done anything."

Frank slapped a hand on Grimshaw's shoulder. "I'll be seeing you."

As Grimshaw strolled away and Marshal Price continued hurrying toward Frank, The Drifter's thoughts went back to the last time he had seen Jack Grimshaw.

"They'll be comin' soon," Grimshaw said as he crouched next to the window in the ramshackle old cabin. "You ready, Frank?"

"Ready as I'll ever be," Frank replied with a nod. He was next to the window on the other side of the cabin's only door. Whenever he risked a glance out that window, he could see a magnificent vista of Wyoming mountains spread out before him.

Unfortunately, hidden out there in the trees and the brush were nearly a dozen hardened gunmen who wanted to kill Frank and Jack Grimshaw because Frank and Grimshaw rode for one side in the deadly war that had spread across this part of the territory and they rode for the other.

It was as simple as that. A fella took money from one man, and he became mortal enemies with the hombres who took money from another man. That was crazy, Frank had been known to think, but it was the way of the West and had been ever since the great cattle barons had begun clashing over the rich rangeland.

Of course, for some men, things were a little more complicated. Frank himself had never sold his gun strictly for cash, despite the reputation that had attached itself to him over the years. The only causes he fought for were the ones he believed in.

In this case, he had allied himself with a rancher named Maynard Pollinger, an Englishman who had come to this country to make a new life for himself because he'd had the misfortune to be born the second son in an aristocratic British family. Pollinger wasn't looking for trouble, but his MP spread had grown to be successful enough that it attracted the attention of Pete Dwyer, the boss of the Diamond D. Dwyer regarded Pollinger as a threat, and so he had started trying to run him out of the territory, sending hired guns to ambush Pollinger's cowboys, poison his water holes, and stampede his stock.

Pollinger had had no choice but to fight back using the same methods. Jack Grimshaw was one of the men he had hired. Frank was another. They had been riding Pollinger's range today when they'd been ambushed by a group of Dwyer's gunwolves. Forced to flee, they had taken shelter in this old line shack.

But even as they forted up inside the shack, both men had known that it would be only a matter of time before their enemies rushed them. The numbers were on the side of Dwyer's men. They would lose a few, without any doubt, but in the end they would overrun the cabin and kill Frank and Grimshaw.

As Frank waited beside the window, a six-gun in each hand, ready to sell his life as dearly as possible, he suddenly heard a thump on the roof overhead. So did Grimshaw, who looked up and exclaimed bitterly, "Damn it!"

A couple of seconds later, both of them smelled smoke. That didn't come as a surprise to either Frank or Grimshaw. Dwyer's men had decided they didn't want to lose anybody. One of them had gotten behind the line shack and tossed a torch onto the roof. They were going to smoke out their quarry.

Grimshaw's lips drew back from his teeth in a grimace as he looked over at Frank. "We go out shootin'?" he asked.

"Only way to go," Frank said.

"You know . . . you might have a better chance of gettin' away if I drew their fire first . . ."

"We go together, or not at all."

Grimshaw chuckled, said, "To hell with that," and before Frank could even move, his companion had bounded out the door and was running toward the trees. The irons in Grimshaw's hands blazed as they threw out a storm of lead.

"Blast it!" Frank exclaimed as he darted through the door as well. He saw men to either side of the cabin and fired in both directions at once. He saw several of Dwyer's killers go down, felt the tug of bullets on his shirt.

Up ahead, Jack Grimshaw stumbled, twisted, went down. Crimson flowers bloomed on Grimshaw's shirt. Frank ran to him, stood over him, and kept firing, expecting to feel lead smashing into him, too, at any second.

Then, the sudden pounding of hoofbeats

and a fresh rattle of gunfire changed things. A group of riders led by Maynard Pollinger swept down out of the hills toward the burning line shack, and that tipped the balance. The newcomers' bullets riddled Dwyer's men, except for a couple who fled frantically.

Safe again and miraculously unhit, Frank dropped to a knee beside Grimshaw and rolled the man onto his back. "Jack, damn it," Frank said, "if you'd just waited a minute, help was on the way."

Grimshaw was conscious. He looked up at Frank, his face gray and drawn, and rasped, "Well, we didn't . . . know that . . . did we?"

"If you hadn't been trying to give me a better chance —"

"Hell," Grimshaw cut in. "I always figured to . . . go out shootin' . . . anyway."

Maynard Pollinger rode up and quickly dismounted. "How badly is he hit, Frank?"

"Shot through the body three or four times, looks like," Frank told the Englishman.

"We'll take him back to the ranch. I'll send a man right now to fetch the doctor from town. We'll do everything we can to save his life. I give you my word on that."

Frank looked down at Grimshaw's gaunt,

gray face and figured it was too late for that.

He'd been wrong, though. Maynard Pollinger was true to his word. He got the best medical attention possible for Grimshaw, nursed the gunman through the critical first few days, then took him to the doctor's house in Laramie as soon as Grimshaw was strong enough to stand the trip. Frank heard later that Grimshaw had been laid up for eight months, but eventually he had made a full recovery. Frank had seen the proof of that with his own eyes, here in Eureka.

The range war between the MP and the Diamond D had ended in rather prosaic fashion only a couple of weeks after the fight at the line shack. A horse had kicked Pete Dwyer in the head, and after a couple of days of lingering in unconsciousness, the cattle baron had died. His grieving widow didn't have the stomach to continue the war. In fact, she had sold the ranch and left Wyoming Territory, and after that, things had become downright peaceful in the region. All the hired gunmen drifted on, including Frank, once he had satisfied himself that Grimshaw was getting the best care possible.

Those memories flashed through Frank's mind in a second as he stood there in

Eureka's main street. The history between Frank Morgan and Jack Grimshaw went back a lot further than that range war in Wyoming, though. They had known each other as boys growing up near Weatherford, Texas, and had spent a considerable amount of time fishing, as Grimshaw had mentioned. They had ridden hell-for-leather across the wooded hills of the Cross Timbers as wild young cowboys.

Frank had gone on the drift after the war, when he began to get a reputation for being fast on the draw. As far as he knew at the time, Grimshaw had remained behind to continue working as a cowhand.

A few years later, though, he had run into his friend in Santa Fe and discovered that Grimshaw had abandoned ranch life, too, and was now walking the thin line that divided the law-abiding from the outlaws. He wasn't as slick with a gun as Frank, but he was fast enough to stay alive. As fellow members of the gunfighting fraternity, they had run into each other several times over the years. The West, for all its untamed vastness, was a small place in many ways. The two of them had fought on the same side more than once. Grimshaw had saved Frank's life in a fight in Wichita, and Frank had returned the favor during a dustup at

Yankton.

Now, Frank was pleased to see Grimshaw again, pleased that Grimshaw seemed to be doing all right. He put the thoughts of his old friend out of his mind, though, because now Marshal Gene Price was standing in front of him, an angry look on his face.

"What the hell's all this?" the lawman demanded as he swept a hand toward the body on the travois.

"I was hoping you could tell me, Marshal. I found this man out in the woods. Looks like the Terror got him."

An expression like he had just bitten into something extremely unpleasant appeared on Price's face. "The Terror, eh?"

"His back is clawed up pretty bad. I reckon he died from losing so much blood. Have you ever seen him before?"

Price frowned and studied the dead man's face. After a moment, the marshal said, "Maybe. I think I've seen him around town. I don't know his name, though."

"Or what he was doing here?"

Price gave a disgusted snort. "Doing the same thing as every other damn fool in these parts, I reckon. Hunting that monster." Price turned toward Frank again. "Or maybe I should say, that's what they were doing until you came along, Morgan. You've sort of taken over that job, haven't you?"

"I just figured it would be a good idea if the woods weren't full of men shooting at anything that moves."

"Yeah. And if you earn yourself ten thousand dollars in the process, then so much the better, eh?"

Frank knew the lawman didn't like him. Fortunately, he didn't care one way or the other about Gene Price's opinion of him. He said, "I'm going to take the body on down to the undertaking parlor and spread the word that folks should go by there and see if they can identify it. Maybe somebody will claim the body."

"I wouldn't count on it. Hardcases like that usually don't have many friends."

That was true enough, Frank thought, and there was another angle to consider, too. If the dead man was part of the group that had attacked the logging camp, the men who had been with him weren't likely to come forward and identify him, let alone claim the body and give it a proper burial. They would want to keep any connection with the dead man concealed, to avoid any awkward questions from the law.

In fact, Frank would have been willing to bet that any time the gang got together here in town, they would do so in secret if possible, so people wouldn't get the idea they were working together. If Emmett Bosworth actually was behind the atrocity at the logging camp, as Frank suspected, he would want to avoid as much suspicion as possible, so he wouldn't want his men to be noticed.

Frank took up Goldy's reins and began leading the horse along the street. Price walked alongside him, and as they went toward the undertaker's place, the marshal shooed away the curious townsmen who wanted to gawk at the corpse.

"I don't see why it matters to you who he is," Price commented to Frank.

"Just curious, I guess," Frank replied with a shrug of his shoulders. "I don't think there's any connection between the Terror's victims. They're just hombres who were unlucky to run into the thing. But you never know. I might find out something that would help me track it down."

Price glanced over at Frank, his eyes narrowing. "Seems to me that you've been mighty close to the thing several times now, and it hasn't come after *you*. Maybe there's some connection between you and it."

"You're barking up the wrong redwood, Marshal," Frank said with a smile. "I'd never even heard of the Terror until yesterday. I don't know what it is. I just want to put a stop to the killing."

"A gunfighter, wanting to put a stop to killing." Sarcasm dripped from Price's voice. "If that don't beat all."

Frank suppressed the flash of annoyance he felt at the marshal's attitude. Price was just trying to put a burr under his saddle, and Frank wasn't going to let him do that.

They reached the undertaking parlor and found the proprietor, a fat man with a round, unaccountably jolly face, waiting for them. "Take the deceased around back," the undertaker told Frank. "I heard about you bringing a body into town, Mr. Morgan, so I have a couple of my assistants waiting back there to take charge of the remains."

"Before I do that," Frank said, "do you recognize this hombre?"

The undertaker studied the dead man's face for a moment, then shook his head. "Can't say as I do. But then, I don't pay much attention to what folks look like until I see them under these circumstances, when they're never at their best."

Frank turned the dead man over the undertaker's assistants. As they left the place, Marshal Price asked, "What are you going to do now, Morgan?"

"I thought I'd get some lunch, and then I plan to go out and try to pick up the Terror's trail again."

"How do you figure to kill a thing that can do" — Price jerked his head toward the undertaking parlor to indicate the corpse they had just left there — "*that?*"

"Reckon I'll figure that out when the time comes," Frank said. He didn't mention the fact that he didn't plan to kill the Terror as long as there was a chance the thing was really Ben Chamberlain. He had given his word to Nancy Chamberlain.

So what he really had to figure out was a way to trap a creature that could tear a man limb from limb and move through the woods with the speed and stealth of a ghost.

That was all.

CHAPTER 15

Grimshaw looked around as he went into the Bull o' the Woods Saloon. His men were scattered around the establishment's big main room, drinking in groups of two or three, but not clustered together so it was obvious that they knew each other. That was the way Emmett Bosworth wanted it. The timber magnate didn't want anyone in Eureka suspecting that he had assembled a gang of hired killers.

As Grimshaw went to the bar, he caught the eye of the man on the other side of the hardwood. He gave the bartender a tiny nod and then said, "Give me a beer, Harry."

The drink juggler drew the beer, wiped the bar in front of Grimshaw with his rag, and then set down the foaming mug. When Grimshaw picked up the mug, his other hand moved smoothly to rest on the spot where the beer had been. That move with the rag had allowed Harry the bartender to slip a key under the mug, and now Grimshaw's hand rested on it without anyone being the wiser. When he moved his hand, the key went with it.

The key unlocked a door that opened from the alley behind the Bull o' the Woods into the saloon's back room. There was nothing in that room except a table and some chairs. From time to time, private poker games took place there. Months ago, Grimshaw had slipped Harry a tidy little sum to insure that he and the other men working for Bosworth would have a place to meet where no one could observe them together.

Grimshaw drank about half the beer, then left the rest and walked out of the saloon after tossing a coin on the bar to pay for the drink. The others knew what to do. After making sure that no one on the street was paying any attention to him, he stepped into the narrow passage beside the building and made his way to the alley in back. He unlocked the door, stepped into the private room. It had one window, but the shade was tightly drawn.

Within minutes, the first of the other men showed up, seeking entrance with a discreet knock. One by one, they filtered into the meeting place until all thirteen remaining members of the gang were there.

"You got it?" Hooley asked eagerly. "You got the money?"

Grimshaw took the roll of bills from inside his shirt. He had already discreetly peeled off his share and stashed it in one of his pockets. As he tossed the money on the table, he said, "What do you think? There it is, boys. Twenty-eight hundred dollars, as promised."

"Wait a minute," Radburn said. "There's only thirteen of us here, not countin' you, Jack. What about Nichols?"

Grimshaw shook his head. "Nichols won't be collecting his share." They would hear about it sooner or later anyway, so he thought he might as well go ahead and tell them the news. "The Terror got him. Frank Morgan brought his body in from the woods."

"Morgan!" one of the men said. "I heard he was in these parts. How do you know Morgan didn't kill Nichols?"

"Because he wasn't shot," Grimshaw replied flatly. "His back was clawed so wide open that most of his blood spilled out."

"Son of a bitch," Radburn said in a soft, awed voice. He turned his head to look at Hooley. So did several of the other men.

"What?" Hooley demanded. "You think I

209

should have stayed there and got ripped open, too?" He started to cough, and had to cover his mouth with his hand.

"What's done is done," Grimshaw said in a hard, emotionless voice. "What it amounts to is that there's an extra two hundred bucks in that roll. You fellas can split it up any way you want to."

"I don't really care," one man said, "as long as Hooley don't get any of the extra."

Another man jerked his head in a curt nod. "Yeah, that sounds good to me, too." Mutters of agreement came from several of the others.

For a moment, Hooley looked like he was going to fly into a rage. But then he controlled himself with a visible effort and his lip curled in a snarl.

"Take it," he snapped. "I don't want any of the damned money except my share."

"Fine," Radburn said. He scooped up the roll from the table and began passing out the bills. One of the men was pretty good at ciphering, so he figured out that if they split the extra money evenly, everybody would get an extra $16.66.

"How the hell are we gonna do that?" one man demanded. "These are twenty-dollar bills."

Grimshaw took a couple of double eagles

from his pocket and slapped the gold pieces down on the table. "There you go, boys," he said. "That'll make it come out even, an extra twenty apiece."

"We're obliged, Jack," Radburn said. "You didn't have to do that."

"We're all in this together, ain't we?"

Radburn gave Hooley a significant look. "Most of us are anyway."

Grimshaw laughed and clapped a hand on Radburn's shoulder. "You were playin' peacemaker earlier, so don't go stirrin' up trouble now," he advised. Then he addressed the whole group. "The boss said he'd have some more work for us in a while. Until then, just lie low. You can have a good time, but stay out of trouble. And whatever you do, watch what you say. No talking about anything that happened today."

Radburn shook his head. "I don't reckon any of us would much want to talk about that anyway, Jack."

Grimshaw knew exactly what his fellow gunman meant. Bushwhacking was one thing, but mutilating a bunch of corpses was something else entirely. There was a time in his life when he would have said no to such a job and ridden away.

But that time was gone. Grimshaw didn't have any family left, no home to return to, damn few friends. He had his job, and by God, he was going to do it, no matter how unpleasant it got sometimes.

At least Frank Morgan was in town. It would be nice to sit and talk about old times with good ol' Frank.

After leaving the undertaking parlor with Marshal Price, Frank said good-bye to the lawman and led Goldy toward the livery stable, with Dog padding along behind them. Patterson greeted the three of them with a friendly grin and set aside a wagon wheel hub he was greasing.

The liveryman grew more serious as he said, "Heard you found another fella in the woods who'd been unlucky enough to run into the Terror."

Frank nodded. "Yeah, that's right. His body's down at the undertaker's. I'd be obliged if you'd go down there and take a look at it if you get a chance."

"Me?" Patterson asked with a surprised frown. "Why me?"

"Because you have the best livery stable in town, from what I've seen, and probably a lot of strangers come here first when they get to Eureka. I'd like to know if you've seen this fella around, and more importantly, if you've seen him with anybody else."

Patterson scratched at his close-cropped beard. "Well, I reckon that makes sense. Sure, I'll mosey down there after a while and have a look. Can't say as I'm real eager to take a gander at a corpse, though."

"I don't blame you for that," Frank said.

He led Goldy into the stall where the horse had spent the night and started unsaddling him. When he returned to the forest this afternoon, he would take Stormy. Having two superb mounts enabled him to switch out between them and keep both horses fresher.

When he was finished with that chore, he walked back to the front of the barn. He had his bedroll in his hands.

"I'm hoping you can tell me who the best doctor in town is, if there's more than one."

Patterson looked surprised again. "You sick or hurt?"

"No, I just need to ask him a couple of questions."

"We got three doctors here in Eureka, that I know of . . . but I'd say Dr. Connelly is the best one." Patterson told Frank how to find the physician's office, which was on a side street at the other end of town. Frank thanked him, and then Patterson added, "Why don't you just leave the dog here? I was about to step out back and eat some

213

lunch, and he seems mighty fond of my table scraps."

Frank grinned. "Sure. Stay, Dog. I'll see you later."

Carrying the bedroll, he headed along the street toward Dr. Connelly's office. As he did, he thought about Jack Grimshaw and wondered what his old comrade in arms was doing in this part of the world. A disturbing possibility occurred to him. If Emmett Bosworth had indeed hired a gang of killers to go after Chamberlain's men, then Grimshaw could be one of them. Even though they had been friends, Frank was honest enough with himself to realize that Grimshaw had always been more willing than he was to sign on for a job strictly for the money. Over the years, Frank had heard rumors that Grimshaw was mixed up in some pretty shady deals.

But a little freelance outlawry was different from bushwhacking innocent men and then chopping them up with axes, Frank told himself. He didn't want to believe that Jack Grimshaw was capable of such a thing, and until he saw proof of it with his own eyes, he wasn't going to believe it.

Dr. Patrick Connelly's practice consisted of a neat little cottage containing his surgery and examination rooms, backed up by a larger house that was obviously the doctor's home. No one answered Frank's knock on the office door, so he walked around back to the doctor's living quarters.

The door there was opened by an attractive woman in her thirties with auburn hair and green eyes. "The doctor's having his dinner," she said in a tart voice. "He's not seeing any patients right now. You can wait on the front porch of the office if you'd like."

"I'm not a patient," Frank said, "and I hate to disturb a man's dinner, but I need to ask him a question. Shouldn't take but a minute, and then I'll let him get back to his meal."

The woman got a stubborn look on her pretty face. She wore a wedding band on her left ring finger, so Frank figured she was Connelly's wife. She was about to dig in her heels and tell Frank to go away, when a man's voice came from somewhere else in the house.

"Who is it, Molly?"

The woman turned her head and called back, "Just an old cowboy. Nothing for you to concern yourself with, Patrick."

Frank heard footsteps, and then someone opened the door wider. The man who stood there was burly, built more like a prizefighter than a physician. He had a shock of gray hair and a salt-and-pepper beard.

"I heard you say you have a question for me, sir," he said. "I hope for both of our sakes that it's a good one. Otherwise, we're both risking the wrath of my wife here."

"I think it's a good one," Frank said.

The man raised his rather bushy eyebrows when Frank paused.

"It's about a bone."

Interest sparked in the man's eyes. He stepped back and said, "Come in."

Molly Connelly blew out her breath disgustedly, shook her head, and retreated out of the room. "It's a poor doctor who doesn't take care of himself first," she said over her shoulder.

Connelly grinned and waited until she was gone before he said quietly, "My wife thinks my practice causes me to miss too many meals." He patted his thick belly. "You couldn't tell it to look at me, though, could you?" He ushered Frank into a parlor and then said, "Now what's this about a bone?"

Frank nodded toward a divan and said, "I need to unwrap it."

"By all means."

He set the bedroll on the divan and unrolled it. When he lifted the bone and held it up where the doctor could see it, Connelly's eyes widened.

"You were right, my friend. That's definitely a bone."

"Human, isn't it?" Frank asked.

"Yes. That's the radius, one of two bones that form the skeletal structure of a man's forearm. Or a woman's, although judging by the length and diameter of that one, I'd say it came from a man." Connelly turned toward a bookcase that sat against one wall. "Let me show you . . ."

He took a thick, leather-bound volume from one of the shelves and began flipping through it.

"*Gray's Anatomy?*" Frank asked.

Connelly glanced up in surprise. "You're familiar with it? You've had medical training?"

Frank shook his head. "Only enough practical experience to patch up a bullet wound or a knife slash or set a broken bone. But I do a considerable amount of reading when I get the chance, in all subjects."

Connelly took a long look at Frank and then nodded. "Yes, I'd venture a guess that you've encountered more wounds of violence than an average man." He flipped a couple more pages in the book, found what he was looking for, and jabbed a finger at one of the illustrations. "You see, here's a man's arm. The upper bone, between the shoulder and the elbow, is the humerus. The two lower bones, between the elbow and the wrist, are the radius and the ulna. What you have there is a radius, as I said. Where did you get it?"

Before Frank could answer, Molly Connelly appeared in the doorway. "It would only take a minute, you said," she told Frank in an accusatory tone. "Patrick, your food is getting cold."

"I'm sorry, my dear," Connelly said. "Our visitor . . . By the way, what *is* your name, sir?"

"Morgan. Frank Morgan."

"Mr. Morgan has brought me a very intriguing artifact."

Molly snorted. "That? That's just an old bone."

"Indeed. And Mr. Morgan was about to tell me where he got it."

Molly shook her head and left the room again. Frank smiled and said, "Reckon I've caused some trouble in your household."

Connelly waved a hand. "Don't let it worry you. Molly is quick to anger, but even quicker to forgive. *And* she's an excellent nurse, not to mention easy on the eyes." He put out his hand, palm up. "May I?"

Frank gave him the bone. As Connelly brought it close to his face and studied it

218

intently, Frank said, "I found it in a cabin out in the woods."

"It was by itself?" Connelly murmured. "No other remains?"

"Nope. Just the one bone. And it was stuck almost out of sight, where it would be easy to overlook."

Connelly glanced up. "Then someone took the rest of the skeleton and left this bone by accident."

"That's what I'm wondering about," Frank said with a nod.

"One thing we can be certain of . . . The other bones didn't get up and walk away by themselves." The doctor's manner became more brisk. "What is it you want from me, Mr. Morgan? A simple confirmation that this bone came from a human skeleton? The answer is yes."

"It doesn't look like it's been . . . damaged."

"Gnawed on, you mean?" Connelly looked at the bone again. "I agree. I don't see any teeth marks. I'd say it was picked clean by insects, not cannibals." Connelly smiled. "That thought *did* enter your mind, didn't it, Mr. Morgan?"

Frank shrugged. "Maybe."

"Wait a minute," Connelly said with a sudden frown. "Morgan, Morgan . . . You're the man Rutherford Chamberlain hired to go after the Terror. The gunfighter. You're the talk of the town . . . along with the Terror itself, of course." He waved the bone in the air. "Does *this* have something to do with the Terror?"

"I don't know yet," Frank replied honestly. Even though he instinctively liked and trusted the doctor, he wasn't ready to reveal all his secrets and theories to the man. "I'd like to ask you, though, as a man of science . . . do you believe all the stories that have been told about the Terror?"

For a long moment, Connelly didn't reply. Then he said, "There have been reports of strange, unknown animals from around the world for years, Mr. Morgan, perhaps even for centuries. Did you know that in Africa, there are creatures called gorillas, who are supposed to be half-man, half-ape? I'd love to see one someday."

Connelly was straying from the subject at hand. "What about the Terror?" Frank prodded. "Could it really be some sort of monster, instead of, say, a man?"

The doctor frowned. "I've seen some of the damage done by the Terror, Mr. Morgan."

"So have I."

"Do *you* think a man did that?"

It was a fair question, but to be honest, Frank couldn't be sure. He was about to say as much when someone pounded violently on the front door of the doctor's house.

"Doc! Doc! Come quick!" a man yelled. "There's trouble!"

Molly appeared in the doorway to the kitchen again. "Now what's all this disturbance?" she asked hotly. "At this rate, you'll never finish your dinner, Patrick!"

"Occupational hazard, my dear, occupational hazard." Connelly strode over to the front door and pulled it open. A red-faced townie stood there, breathing hard. "What's all the excitement about, Bert?"

"You got to come downtown, Doc," the man said. "A couple of Chamberlain's loggers just brought in a wagon, and it's plumb full of men who are all tore up!"

CHAPTER 16

Frank wasn't surprised by that breathless announcement. If anything, he had sort of expected some of Chamberlain's men to discover the massacre at the logging camp and bring the grisly news to town before now.

Evidently, they had brought more than the news. They had brought the gruesome evidence of the killings as well.

"Settle down, Bert," Connelly said. "These men are all dead?"

"Yeah. They're all tore up!"

"Yes, you said that. It seems that they'd be more in need of the undertaker's attention than mine."

"All I know, Doc, is that Marshal Price told me to fetch you."

"Very well." Connelly still held the bone in his hand. As he turned toward Frank, he lifted it and asked, "Do you mind if I hang on to this for the time being, Mr. Morgan?

I might be able to determine a little more about it if I have time to study it."

Frank nodded. "That's fine, Doctor. Just keep it somewhere safe."

Connelly laid the bone on a small table where he had placed the copy of *Gray's Anatomy*. He reached for his coat and hat, which hung on hooks next to the door, and as he put them on, he said to his wife, "I'll be back as soon as I can, Molly. I doubt if there's any reason to keep my dinner warm, though. I expect I'll be downtown for a while."

She sighed and gave him a resigned nod.

Frank followed Connelly out of the house. Bert, the townie who had brought the news, was too excited to move at a normal pace. He broke into a run, obviously anxious to return to the main street.

"Man's morbid curiosity," Connelly said as he and Frank strode along side by side. "I see it all the time. There's nothing more intriguing than death, probably because of its universality and inevitability."

"Yeah, I expect there'll be quite a crowd gathered around that wagon."

Frank's prediction proved to be accurate. So many people were in the street that it was difficult to see the wagon itself. He spotted the man sitting on the seat holding the reins, though, and recognized Karl Wilcox, the logger he had met the day before. Wilcox looked pale and shaken, which wasn't surprising considering his cargo.

Marshal Gene Price was on hand, too. When he saw Frank and Dr. Connelly approaching, he raised his voice and ordered, "All right, everybody get back! Get back, there! Let the doctor through!"

On the wagon seat, Wilcox rubbed a shaky hand over his face and said, "It's too late for a sawbones, Marshal. Way too late."

Frank knew that was true, and Price must have as well. Still, the marshal took hold of Connelly's arm and steered the physician to the wagon. "Take a look, Doc, and see what you think."

Connelly had to know what to expect, but he blanched anyway as he studied the grisly remains in the back of the wagon. "I think this gentleman is right," he said with a nod toward Wilcox. "The time when my services might have come in handy has long since passed."

"You've seen some of the other bodies that have been brought into town from the woods," Price said. "Are these killings the work of the same creature?"

Frank was particularly interested in hearing Connelly's answer. He had determined to his own satisfaction that men were responsible for this outrage, not some monster. However, his discovery of the other body indicated that the Terror *had* been in the vicinity of the logging camp when the massacre took place.

Connelly said, "I couldn't tell you that, Marshal, without a closer examination of the bodies. What I *can* say is that you should get them off the street. There's no need for this grotesque display. Take them down to the undertaking parlor, and I'll have a better look at them there."

Price nodded and made a curt gesture to Wilcox. "You heard the doc," he said. The lawman stepped away from the wagon and waved his arms. "Let's have some room here, damn it!"

Reluctantly, the crowd moved back far enough so that Wilcox could flap the reins and get the team of mules moving again. Connelly followed the vehicle toward the undertaking parlor.

Price hung back and frowned at Frank. "I saw you come up with the doctor, Morgan," he said. "You sick or something?"

"No, but I was discussing some medical matters with him."

Price looked like he was waiting for Frank to go on, but Frank didn't elaborate. After a

225

moment, the marshal said, "If you're going to hunt down that creature, Morgan, I hope you do it soon. Even though these killings aren't happening in my jurisdiction, I don't like seeing all these bodies brought into my town."

"I'll be riding out again, right after I get something to eat," Frank said.

Price grunted and inclined his head toward the wagon, which was still rolling down the street toward the undertaker's. "You've got an appetite after seeing that?"

Frank smiled thinly. "A man's got to keep his strength up if he's going to be hunting monsters."

After leaving a grim-looking Marshal Price in the street, Frank headed for Peter Lee's hash house. The proprietor, his pretty wife, and their two children were busy at this time of day, but Frank found an empty stool at the counter and ordered the lunch special — steak, potatoes, greens, and apple pie. When Lee put the plate in front of Frank, he nodded toward the window and said, "Lots of excitement out there in the street a little while ago. I figured it would be better if I kept my wife and the little ones in here while it was going on."

"You were right about that," Frank told him.

Lee lowered his voice. "They say more men were killed by the Terror."

"That's what it looked like, all right."

Frank didn't add that that was what it was *supposed* to look like. He knew better, though. He suspected that by this time, so did Dr. Patrick Connelly. He couldn't imagine the doctor overlooking the slight discrepancies between the wounds these latest victims had suffered and the earlier ones actually inflicted by the Terror.

The question was, would Connelly say anything about it to Marshal Price?

"A little while ago, I saw those men who came in here and caused all that trouble last night," Lee went on. "They went by the window. I think they were headed into the Bull o' the Woods."

"Any of them appear to be hurt?" Frank asked as a theory came to his mind.

"One of them had a bloody rag tied around his arm, and another was walking really funny, like there was something wrong with his, well, his rear end."

Frank tried not to grin. That was enough to tell him his hunch was probably right. The fella with the bandaged arm was the one he'd nicked, and the other one had

227

probably made the acquaintance of Dog's sharp fangs, up close and personal.

So the three would-be monster hunters, as well as the three loggers who had thrown in with them, had followed him into the woods and bushwhacked him. That didn't come as any real surprise to Frank. They were filled with greed and anger, and they figured that killing him would not only settle the score for the damage he'd dealt out in that fracas, but also open the door for Chamberlain to reinstate the bounty on the Terror. A bounty that, in their confidence bordering on arrogance, they intended to collect.

So this morning there had been two separate gangs of gunmen in the forest — Erickson and his cronies, and the men who had wiped out the loggers at that camp and mutilated the bodies. Frank knew Erickson's bunch hadn't done that. There weren't enough of them.

Plus the Terror had been in the vicinity, too. Frank's earlier thought about the woods being crowded today was looking more and more right.

"If Erickson and the rest of those men bother you, Peter, you let me know," Frank said. "I don't think they will, though. Their grudge is against me, not you."

"Don't worry." Lee leaned forward and lowered his voice. "I have a shotgun here under the counter in case of trouble. Those varmints come in here and try to start anything, they'll wish they hadn't when they get a faceful of buckshot."

Frank had to grin. If there were more people like Peter Lee around who were willing to do what was necessary in order to protect themselves and their families, the world would be a better place.

Frank enjoyed his lunch. He could see why the hash house did such good business. The food was delicious. There wasn't much *ambience*, as highfalutin folks in cities like San Francisco and Boston liked to talk about, but a man couldn't fill his belly with ambience, now could he?

He was cleaning up the last of his apple pie when Lee paused in front of him, nodded toward the front window, and said, "Look there, Mr. Morgan."

Frank turned his head and looked out the window as a large black carriage rolled past, pulled by a pair of big black horses in fancy silver rigging. The carriage had a lot of silver trim on it, too.

"Looks almost like a hearse," Frank commented.

Lee shook his head. "No, that's no hearse.

That's Mr. Rutherford Chamberlain's carriage."

Frank wondered for a second what Chamberlain was doing in town. According to what he had been told, the timber baron seldom, if ever, left that huge redwood mansion in the forest these days.

Then he realized that word must have reached Chamberlain about the slaughter at his logging camp. That would have been enough to budge the man from his sanctum.

Frank set his fork on the empty saucer where the pie had been and stood up. He slid a coin onto the counter to pay for his meal, and when Lee said, "I'll get your change," he waved it off.

"See you later, Peter," he said as he settled his hat on his head.

"Be careful, Mr. Morgan. I have a feeling that there are a lot of people around here who harbor ill wishes for you."

Frank chuckled, but there wasn't much actual humor in the sound. "That's been true just about every place I've gone in my life."

He stepped out of the hash house and looked up the street. The carriage had come to a stop in front of the hotel. Frank's powerful stride carried him in that direction.

He was passing the vehicle when he heard a woman's voice say, "Mr. Morgan?"

Frank paused and looked over at the carriage. It had fine silk curtains over the windows to keep out the dust, but those curtains had been pushed back at one window and Nancy Chamberlain peered out at Frank with a worried expression on her pretty face.

"Mr. Morgan," she said in a half whisper, "have you found out anything about . . . about . . ."

Frank moved closer to the window and glanced at the driver's seat on the front of the carriage. It was empty at the moment, and he wondered if the driver was in one of the saloons wetting his whistle. That didn't really matter. What was important was that he had a moment here to speak privately with Nancy.

"Miss Chamberlain," he said with a polite nod. "What brings you and your father to town? I assume he came along, too?"

"He's in the hotel," she said. "He's looking for you. He's furious, Mr. Morgan. One of his workers came to the house and told him that eleven more men had been killed at one of our camps this morning. Killed by . . . by the Terror." Her pale fingers clutched the edge of the window. "I can't

231

believe that. Do . . . do you know if it really happened, or is it just some terrible rumor?"

Frank wished he could have spared her what she was bound to be thinking, but he couldn't. "Those men were killed, all right," he said with a grim nod. "I saw their bodies when they were brought in."

Nancy closed her eyes and flinched as if she'd been struck a physical blow. "Oh, dear Lord," she murmured.

For a moment, Frank thought about telling her he was convinced that the Terror — whatever it was, whether Nancy's brother or not — hadn't been responsible for these latest killings. But then he remembered his decision to play that card close to his chest, and so he kept silent.

Nancy opened her eyes and looked imploringly at him. "Have you found out anything yet? Found any sign of . . . of . . ."

"I found that cabin you told me about," Frank said. "It looked like nobody had been there for months."

"Yes, he started shunning it for some reason. Almost like something happened there that upset him."

Something that left a human bone in the cabin, Frank thought. Was that where Ben Chamberlain had carried out his first killing? Was that where he had begun his descent into madness, his transformation into a monster?

Frank didn't know yet, but he was determined to have those answers. He had given his word to Nancy, and he was starting to feel like he owed it to all the men who had died to uncover the truth, too.

"Father flew into a rage when he heard about the latest deaths," Nancy went on. "He even ordered the servants to get the carriage ready and said we were coming to town. He's looking for you, Mr. Morgan. He wants the Terror killed *now*, and if you can't do it, he's going to reinstate the bounty."

A frown creased Frank's forehead. "That's not a good idea. He needs to give me more time —"

"Morgan!"

The angry roar came from the front porch of the hotel. Despite Rutherford Chamberlain's gaunt, wasted frame, he still possessed the deep, rumbling voice of a much more powerful man. Frank turned to see Chamberlain standing there, a look of impatient rage on his face.

From the carriage window, Nancy said softly, "I think your time has run out, Mr. Morgan."

CHAPTER 17

Frank thought Nancy was probably right about that. Rutherford Chamberlain looked mad enough to chew nails or bite somebody's head off.

Chamberlain stomped down from the porch and came toward the carriage. He wore a white suit today, with a flat-crowned white hat, and looked more like a Southern plantation owner than a timber baron. He came to a stop in front of Frank, glared at him, and demanded, "What the devil are you doing talking to my daughter?"

"Just saying hello to the young lady," Frank responded. "She told me you were looking for me. I was about to go into the hotel and find you."

Chamberlain snorted. "Somehow I doubt that. You'd have to explain yourself, sir."

"Explain what?"

"Why you haven't killed that unholy creature yet!"

Frank took a deep breath and kept a tight rein on his temper. "It's been less than twenty-four hours since we came to our agreement, Mr. Chamberlain. I don't reckon that's really giving me a fair chance to do the job, now is it?"

"You haven't had time to find the Terror and kill it, but the monster has had time to slaughter a dozen more of my men! Is *that* fair?"

"I was in the woods this morning," Frank explained. "I found one of the victims and brought him in. You didn't know about that, did you?"

Chamberlain continued glowering at him and snapped, "It doesn't matter. That creature has to be found and killed — now! Several of my foremen came to the house just before Nancy and I left and told me that the loggers don't want to leave their barracks anymore. They're afraid to do their work. I can't allow that, Morgan. My business will collapse if the men won't go into the woods."

And that was probably the exact reaction Emmett Bosworth had been hoping for when he hired that crew of gun-wolves, Frank thought. Once again, the image of Jack Grimshaw flashed through his mind. He still hated to think that Grimshaw might

235

be involved in that, but he was coming to the realization that he was going to have to talk to his old friend and try to get the truth out of him.

"Just give me some more time," Frank told Chamberlain.

"How much time? Until every man jack who works for me has been ripped to shreds?"

"Give me another twenty-four hours," Frank said.

"And if you haven't found the Terror by then?"

"I reckon you'll do whatever it is you think you have to do."

Chamberlain snorted in disgust. "I'll put that bounty back on the monster's head," he declared. "Only, it won't be ten thousand dollars next time. It'll be twenty thousand!"

Frank bit back a curse. Quite a few people had gathered around to watch the angry confrontation between him and Chamberlain, and they all heard what the timber baron had just said. Gasps of surprise came from several of them, followed by excited murmuring. In half an hour, maybe less, nearly everybody in Eureka would know that Chamberlain was talking about reinstating the bounty — and doubling it.

To men like Erickson and his pards, that

would mean Frank was the only thing standing between them and a chance at twenty grand.

Chamberlain had just painted an even bigger target on Frank's back than the one Frank usually wore there just because he was the infamous Drifter.

"Twenty-four hours," he said, pressing Chamberlain. "We have a deal?"

Chamberlain hesitated, then jerked his head in a curt nod. "All right. Twenty-four hours. But not a minute more. And if you haven't brought that monster's head to me by that time, you're finished, Morgan."

Frank glanced at the carriage window, where Nancy Chamberlain's pale, drawn face peered out. He gave her a tiny nod, trying to let her know that everything was going to be all right. He would find the Terror, determine whether or not it was really her brother, and act accordingly from there. Exposing Emmett Bosworth's scheming would just have to wait.

Chamberlain turned away and started hollering for his driver. Frank nodded at Nancy again, then went into the hotel. He wanted to gather some extra gear. Once he went into the woods the next time, he wouldn't be coming out again until he had found what he was looking for.

When he came back downstairs a short time later with a pair of full saddlebags draped over his shoulder, he found Dr. Patrick Connelly waiting in the lobby. Frank frowned in surprise as Connelly lifted a hand in greeting and said, "Could I have a moment of your time, Mr. Morgan?"

"Sure. I was on my way to the livery stable, if you'd like to walk along with me."

"That will be fine."

As they headed toward Patterson's, Frank asked, "What can I do for you, Doctor?"

"A short time ago, you asked me to confirm something for you, Mr. Morgan. Now, I'd like for you to confirm something for me. You strike me as an observant, intelligent man, and even though you've only been in this area for a short time, you've seen several of the victims attributed to this so-called Terror."

Frank laughed. "Funny how people keep putting *so-called* in front of the thing's name. I've done it myself."

"That's because at this point, no one is certain what it really is. We can't be, until it's killed . . . or captured."

"Seems like a man would have a mighty tough chore on his hands if he set out to capture a thing like that."

"Indeed. But my point, Mr. Morgan, is

238

that these bodies today struck me as being slightly different from the previous victims. I was wondering if you noticed the same thing."

Frank stopped and looked around. No one was close enough to overhear him as he lowered his voice and said, "You don't think the Terror killed those men Wilcox brought in from the logging camp."

Connelly shook his head slowly. "Not unless it's learned how to wield an ax. Those poor devils were chopped apart, not torn apart. I suspect that they were shot first as well, so the mutilation was postmortem, but I'd have to dig into their bodies and find the bullets to prove that. Whoever took an ax to them was careful to obliterate the gunshot wounds."

"Have you told anybody else about this, like the marshal?"

Connelly grimaced. "Gene Price is an honest man, a good man despite his gruff nature. And he does a good job of keeping the peace here in town. But dealing with violence on this scale, with cold-blooded mass murder . . . that's a little beyond him, I'm afraid. There's enough panic in the region already because of the Terror. If people knew that a gang of vicious murderers was roaming the countryside as well . . ."

The doctor shook his head. "It wouldn't take much to set off riots among the loggers, and that could easily spread to the town."

"That's what I thought," Frank said with a nod. "That's why I've kept quiet about it."

"Who do you think could be responsible for such an atrocity?"

"Only one man I can think of. Chamberlain's competition. Emmett Bosworth."

"Bosworth," Connelly said softly. "He's in town, you know."

"He is?"

The physician nodded. "He's staying at the Eureka House. Has the big suite, right up in front on the second floor. He's been here, off and on, for months. He has a small timber lease up the coast, so it's not unreasonable for him to be here to check on his holdings. Everyone knows he's got his eye on Chamberlain's trees, though."

"I'd like to talk to him," Frank said, "but I don't have time right now."

"Ah, yes, Mr. Chamberlain's deadline. I heard about that. Do you believe you can find the Terror in that amount of time?"

"I'm going to try, that's for sure." Frank turned toward the livery stable again. He was glad he'd had this chance to talk to

Connelly, but now he needed to get started on the hunt again.

"Mr. Morgan . . . that bone you showed me? Does *that* have something to do with the Terror?"

"It might," Frank admitted. "I don't know yet."

"I have a safe in my office. I'll lock it up, so that it'll be secure."

Frank nodded. "I'd appreciate that." He shook hands with Connelly. "So long, Doctor."

"Good luck, Mr. Morgan . . . or should I say, good hunting?"

Frank headed for the livery stable, leaving Connelly there in the street. He glanced toward the Eureka House and thought about Emmett Bosworth. He was leaving a lot of things hanging fire here, but he had no choice. If he didn't find the Terror in the next twenty-four hours, Rutherford Chamberlain would put that twenty-thousand-dollar bounty on its head, and the whole countryside would explode in violence, Frank reckoned. The only way to stop that was to bring in the creature himself.

One showdown at a time, he thought as a grim smile tugged at the corners of his mouth.

■ ■ ■ ■

"Son of a bitch," Emmett Bosworth said as he let the curtain fall closed over the window. He'd had it pushed back only a few inches, leaving a small gap through which he could watch as Frank Morgan carried on an earnest conversation with Dr. Patrick Connelly. Bosworth knew Connelly from the time he had spent here in Eureka, and he had heard a great deal about Frank Morgan. Supposedly, Rutherford Chamberlain had hired the notorious gunfighter to find the Terror, and according to the conversations Bosworth had overheard in the hotel dining room a few minutes earlier, Chamberlain had now given Morgan a twenty-four-hour deadline to kill the creature.

That wouldn't do at all. For his plans to succeed, he needed the Terror, whatever it was, to continue its occasional depredations. That way, the Terror would be blamed for the things Bosworth's men were actually doing.

The Eureka House had a bell system, so that all Bosworth had to do to summon a porter was to push a button. He did so now, and a few minutes later, a soft knock came on the door. Bosworth opened it to see an elderly black man in a red jacket waiting in the hallway.

"Can I do somethin' for you, Mr. Bosworth, sir?" the porter asked.

"Do you know a man named Jack Grimshaw?"

"Seen him around, yes, sir."

"Find him," Bosworth snapped. "Tell him I need to talk to him as soon as possible." He took a silver dollar from his pocket and flipped it to the old man. "There'll be another one of those for you if you don't say a word to anyone about this ever. You understand?"

The coin disappeared smoothly into a pocket of the red jacket. "Yes, sir."

"And if you do go shooting off your mouth, I'll make you sorry that Abe Lincoln ever set you free."

"No, sir. That won't happen."

Bosworth nodded curtly and shut the door. He took a cigar from his vest pocket, clipped off the end of it, lit it, and then paced back and forth and smoked for the next fifteen minutes while he waited for Grimshaw.

When a knock sounded on the door again, Bosworth stalked over to it and jerked it open. Grimshaw stood there, a puzzled look on his rugged face.

"You wanted to see me, Mr. Bosworth?" the gunman asked.

Bosworth jerked his head and said, "Come inside." He closed the door behind Grimshaw and didn't offer him a drink this time. "Have you ever heard of a man named Frank Morgan?"

Grimshaw's eyebrows went up in surprise. "Morgan? You mean The Drifter? Yeah, sure, I've heard of him. Just about everybody west of the Mississippi has."

"I thought you might know who he was, since you're in the same line of work. Are you actually acquainted with him?"

"We've crossed trails a time or two over the years," Grimshaw replied, his voice wary.

"Is he the sort of man who can be paid off?"

"Paid off to do what?"

"To go away and mind his own business."

Grimshaw looked at Bosworth in silence for a moment, then burst out with a harsh laugh. "Frank Morgan? Paid to give up a job he's agreed to do?" Grimshaw shook his head. "Not hardly."

"You're sure of that?"

"I'd stake my life on it," Grimshaw said flatly.

Bosworth sighed. He stuck the cigar back in his mouth and bit down hard on the end.

"Very well then," he said around the cylinder of tobacco. "I have a new job for you and your men, Grimshaw."

"Thought you said you wouldn't be needin' us for a while," Grimshaw said with a frown.

"That was before other matters came up. You'll have to leave this afternoon."

"Where are we goin'? What's the job?"

Bosworth puffed on the cigar for a second, then took it out of his mouth and said, "You're going to follow Frank Morgan into the woods . . . and kill him."

CHAPTER 18

Jack Grimshaw had been worried that was what Bosworth was going to say. The timber baron wouldn't have started asking about Morgan if he wasn't concerned about The Drifter for some reason.

But Grimshaw wasn't going to just accept this new job without finding out what it was all about either.

"Why do you want Morgan dead?" he asked.

Bosworth flushed with anger at the blunt question. "I'm not in the habit of having my orders questioned, Grimshaw, or of explaining myself."

Grimshaw didn't back down. He said, "Yeah, well, you never sent me after a man like Morgan either. You know, sometimes folks have another name for him besides The Drifter. They call him The Last Gunfighter."

Bosworth gave a contemptuous snort.

"That's preposterous. There are scores of gunfighters left in the West. Hundreds perhaps. You're one yourself, and so are the men who ride with you."

"Not the same thing," Grimshaw replied with a shake of his head. "Yeah, I'm pretty slick on the draw, and I hit what I shoot at. Those other boys, they're the same way. But Frank Morgan . . . well, he's in a class by himself. Ben Thompson and Wes Hardin are dead. Smoke Jensen, Falcon McAllister, Matt Bodine . . . they've all hung up their guns, and they're makin' it stick somehow. That old-timer called Preacher . . . well, hell, he's *got* to be dead by now, even though I never heard anybody who knew for sure say that he is. But Morgan, he's still in the game, and still as good as he ever was, from what I've heard."

Bosworth had listened to Grimshaw's words with growing impatience on his face. He took the cigar out of his mouth, waved it in the air, and with his lip curled in a sneer, said, "So what you're telling me is that you're *afraid* of this man?"

Grimshaw suppressed the impulse to knock that sneer off of Bosworth's face. That wouldn't solve anything in the long run. Instead, he said, "I'm tellin' you that Frank Morgan is a mighty dangerous man,

247

and I respect that. I'd be a damn fool not to, and my mama back in Texas didn't raise any fools."

"More dangerous than fifteen men who are supposed to be good with their guns?"

"Fourteen," Grimshaw reminded him. "We lost Nichols this morning."

Bosworth waved that away. "So the odds are fourteen to one, and yet you hesitate to go after Morgan?"

"I didn't say we wouldn't do it," Grimshaw snapped.

"Ah!" Understanding appeared on Bosworth's face. "You want more than your usual pay."

"What I want is to know why. What's so important about Morgan that you have to send us after him?"

Bosworth snorted. "Isn't it obvious? Chamberlain has given him the job of tracking down the Terror and killing it. If this man Morgan is actually as dangerous as you claim he is, he might succeed. We can't allow that."

"Because you need the Terror to stay out there in the woods, so he'll get blamed for anything me and the rest of the men do for you."

"Exactly!" Bosworth puffed on the cheroot. "Perhaps your mother really didn't raise any fools, although I'd say that the jury is still out on that question."

Grimshaw allowed himself a second's luxury to wonder how it was that an arrogant son of a bitch like Bosworth had managed to live this long without anybody shooting him or beating him to death with a two-by-four. Then he said, "It didn't bother you when Chamberlain had that ten-grand bounty on the critter and there were men all over the woods looking for it."

"The chances of any of those men actually finding and killing the Terror, or even of surviving the encounter, were so slim that I wasn't worried. But as you yourself say, Morgan is different."

Even though Grimshaw didn't want to admit it, Bosworth had a point. If there was anybody who might actually corral the Terror, it was Frank. And if that happened, Bosworth's long-range plans would indeed be ruined.

But this was *Frank* that Bosworth was talking about. Sure, they hadn't been all that close over the years, but they had fought side by side on more than one occasion. They had saved each other's life. They'd fished and gone swimming in the Brazos River and run wild as kids together. Forget for a minute about the dangers involved in trying to kill Frank Morgan. Think about betraying an old friend . . .

"Five thousand," Bosworth said.

Grimshaw blinked. "What? You mean you'll give us five thousand for this job?"

Bosworth shook his head. "No. I'll give *you* five thousand, and five thousand more to split among your men. Chamberlain put up a bounty of ten thousand dollars for the man who kills the Terror. It's worth that much to me to keep the thing alive for a while longer."

"Chamberlain's talkin' about doublin' it to twenty grand, you know."

"Don't push it, Grimshaw. That's my offer. Five to you, five to your men."

"And if I don't take it?"

"Then I'll make the same offer to, say, Radburn. He seems like a tough, competent man."

There was no getting around it, Grimshaw realized. That was too much money to turn down, and if he *did* refuse it, then Bosworth was right — Radburn wouldn't. The men would go after Frank either way.

But they'd be more likely to succeed if Grimshaw was along, he told himself. He knew Frank Morgan better than anybody else in these parts. The group would have the best chance of bringing him down, and losing fewer men in the process, if Grimshaw was part of the effort. And he did owe some loyalty to his current partners, didn't he?

"All right," he said heavily. "It's a deal."

"Good." Bosworth glanced out the window, then lifted a hand and summoned Grimshaw over. "There he is now, leaving the livery barn. He'll be riding out of town. Follow him. Kill him. Simple as that. When you come back, I'll have ten thousand dollars in cold, hard cash waiting for you."

Grimshaw nodded and turned toward the door. Normally, he shook hands to seal a deal, but he didn't particularly want to shake Emmett Bosworth's hand.

And Bosworth probably didn't want to shake the hand of a man who would betray an old friend either, Grimshaw thought as he put a stony expression on his face and left the hotel room.

"Well, better you than me goin' out there," Patterson said as Frank walked out of the livery stable leading Stormy and Goldy.

The rangy gray stallion wore the saddle right now, but Frank intended to take both horses along on this trip, despite the fact that he had ridden Goldy that morning. He didn't know how long he would be away

251

from town. He had packed supplies to last for several days. If he didn't find the Terror before the deadline Chamberlain had given him, that didn't mean he was going to abandon the search. He intended to keep looking until he located the creature and determined once and for all whether Nancy Chamberlain was right about it being her brother.

If it wasn't — if it was some sort of animal — Frank intended to kill it. Even though the Terror wasn't guilty of all the charges that had been leveled against it, there was no doubt that it had attacked and killed more than a dozen men. Either way, it had to be stopped.

"I appreciate the good care you've taken of my friends," Frank said as he held out his hand to the liveryman. "We'll see you when we get back to town."

"Sure thing," Patterson said. "By the way, I went down to the undertaker's and had a look at that dead fella, the way you asked me to."

"Did you recognize him?"

"Yeah, I think he kept his horse here for a few nights when he first got to town. That was a while back, a couple of months ago maybe, so I can't be completely sure, but I believe I'm right."

"Do you remember if he was traveling with anybody else?"

Patterson shook his head. "Not really. Like I said, it's been a while."

"Well, I appreciate it anyway. You say he only kept his horse here for a few nights?"

"Right. I reckon he found some place permanent to stay and was able to keep his horse there. That's just a guess, but it's all I've got, Mr. Morgan."

"I'm obliged," Frank said with a nod. He mounted up and lifted a hand in farewell, then turned the horses toward the end of the street. Dog trotted alongside as Frank rode out of Eureka.

He headed southwest, toward the thick band of timber that ran for miles along the Pacific coast, south of Humboldt Bay. Thick clouds were forming over the ocean, Frank saw. They didn't look particularly threatening, but they would block some of the sunlight and make the twilight world under the redwoods more shadowy than ever. No telling what might be lurking in that gloom . . .

The Terror wasn't the only thing he had to worry about, he reminded himself. He'd been shot at several times during the twenty-four hours he had been in this part of the country, including the previous afternoon when he first visited Ben Chamberlain's cabin. That incident had been lurking in the back of his mind. Something about it didn't quite jibe, and as he rode along the logging road now, penetrating deeper into the woods, he thought about what had happened at the cabin. That was before the ruckus with Erickson and his friends, before it was even widely known that Rutherford Chamberlain had given him the job of finding the Terror.

So who had taken those potshots at him when he stepped out of the cabin?

Frank had no answer for that, but it was one more mystery to solve once he had taken care of his more pressing problem.

"Stay alert, Dog," he said unnecessarily to the big cur as they entered the towering trees. Dog's senses always operated at peak efficiency.

Frank had recognized a landmark, a particular tree with a long blaze down its side from a lightning strike. The tree had survived, but it would be marked for all eternity by what had happened to it.

One more way trees and men were alike, Frank reflected as he rode past the redwood.

"Twenty grand," Treadwell said. "A big share of that bounty would go a long way toward making things all right again."

"Yeah, your balls wouldn't ache as much if you had a pocket full of *dinero*, would they?" Erickson asked with a grin.

"Let's leave my balls outta this. And Sutherland's ass and Roylston's nose, too. Let's face it, all of us have plenty of reasons for wantin' that bastard Morgan dead, even without the bounty."

Dawson said, "But twenty grand always helps."

None of the six men could argue with that.

They had ridden out of Eureka about half an hour after Frank Morgan left town. Roylston, Jenkins, and Sutherland had all worked for Rutherford Chamberlain before the danger from the Terror had spooked them into quitting, so they knew the woods quite well. Erickson intended to put that knowledge to good use.

In fact, he had gotten Jenkins, the smartest of the trio, to draw a map of the timberland southwest of the settlement. There was a low range of hills to the east, the Pacific to the west, and the Eel River running into the ocean about twenty miles south of Eureka. Within those boundaries were some of the biggest trees in the world, and those were also the stomping grounds of the Terror. The three loggers knew every place the monster had struck. Chances are Morgan would be scouting around those same locations. And Erickson and his companions would be scouting for Morgan.

"Here's what we'll do," Erickson mused as they rode along. "Once we've taken care of Morgan, we'll go ahead and start looking for the Terror. If we find it, we can kill it and hide the body somewhere. Then we'll go back to town to wait until Old Man Chamberlain has given up on Morgan and posted that twenty-thousand-dollar bounty. *Then* we'll go back to wherever we stashed the body, cut off the head, and take it back to collect." He grinned at the others. "How's that sound?"

"It sounds like you ain't hurtin' for confidence," Treadwell said with a dour look. "Hell, it ain't the middle of the afternoon yet. Plenty of time to hunt down and kill Morgan *and* the Terror."

Erickson frowned. "I'm just sayin', if it works out that way, that's how we'll do it."

"Sounds good to me," Dawson said. "I'd just as soon get this over with as quick as we can." He looked at the trees that had started to close in around them. "I don't much like it out here."

Neither did Erickson, but he wasn't going to let the others see that. He kept the

confident look on his face as he rode forward.

The wind picked up a short time later.
They really couldn't feel it much where they
were, but they could hear it sighing through
the branches far overhead, and see the trees
swaying a little, too, if they looked up. Dawson asked, "Is it gonna storm?"

"No, those weren't storm clouds comin'
in from the ocean," Roylston said. "It might
drizzle a little, that's all. You'd hardly feel it
under here."

"I wouldn't want to get caught in these
trees during a thunderstorm. Too much
lightnin'."

"Hell, you'd be safe." Roylston waved a
hand at the redwoods. "Everything around
here is a whole heap taller'n a man. What
you have to worry about with lightning is it
starting a fire, and we've had enough rain
lately so that's not a real threat right now."

Erickson took the map Jenkins had drawn
out of his shirt pocket and unfolded it to
study it. He motioned Jenkins up alongside
him, conferred with the former logger for a
moment, then said, "How about we all shut
up for a while? We're gettin' to an area
where the Terror's been spotted several
times. In fact, the damn thing killed a man
not far from here. We don't want it sneakin'

257

up on us while we're busy runnin' our mouths, do we?"

The men shook their heads as Erickson looked at them one by one. He had just gotten that response from Sutherland when something came flashing out from behind a tree and jerked the man right out of the saddle.

CHAPTER 19

Frank heard the gunshots from somewhere behind him and reined Stormy to a halt. He hipped around in the saddle to peer through the trees, but of course, he couldn't see more than about fifty yards in any direction because of all the thick redwood trunks.

Frantic shouts accompanied the gunfire. Those sounds were all too familiar to Frank.

They were the sounds of the Terror going about its bloody business.

Dog had turned around, too, and pricked his ears forward. The hair on the back of his neck was ruffled up, and a low growl came from him.

"Yeah, Dog, that sounds like what we're looking for," Frank said. "Go get it!"

Dog took off like a shot. Frank rode after him, leading Goldy and trusting Stormy to find the fastest route through the woods. The shots and the yelling grew louder. It sounded like the men were coming toward

Frank at the same time he was headed toward them.

Up ahead somewhere in the brush, Dog suddenly snapped and snarled and then yelped wildly. "Dog!" Frank bellowed. He jerked the Winchester from its saddle sheath and worked the rifle's lever.

At that same instant, something came crashing through the undergrowth and burst out right in front of Frank. One second it wasn't there, the next second it was. He didn't have time to even try to bring Stormy to a halt. The big gray collided with whatever the thing was. Frank caught only a glimpse of it before Stormy went down and he was sent sailing through the air. In that brief second, though, he was aware of its massive size, its shaggy pelt, and its blinding speed as it ran upright with something slung over one shoulder.

Frank thought that something was a man.

Then he crashed into a tree trunk, bounced off, and went rolling across the ground. The impact stunned him, and although a part of his brain cried out for him to get up and find the Winchester he had just dropped, his muscles refused to respond. All he could do was lie there with the world spinning crazily around him.

He was at the mercy of the Terror.

There was no doubt in Frank's mind that was what he had just seen. The huge, hairy beast was what had been killing men all through these woods for months. This encounter contained something new, though. The Terror had had a prisoner. Maybe that was keeping it occupied. Maybe that was why it hadn't fallen on Frank already and ripped him limb from limb.

Frank suddenly felt coarse hair against his face. He jerked away from it, some deep, atavistic instinct finally forcing his muscles to work again.

Then relief washed through him as he saw Dog's face only inches away from his own. The big cur peered intently at him with a mixture of curiosity and concern.

Frank's muscles were starting to work again after the shock of slamming into the tree like that. He reached up, looped an arm over Dog's sturdy back, and braced himself that way as he pulled himself into a sitting position. Dog licked his face happily. Frank recalled the animal's yelp a few minutes earlier, and looked him over for any sign of an injury. He didn't see any blood. Maybe Dog had just been scared. Such a thing was mighty rare, but not impossible.

Frank had felt some fear of his own during that instant when he'd gotten a close-up look at the Terror.

Unfortunately, everything had happened so fast that he still didn't know if it was man or beast. The shaggy pelt said animal, but he had never seen an animal move that fast on two legs.

Whatever it was, it was gone now. He didn't see it anywhere.

He was about to have other company, though. Horses pounded and crashed through the woods somewhere nearby, and a man shouted, "Sutherland! Damn it, Sutherland, can you hear me?"

Sutherland — if that was the name of the man the Terror had been carrying — couldn't hear him. Sutherland was either dead or a long way off by now, the way the Terror had been moving.

Another man called, "Erickson, did you *see* that thing? The way it snatched Sutherland off his horse . . . I . . . I never saw anything like that in my life."

Erickson, Frank thought. The men coming toward him wanted him dead. Might be a good idea not to be just sitting here in the forest when they came along.

He glanced around for Stormy and Goldy, but didn't see either of the horses. They would be somewhere close by, he knew, and would come if he whistled for them. It

might be better to just let them stay wherever they were, though, at least for the moment.

He spotted his Winchester and his hat lying nearby and reached for them, wincing
as pain shot through him when he leaned
over. He might have cracked a rib or two,
he thought. Getting hold of the rifle's barrel, he drew the weapon toward him and
then planted the butt against the ground.
He used it as a makeshift crutch to lever
himself to his feet, being careful not to let
the barrel point at him as he did so.

When he was standing again, he hobbled
toward the closest redwood. The sounds of
horses and men were very close now. Erickson and his cronies would be coming in
sight at any moment. Frank hurried as
much as he could, motioning for Dog to
follow him.

They went around the tree, which was
about twelve feet wide at the base, and then
Frank stopped and leaned back against the
trunk. He stood there with the Winchester
slanted across his chest, ready to fight if he
had to. Dog sat at his feet, still and silent
except for an occasional tiny whine that
showed how much he wanted to tear into
the hombres searching through the woods.

Frank would shoot it out with Erickson's

bunch if he had to, but shaken up and on foot as he was, it would be better if they didn't find him right now. To increase the chances of that, he stayed absolutely still, barely even breathing, as the searchers moved closer and closer. The wind sighed through the treetops high overhead. Frank felt a few drops of drizzle on his face as the moisture filtered down through the thick canopy of branches.

Then a couple of riders passed by not more than twenty feet away from him. All they would have had to do to see him was turn their heads, but they never looked in his direction. He recognized the big, red-bearded Erickson and one of the other men whose name he hadn't heard. The other man was saying, "Sutherland's gone. We're never gonna see him again, Erickson."

"We don't know that —" Erickson began.

"The hell we don't. You saw that thing carry him off. It's gonna eat him, that's what it's gonna do. You know how loco an animal is once it gets a taste for human flesh."

"Shut up!" Erickson snapped. "I don't want to hear that kind of talk."

"Why else would it carry him off instead of just killin' him? We know Sutherland was alive the last time we saw him. He was still hollerin'. Damn beast'll probably keep him alive and just eat him a little bit at a time."

"Jenkins, I told you . . . shut . . . the hell . . . up."

Erickson spoke through clenched teeth as the men passed on out of sight. Frank didn't relax because they were gone, however. He knew there were probably several other men in the group, and they'd be moving around in the area, searching for the missing man, too.

He could have eased their minds a little, Frank thought. He hadn't seen any sign that the Terror ever consumed its victims. The bone he had found at the primitive cabin seemed to indicate that the creature didn't indulge in such grim appetites.

But he didn't care about easing their minds. The varmints wanted to kill him, so let them worry.

A moment later, he heard the other men off to his left, but they didn't come as close to him as Erickson and Jenkins had. They moved on into the forest, searching for the long-gone Sutherland. Even though Frank didn't believe that the Terror was going to eat its prisoner, he wouldn't bet a hat — or anything else — that Sutherland would survive being captured by the creature.

Frank waited until all the men were gone,

then whistled softly. It took him a couple of tries before noises in the brush told him that Stormy and Goldy were responding. The horses pushed through the undergrowth and emerged near the tree where Frank waited. He still leaned against the trunk because it hurt when he tried to straighten up.

Stormy came over to him, nuzzled his shoulder. "Good fella," Frank murmured. He slid the Winchester back in its sheath, then grasped the saddle horn with both hands. He got his left foot in the stirrup and pulled himself up into the saddle. Pain shot through him again, but he told himself to ignore it. More than likely, those ribs were just bruised. He just needed to take it easy for a while.

Unfortunately, there was no time for that. Not with the Terror still on the loose and the time that Rutherford Chamberlain had given him running out.

Frank didn't bother with Goldy's reins. He knew the horse would follow Stormy.

"Get the scent, Dog," he told the big cur. "The critter ran right through here. You can pick up his trail."

Dog cast back and forth, nose to the ground, for a couple of minutes, then stood stiff-legged and growled, signifying that he had found the scent of something that bothered him. He had reacted the same way to the Terror's scent earlier, so Frank said, "Good boy. Trail, Dog!"

Dog took off through the brush. Frank followed. Sometimes he had to detour the horses around some obstacle that Dog could slip under or over, and when that happened, Dog always waited until Frank, Stormy, and Goldy caught up. The four of them made a fine team. It had been that way for a long time, and things would stay like that for a long time to come, God willing, Frank thought.

The chore facing them this afternoon had gotten harder. Not only did he have to worry about finding the Terror and dealing with it, but now he knew for sure that Erickson and the others were out here in the woods, too, hunting for *him*.

What about the men he suspected were working for Bosworth, the ones who had attacked the logging camp that morning? It was unlikely they would return to the forest this soon, Frank reasoned, so at least he didn't have to concern himself with *them*.

A fine mist continued to fall. The trees shielded Frank from most of it, but he felt its wet touch on his face from time to time. Actually, it was sort of refreshing, so he didn't care about the rain. It wasn't coming down hard enough to wash away the scent that Dog was following.

Every so often, he heard shouting in the distance. Erickson and his companions were still looking for the missing Sutherland. But the trail Dog was following veered more toward the ocean, taking him and Frank away from the area where Erickson and the others were. The Terror had changed direction as it charged through the woods. Erickson and his friends didn't know that because they didn't have Dog's sensitive nose to tell them.

Frank called soft encouragement to the big cur, who began to pick up speed as if the scent were getting stronger. But then Dog slowed suddenly and came to a stop with his hackles raised. Frank reined Stormy to a halt, drew the Winchester, and looked around.

He didn't see anything moving. Dog was gazing intently at a spot a few yards ahead, at the thick base of a tree. Frank looked at the same place, but didn't see a thing other than a few dark spots on the ground. Dog started to growl.

"Hush, Dog," Frank said quietly. "Hush."

Dog obeyed, and thick silence closed in around them. Frank listened. He didn't hear anything except a faint *plop*, the sound a big drop of rain made when it fell and landed. But there weren't any big raindrops today, only the fine mist.

But there was another dark spot at the base of the tree now, Frank noticed as a little shock ran through him.

He tilted his head back and looked up, his gaze following the trunk of the redwood until it reached the spot where branches began protruding from the tree.

Crammed into the angle between one of those lower branches and the trunk itself was the body of a man. It dangled there precariously, and as Frank watched, another huge drop of blood fell like crimson rain and splattered at the base of the tree.

He reckoned he'd found the missing Sutherland.

How in the world had the Terror gotten the body up there? At the tree's base, the trunk was much too big for a man to wrap his arms and legs around it and shinny up, although it narrowed considerably by the area where the branches began growing. The trunk wasn't smooth; the bark that covered it was rough and seamed with fissures. But it would take an incredible amount of strength to seek out handholds and footholds and scale the tree that way, at the same time carrying a man's corpse.

One thing the Terror didn't seem to lack for, Frank reminded himself, was strength. A creature that could rip a man's arms off his body was capable of some prodigious feats.

Why climb up and hide the body in the tree, though? What purpose did that serve?

But again, this was the Terror, an irrational being if ever there was one. It didn't do any good to questions its motives as you would those of a normal man. The creature seemed to operate on pure, destructive rage.

It hadn't done a very good job of wedging the corpse into place either. As Frank watched, the body began to slip. There was nothing he could do to prevent it from falling, so he lifted the reins and backed Stormy away from the tree, getting well out of the way.

"Come on, Dog," he said.

Goldy retreated as well. A few moments later, the body slipped free. It plummeted toward the earth, turning over once as it fell. It landed with a heavy thud at the base of the tree, in the same place where the blood drops had landed.

Frank edged Stormy forward. He dismounted and walked over to the dead man, carrying the Winchester with him. The man had landed facedown. Frank hooked a toe under his shoulder and rolled him onto his back. The body moved limply. The fall seemed to have broken numerous bones. The man's throat was torn open, and there were deep wounds on his chest as well. His face was relatively unmarked, though. Frank recognized him as one of the loggers who had come into Peter Lee's place with Erickson and the others the night before.

So now there were only five men out here hunting for him. Still respectable odds, Frank mused, but nothing he hadn't handled on many occasions in the past.

Frank left the body where it had fallen. There was nothing else he could do. Mounting up again, he called out to Dog, "Find that scent again, boy. Find the critter."

Dog circled wide around the tree where the corpse lay, and then trotted back and forth until he picked up the scent again. Then he took off eagerly, still heading toward the coast.

Fifteen minutes later, Frank rode out into a clearing that ran along the top of a cliff. The open area was narrow, only fifty yards or so wide, but it ran for hundreds of yards, as far as Frank could see in both directions.

And directly in front of him, stretching out endlessly, was the gray, restless sea. He heard the never-ceasing waves pounding against the rocks at the bottom of the cliff, a hundred feet below.

The clearing had a nice carpet of grass on it. Frank rode across it toward the sheer rock face where land ended and sea began. He had seen the Pacific before, on numerous occasions, but it never failed to impress him. Even though he was much more comfortable on land, he could see why some men talked about the ocean's majesty. It was bleak today, but no less majestic.

Dog had trotted right over to the brink, and now stood there staring out at the ocean, the wind ruffling his thick coat. The wind blew harder here, without the trees to block it. Frank rode up to join Dog. He dismounted and peered over the cliff as he hung on to Stormy's reins. He had no special fear of heights, but he believed in giving natural dangers the respect they deserved.

"Nothing down there but rocks," Frank said. The constant action of the waves had rounded the large gray stones. Waves foamed and hissed around them. It was an impressive scene. Frank didn't see what it had to do with his quarry, though. The Terror wasn't down there, and there was no place for the thing to hide along this rugged cliff.

Had it come here, to stand and gaze out over the water, as Frank was doing now? He couldn't help but wonder about that. Everything he had seen so far suggested that the Terror was nothing more than a mindless monster, whether it had started out as human or not.

But if Nancy was right and the Terror really was her brother, was it possible that a spark of humanity was still buried somewhere inside the creature? In the midst of all the brutality and killing, were there occasional moments of reflection as well?

Frank didn't know, and considered it highly unlikely that he would ever find out. And as starkly beautiful as this scene was, he didn't have time to stand around appreciating it.

"Where did it go, Dog? Find the scent. Hunt, Dog."

The big cur started searching for the scent again. He seemed to have it in short order and began trotting along the edge of the cliff. Frank mounted up and followed. After a hundred yards or so, Dog turned and headed toward the trees again.

So the Terror had come out here, stood at the edge of the ocean for a time, and then gone back to its woodland home. Frank didn't think the creature was all that far ahead of him now, and he hoped that the chase wouldn't last much longer.

Frank had just pulled Stormy's head around to start after Dog when flame suddenly lanced out from the shadows underneath the big trees. He heard the crack of a rifle, the whistle of a slug past his ear. Then more shots blasted from the trees, a whole volley of them, and as Frank braced himself for the horrible impact of bullets smashing into his body, he knew that out here at the edge of the world, with bushwhackers in front of him and the endless sea behind him, there was no cover, no place to fort up.

He was trapped.

CHAPTER 20

Frank kicked his feet free of the stirrups and threw himself out of the saddle as lead stormed around him. He felt a couple of bullets tug on his shirt, and heard the wind-rip of another as it passed close by his ear. Miraculously, though, he hit the ground without being wounded.

"Go!" he shouted at the horses. "Stormy! Goldy! Get out of here!"

Both of them took off at a gallop as they recognized the command Frank had given them. At the same time, Dog turned around and started to come back toward him.

"No, Dog!" he called. "Into the woods! Go!"

Dog hesitated, then whirled around and raced toward the trees, angling away from the gunfire as he stretched out in a dead run. Bullets kicked up dirt around his paws, but didn't slow him down. He vanished into the thick shadows under the redwoods.

By this time, Frank was rolling desperately toward the edge of the cliff, toward a spot where the ground sloped slightly toward the brink. He had caught sight of it as he was diving off Stormy's back, and he knew it represented the closest thing to any cover he was going to find out here. Bullets still sizzled through the air around him.

Pain suddenly lanced into his left arm, and he knew he was hit. He gritted his teeth and tried to ignore it, just as he had been ignoring the pain from those bruised ribs. He reached the place where the ground fell away toward the cliff, and rolled onto it. It was no more than ten feet by ten feet, just a slight depression, but it was enough to put some earth between him and the men trying to kill him.

Unfortunately, there was nowhere to go from here. He was pinned down about as securely as a man could be.

But he still had hold of his rifle and had quite a bit of ammunition in his pockets, so if those gunmen hidden under the trees decided to rush him, he could make them pay a price for killing him.

Frank lay stretched out on his belly on the damp grass, which grew all the way to the cliff's edge. He tried not to think about the fact that only a couple of feet behind him lay yawning, deadly emptiness with rocks and sea at the bottom.

As the mist continued to fall and make his clothes even wetter, he looked over at his left arm to see how badly he was hit. Blood stained the sleeve of his shirt about halfway between his shoulder and elbow. Frank moved the arm, and even though doing so hurt like blazes, the muscles still obeyed him and he didn't feel anything grating together.

So the bullet had missed the bone, he thought — the humerus, he remembered Dr. Patrick Connelly calling it — and had just torn through flesh. And it had gone all the way through as well, Frank knew, because he could feel distinct entry and exit wounds as they throbbed.

The loss of blood could still be dangerous, but from the rate at which the crimson fluid leaked onto his shirt, he could tell that the slug hadn't nicked any veins or arteries. With even rudimentary medical attention, the wounds ought to heal. His arm should be fine.

Of course, there was still a little matter of surviving this ambush.

The shots died away as the men in the trees realized that they couldn't see him anymore. Now they would be debating what they ought to do next, whether to rush him or try to wait him out.

Frank cast a glance at the sky, which was completely gray and overcast by now. There were still a number of hours of daylight left, but if the bushwhackers waited too long and night fell, Frank might be able to slip away in the darkness. They had to be as aware of that as he was.

He wondered who they were. Erickson and his friends were the most likely suspects, but they had been going in a different direction the last time Frank heard their shouts in the distance.

And although it was difficult to tell because everything had happened so fast, he would have sworn that more than five men had been shooting at him, too. More like twice that many, maybe more.

It was possible that Erickson and the others had run into some other would-be monster hunters who wanted Frank dead and had thrown in with them. A lot of folks had been upset about Chamberlain lifting the ten-grand bounty, and today those same hombres were licking their chops over the prospect of a bounty twice that size, with only Frank Morgan standing in the way of it.

Another possibility was that the killers

hired by Bosworth had ventured back into the woods today after all. But if that were the case, why would they be after him? Frank wondered.

There was one good reason, he realized as he thought about it, and it tied in with other things he suspected. Bosworth was staying at the Eureka House, according to Dr. Connelly, so it was entirely possible, even likely, that he had heard about Chamberlain giving Frank twenty-four hours to find the Terror. If the men who had wiped out the logging camp that morning worked for Bosworth, as Frank believed, then Bosworth was taking advantage of the fear everyone felt concerning the mysterious monster in the woods.

But if the monster was dead or caught . . . then whatever future atrocities Bosworth had in the works would be ruined, because they couldn't be blamed on the Terror.

Yeah, now that he'd thought it through, it made sense, Frank decided. Bosworth had a different reason for wanting him dead than Erickson and the other would-be monster hunters, but it was no less valid.

Silence still hung over the woods. Frank knew better than to think the bushwhackers were gone, though. They were still there, hidden in the shadows, waiting to kill him if he showed even the slightest glimpse of himself.

"I never saw a man move that fast in my life, Jack," Radburn said to Grimshaw. "With more than a dozen of us openin' fire on him at the same time, how in the hell did he manage not to get hit? He should've been filled full of holes!"

"There's some sort of guardian angel lookin' out for Frank Morgan," Grimshaw replied with a trace of bitterness in his voice. "Always has been, ever since we were kids. Why do you think I always tried to make sure him and me were on the same side every time we got mixed up in some ruckus?" He grunted. "Until now, that is."

Grimshaw had been afraid things would turn out like this. He hadn't wanted to come after Frank Morgan in the first place. Morgan was too slick, too quick-witted, too fast on his feet, to say nothing of his speed with a gun.

But the money Emmett Bosworth was offering was just too damned much to turn down, Grimshaw thought, so he and the other men had left Eureka a short time after Frank, and they had been on his trail ever since. They had been close enough to hear some sort of uproar going on earlier, and when they found a torn-up body at the base of a tree, it hadn't taken much of a guess to know that the Terror was involved somehow. Frank was on the trail of the Terror, but he had danger coming up behind him, too. He just hadn't known it at the time.

Now he did, and Grimshaw couldn't help but regret the fact that they hadn't killed Morgan with their first shots. That would have gotten an unpleasant task over with quickly, before Morgan even knew for sure what was going on.

Letting Frank Morgan know that you were gunning for him, and then failing to kill him, was one of the worst mistakes a man could make.

From behind one of the other trees, Hooley called, "You reckon he fell off the cliff?"

"Well, I don't rightly know," Grimshaw said. "Why don't you mosey out there, Hooley, and see if you can tell?"

Hooley moved slightly, as if he were about to follow Grimshaw's suggestion, but then he stopped short and glared over at the older man.

"You're tryin' to get me killed!"

"Thinnin' the herd," Radburn muttered. Grimshaw could hear him, but Hooley couldn't. Grimshaw chuckled.

"Chances are, Morgan found some cover, even though from here it doesn't look like there is any," Grimshaw added. "He's the best I've ever seen at using whatever luck gives him. The best I've ever seen at anything, period. But he's still human. He can't sprout wings and fly off that cliff, and there's nowhere else for him to go."

"But if we leave these trees, he'll have a clear shot at us," Radburn pointed out. "I don't want to try crossin' fifty yards of open ground while I'm in The Drifter's gunsights. Seems like a good way of committin' suicide."

"None surer," Grimshaw agreed.

"Then how are we gonna get him outta there?" one of the other gunmen asked.

Grimshaw rubbed his jaw and frowned in thought. They had a Mexican standoff here, and he couldn't see any way to resolve it short of charging Morgan's position. If they did that, Grimshaw was confident that Frank would die in the end — but not before quite a few of them got ventilated as well. The rest of the men would be like Radburn; none of them would want to be the one leading the charge.

An idea glimmered to life in Grimshaw's brain. He looked up at the trees towering above them. The redwoods were all at least a hundred and fifty feet tall, and many of them were taller than that.

"Any of you boys know anything about cuttin' down trees?" he asked.

No one spoke up.

"None of you ever worked as a logger before?"

"I always had better things to do with my hands than swing an ax," Hooley said with a sneer in his voice.

"Yeah, I'll bet," one of the other men said, "considerin' how the ladies feel about you."

Hooley turned angrily toward that hombre, but before a squabble could break out, Grimshaw snapped, "Settle down, damn it. We got a real problem here. If we don't deal with Morgan before it gets dark, he'll have a lot better chance of giving us the slip. I want some of you boys to head for that logging camp we hit this morning and bring back all the axes and saws you can carry."

"What if the law's there, or some guards or somebody from Chamberlain's company?" one of the men asked.

"Then wait until they're gone, or find another camp, or figure something out, damn it!" Grimshaw took a deep breath to calm himself. "Just get axes and saws and, oh, yeah, some of those steel wedges loggers drive into the trees when they're cuttin' 'em down. Mallets to drive them, too." He remembered more than he would have thought from the few times he had seen logging crews at work.

"What the hell you got in mind, Jack?" Radburn asked.

Grimshaw nodded toward the trees. "We're gonna use the weapons that the Good Lord was so thoughtful in providin' for us."

Radburn grinned as understanding dawned on him. He said, "How hard can it be to cut down a tree?"

They would soon find out, Grimshaw thought.

An hour went by. Frank's clothes were soaked by now. The fine mist in the air might not amount to much in the way of actual rainfall, but it would get a man wet if he were out in it long enough.

A while earlier, he had heard hoofbeats in the forest, fading into the distance, but he knew better than to think all the bushwhackers were gone. Maybe they were trying to lure him out by making him think they had left, but he doubted that. If they were professional enough to be hired by Emmett Bosworth to commit mass murder, they probably weren't fools, and they wouldn't think he was one either.

Still, the idea that some of them were pulling out was puzzling . . . and a mite worrisome.

Later, the riders came back. Frank heard the horses, although the hoofbeats were muffled by the carpet of needles under the redwoods and the damp, heavy air.

A few minutes after that, he heard the ring of axes biting into wood.

What in blazes were they doing? Cutting down a tree? That was the only explanation for the sounds. The steady *chunk! chunk!* continued until Frank had to risk raising his head just enough to take a look.

As soon as his eyes came over the level of the ground, muzzle fire lanced from several places under the trees as shots cracked out. He ducked and felt the dirt kicked up by the bullets spray over him.

Even that quick glance he had gotten had been enough to tell him that several of the men were working with axes on one of the trees at the very edge of the forest.

Frank studied the tree, tilting his head back enough so that he could run his gaze all the way up the thick trunk to the top. It was close to two hundred feet tall, he estimated, which meant that when it fell, if it toppled in the direction of the cliff, it would reach the spot where he had taken cover . . .

The bastards were going to drop a tree on him!

A grim smile tugged at the corners of his mouth. He'd had folks try to kill him in a heap of different ways, but as far as he could recall, this was the first time anybody had attempted to flatten him with a giant redwood.

That was exactly what would happen, too, if the tree landed on him. He'd be squashed flatter than a flapjack. And if he jumped up to run out of the way when the tree started to fall, the gunmen would be waiting for him, waiting to cut him down with rifle fire, instead of saws and axes.

He had to make them think twice about continuing with their plan. Moving fast, he raised himself enough to thrust the Winchester toward the trees and trigger a shot. That was the only round he got off, though, because the men who weren't working on the tree opened fire as soon as they saw the first flicker of movement from him. He had to hunker down again as bullets slammed into the ground just above him. He had no idea if his shot had come anywhere close to the men cutting down the tree.

The axes continued to ring, and a few

minutes later when they stopped at last, they were replaced within moments by the rasp of a long, crosscut saw.

Frank bit back a curse. They had him trapped good and proper, with no way out that he could see. He edged back a little, so that he could turn and peer over the edge of the cliff. Maybe he could climb down there somehow, work his way along the rocks at the base of the cliff, and find another way up.

He saw instantly that wasn't going to be possible. The cliff was too sheer, too slick, with few if any handholds. And in this mist, it would be even slicker than usual. Trying to climb down was certain death.

But maybe staying here wouldn't be, he saw after a moment. The area that sloped down where he had taken shelter dropped about a foot from front to back. If he stretched out right at the very brink, maybe the surrounding ground would stop the tree from descending all the way into that shallow depression . . .

No, Frank thought, he was grasping at straws. The tree would crush everything in its path when it fell, and that little bit of extra space wouldn't stop it for a second. What he needed was a miracle.

Or some help.

■ ■ ■ ■

"Keep drivin' those wedges in!" Grimshaw called. "We don't want the tree to start bindin' on that saw. If it does, we'll never get it out."

Even though he'd never done anything like this before, cutting down a tree seemed like common sense to Grimshaw. You hewed and sawed through the trunk from both sides, a little lower on the side in the direction you wanted the tree to fall. It was hard, dangerous work, but not all that complicated.

They had started the cuts with axes, but were now using the long, two-man saws. A couple of other men worked driving wedges into the cuts on both sides with wooden mallets. Once the cuts were deeper, the saw on the cliff side would be taken out, and the wedges on that side would be removed as well. Then more wedges would be pounded into the cut on the back side to widen it and tip the tree toward the cliff. When it tipped enough, gravity would take over.

Having a tree dropped on him was a hell of a way for a man like Frank Morgan to die, Grimshaw thought. Ol' Frank ought to go out with his hands full of blazing guns, dealing out death even as it came to him. A shame it couldn't be that way today, but Grimshaw didn't want to lose any more men. Bosworth would have plenty of work for them in the future, and he might wind up needing every gun.

"Keep an eye on Morgan's hidey-hole," Grimshaw reminded the men who had their rifles trained on the edge of the cliff. "You see a whisker move, you open up on it."

He walked around the tree, studying the cuts. They were almost deep enough, he decided, not overlapping but close. "You're doin' fine," he told the men working the crosscut saws. "Another couple of minutes, and we'll be ready to topple the damned thing."

Radburn had one end of a saw. Sweat covered his face. He panted, "I'm sure as hell glad . . . I don't do this . . . for a livin'."

"Yeah, no matter what a man does, there's always something worse," Grimshaw said.

"Give me . . . a gunfight . . . any day."

Grimshaw felt the same way. He had done his share of honest labor when he was a young man. It hadn't taken him long to figure out that he didn't like it. Once he had realized that he could handle a gun pretty well — not anywhere near as good as

Frank Morgan, of course, but better than most men — that was all he'd really needed to know.

Carrying his rifle, he walked around to the back of the tree again. He stood there, watching as the work continued. After a moment, he frowned a little as his nose wrinkled. A funny smell had drifted to him. It wasn't pleasant at all, something like a cross between unwashed flesh and a rotting carcass. It was getting worse, too.

Realizing suddenly what that might mean, Grimshaw stiffened. He jerked his rifle up and whirled around.

And found himself face-to-face with a horror that had surely come crawling up out of the depths of Hell.

CHAPTER 21

Frank heard the yelling and shooting from the trees, and he knew right away the bushwhackers weren't shooting at him. The fast, frantic sound of the gunfire told him the men were fighting for their lives, though.

Then one of them shouted, "Watch out! It's comin' *down!*"

Frank's head jerked up to look at the tree they'd been trying to fell. It was moving, all right, picking up speed as it tilted forward.

He had no choice. He had to get out of that leviathan's way, and hope that the ambushers had their hands too full with something else to gun him down when he came out into the open.

That something else, he thought as he surged to his feet, had to be the Terror. Nothing else out here in these woods could provoke such an uproar.

With a loud cracking sound, the tree began to topple toward the cliff. Frank ran to his right along the rim. Not only did he have to get out of the way of the massive trunk, but he had to avoid the branches, too, some of which were more than big enough to break his bones and knock his brains out if they hit him. As he ran, he snapped shots toward the trees with the Winchester, but he wasn't sure anybody in there was paying attention to him anymore.

The tree came down with a huge crash that caused the earth to shudder. Frank's quick action had carried him well out of its way. He angled toward the trees, thinking that if he could get into that twilight world underneath the redwoods, he would be able to give the bushwhackers the slip.

That is, if any of them survived the battle with the Terror. The yelling and shooting were still going on.

Frank ran into the trees. Instantly, a huge, shaggy shape darted at him. Instinct made Frank swing the Winchester toward the creature, but his finger froze on the trigger before he could pull it. He had recognized Dog, who had obviously been waiting for him.

Dog reared up, put his front paws on Frank's shoulders. Frank winced from the pain that caused in his wounded arm, but he didn't make the big cur get down.

Instead, he looped his arm around the thick, shaggy neck and gave Dog a quick hug, glad to see that his old friend was all right.

"Where are Stormy and Goldy?" he asked. "Take me to 'em, Dog."

Dog got down and started through the trees, glancing back to make sure that Frank was following him. Dog seemed to know where he was going.

A minute later, they came to a small clearing where Stormy and Goldy waited. Frank grabbed Stormy's reins and swung up into the saddle.

"Let's get out of here," he said, but then, before they could even get started, he thought better of it and hauled back on the reins.

He had come out here to find the Terror, he reminded himself. His close call in escaping the ambush attempt didn't really change anything. He still had to deal with the Terror, and the evidence seemed to say that the creature was close by right now. Even though Frank was wounded, it didn't make sense not to try to take advantage of that fact.

He turned Stormy's head toward the sounds of the battle going on nearby.

As he rode, he thumbed fresh cartridges into the rifle's loading gate. When the weapon was fully loaded, he stowed it in the saddle sheath again. If he wound up in the middle of this ruckus, it might be close work, more suited to the Colt on his hip.

Frank weaved around the giant tree trunks. Mist still filtered down through the canopy of branches high overhead. The light was bad, full of shifting shadows.

Then the gunfire stopped. A man yelled, "It went that way!"

"Let it go!" another man bellowed. "Find Morgan! We've still got to kill him!"

Frank's lips drew back from his teeth in a disappointed grimace. He recognized the voice that gave those orders.

It belonged to his old friend Jack Grimshaw.

Frank had hoped that his suspicions about Grimshaw were wrong. Obviously, though, they weren't. Grimshaw worked for Emmett Bosworth. He was part of the group that had slaughtered those loggers at Chamberlain's camp that morning. Given Jack's age and experience, he was probably the ramrod of the bunch. And now Bosworth had given them a new job.

Kill Frank Morgan.

Those were the only conclusions that made any sense. Frank knew what he was facing now, and he knew as well that no matter how much damage the Terror might have done to Bosworth's hired killers, they still probably outnumbered him by quite a bit, and he was in no shape to face them right now. His wounded left arm throbbed, and he could barely use it. His ribs ached. His clothes were soaked, and that had started a chill in his bones. Or maybe the wound in his arm had started a fever brewing inside him. That would account for the chill, too.

Regardless of the cause, he realized that he needed some rest, maybe a fire so that he could dry out, and something to eat, to keep his strength up. He couldn't risk a shootout with a gang of professional killers right now.

So with a sigh, he turned Stormy and motioned for Dog and Goldy to follow him. He had to find a place where he could hole up for the night, a place where Grimshaw and the others wouldn't find him. Then maybe in the morning, he could resume his search for the Terror. He hadn't been thinking straight just now when he'd decided to go after it. Even if he'd found it, he would have been no match for the creature. Even on his best day, he might not be a match for the Terror.

Moving quietly, Frank rode deeper into

the woods. He heard a few sounds of pursuit behind him, but gradually they faded away. It was next to impossible to track somebody in this wilderness unless you had a dog to help you. Frank's confidence that he had given the slip to Grimshaw and the other gun-wolves began to grow.

Damn shame about Grimshaw, Frank mused. Jack had always been one to follow the lure of so-called easy money, though. Frank supposed it was inevitable that if they both lived long enough, sooner or later they would wind up on opposite sides in some fight.

That day had come, and Frank hated to think about what it meant.

More than likely, before this was over he was going to have to kill Jack Grimshaw.

No matter how long he lived, he would never forget the sight that had met his eyes a short time earlier, Grimshaw thought. The image was seared into his brain just as surely as a brand was burned into a cow's hide.

The damn thing had been huge, towering over him — and Grimshaw wasn't a small man. At first glance, it appeared that the creature had some sort of patchwork pelt of different colors and textures. Logic told

Grimshaw that it was really a coat or a robe of some sort, stitched together from the hides of several different kinds of animals. The garment was so shaggy, the creature's hair and beard so long, that it was difficult to tell where one ended and the other began.

But in the midst of all that hair were two burning eyes filled with such hatred that it seemed to blast a path straight through Grimshaw to his soul, which withered for a second under the heat of that baleful gaze. He saw patches of pink scar tissue inside that beard, too, and then a mouth that opened to emit a growl and a wave of even fouler odors as the thing lunged at him.

Grimshaw had never moved faster in his life. He ducked away from the rush, stumbled, fell, rolled, came up with his Colt in his hand spitting fire and lead. Involuntary shouts tore loose from his throat.

The rest of the men had abandoned the tree cutting and swiftly joined the battle, opening fire on the Terror in their midst. Grimshaw knew that Emmett Bosworth wanted the thing to survive, so that it could continue spreading fear and, more importantly, be blamed for any attacks on Chamberlain's operation that Bosworth had Grimshaw and his men carry out.

But knowing that was one thing, and finding yourself under attack by a crazed monster was another. Grimshaw and the others didn't think twice about defending themselves. They just blazed away at the creature.

Problem was, the damn thing was so fast, it seemed to *dodge* the bullets as it rampaged among them, slashing right and left with hands that dealt out as much damage as talons. One man went down with his throat torn open and gushing blood. Another screamed and staggered as his eyeballs were gouged from their sockets and popped from his head like grapes. A third man stumbled backward, his skull crushed and misshapen by the sledgehammer blow that had landed on top of it.

Three men dying in about that many seconds . . . it would have been easy to freeze in fear when confronted with such devastation. Grimshaw's hardcases had been in plenty of fights before, though, even if none of them had ever been like this one. They kept firing, even as the tree toppled on its own, and suddenly the Terror was gone, vanished into the shadows under the redwoods as if it had never been there.

Radburn shouted, "It went that way!" but Grimshaw figured that was just a guess. The Terror had been moving too fast for any of them to see where it had gone.

"Let it go!" he shouted. "Find Morgan! We still have to kill him!"

Grimshaw figured that Frank had slipped out of the trap as soon as all hell broke loose. Holding his Colt at the ready, he ran along the tree trunk to check. Sure enough, when he reached the little hollow at the edge of the cliff where Morgan had taken shelter, it was empty.

The Drifter was gone.

"Mount up!" Grimshaw yelled as he swung around. "We've got to find Morgan!"

Hooley asked, "What about the men that . . . that thing killed?"

"Leave 'em there," Grimshaw replied with a snarl. "We ain't got time to do anything else. Anyway, you left Nichols for the Terror, Hooley, when he was still alive, so don't go gettin' tenderhearted on me now."

For a second, Grimshaw thought Hooley was going to take a shot at him. He would have almost welcomed it. He wanted really badly to kill something right now, and Hooley would do just fine.

But he'd already lost four men today, so he supposed it was better that Hooley got control of his temper and turned away. When you set out after Frank Morgan, you needed the odds on your side to be as high as possible.

The pursuit was delayed even more because some of the horses, badly spooked by the Terror's scent, had broken free and run off. The men whose mounts were still where they had been left had to round up those other horses. By the time they started searching along the cliff, Grimshaw was certain that Frank was long gone.

That was the way it turned out. One of the men thought he had caught a glimpse of Morgan running south along the cliff during the battle with the Terror, but they couldn't be sure about that. And it was next to impossible to follow tracks in the trees.

All they could do was spread out and comb through the forest as best they could. Grimshaw put his men a couple of hundred yards apart and told them to keep their eyes open.

"I don't like it," Hooley said. "What if we run into that monster again? One man alone wouldn't stand a chance against that shaggy bastard."

"Yeah, well, this way he can only kill one of us at a time," Grimshaw pointed out, "instead of wipin' out the whole bunch."

That didn't seem to make Hooley feel a lot better.

The searchers started through the woods, heading south along the coast since that was the only lead they had, and any lead was better than none. As soon as Grimshaw was out of sight of the others, the wet afternoon seemed lonelier than ever. With the trees closing in all around him, he might as well have been the only human being in some strange, primeval world.

"Damn you, Frank," he muttered. "Why couldn't you have just kept riding? Why'd you have to get mixed up in all this?"

Grimshaw wasn't expecting answers, and he didn't get any. Only the whisper of the wind in the trees and the faint dripping of moisture as the drizzle grew harder.

Frank continued working his way inland. He knew there were some hills in that direction that might offer him shelter. Also, he didn't want to get caught with his back to the sea again, with no place to go in case of trouble.

His stomach growled, prompting him to dig a strip of jerky out of his saddlebags and gnaw on it as he rode. He was still feverish, and his left arm now hurt from wrist to shoulder. He shivered in the saddle as chills ran through him again.

Maybe he ought to try to make it back to Eureka, he thought. Dr. Connelly could patch up his arm. Connelly would probably stick him in bed and make him stay there for three or four days, though, and if that happened, Frank wouldn't have any more chances to find the Terror before Rutherford Chamberlain's twenty-thousand-dollar bounty went into effect.

No, he wasn't going back to Eureka, Frank decided. Not until he had finished the job he set out to do.

Gradually, he became aware that the terrain wasn't flat anymore. It had a slope to it. Stormy climbed steadily, still weaving around the massive tree trunks. Dog padded out ahead, while Goldy followed along behind. Because of the late hour and the overcast that was lowering even more, the shadows under the trees were thick enough so that Frank couldn't see more than a few yards in any direction. Tendrils of fog floated among the trees, cutting down on Frank's vision as well.

Suddenly, something huge and black loomed up right in front of them. This wasn't the Terror, Frank sensed immediately. It was too big even for that. After a moment, he realized that it was a low bluff, about thirty feet tall.

And set in it, unless he was mistaken, was the round black mouth of a cave.

He closed his eyes for a second, took a

deep breath. Fate had been kind to him and led him to exactly what he needed: a place to get out of the rain, rest, and spend the night. He urged Stormy forward.

The opening in the bluff was about ten feet tall. Judging by that, the cave might be big enough not only for Frank and Dog, but for Stormy and Goldy as well. Frank hoped that he could find some wood that wasn't too wet to burn. He really wanted to build a fire and dry out.

They were approaching the cave mouth when Dog suddenly planted his feet and started to growl. The two horses stopped short as well and tossed their heads as if reluctant to go any closer.

"Come on," Frank urged. He felt light-headed now, and the fog that crept through the trees seemed to have seeped into his brain as well. His thoughts were sluggish. All he wanted was a place to rest, to be warm again, and his friends who were usually so helpful weren't cooperating this time.

Stormy wouldn't budge, so Frank dismounted, slipping a little and grabbing the saddle horn to keep from falling. He took hold of the reins and tried to lead the rangy gray stallion into the cave. Stormy's hooves were planted firmly on the ground, though.

He wasn't budging. Neither was Dog or Goldy.

"All right," Frank muttered. "Stay out here and get wet then."

Instantly, he felt bad for saying such a thing. He had never had a better friend than Dog, and Stormy and Goldy were almost at the same level as the big cur. Maybe once they saw him go into the cave, they would follow, he thought. He trudged toward the opening.

The smell that came from it made him wrinkle his nose. Something had crawled up in there and died. Maybe more than one something.

But he wasn't going to let a little stink keep him from getting out of the rain. He stepped up to the cave mouth, something nagging at the back of his brain as he did so, and reached into his pocket to fish around for the little waterproof container in which he always kept several matches.

He found it as he moved a couple of steps into the cave. The drizzle wasn't hitting him now. His fingers fumbled to open the container and shake out a match. When he had one, he snapped it to life with his thumbnail.

The match flared up and cast a yellow glow over the interior of the cave. It was rounded, ten or twelve feet high at its tallest, maybe fifteen across and an equal distance deep. Plenty of room for him, Dog, and the two horses, Frank thought. He turned slowly, holding the match higher in his left hand so that the light from it spread all the way to the back of the cave.

That was where he saw what he took at first for a sleeping bear. He stepped back sharply and dropped his right hand to the butt of his gun before he realized what he saw wasn't a bear, wasn't even alive. It was just a pile of animal pelts, dozens of them, from the looks of it. They looked like they had been arranged against the wall to form a bed of sorts. He saw a lot of little bones, too, tossed here and there.

Outside, Stormy and Goldy suddenly let out shrill whinnies of fear. Dog began barking and snarling. Reason finally penetrated Frank's feverish brain, and as he dropped the match and turned, he muttered, "Oh, hell."

Standing there in the cave entrance, silhouetted against the last of the fading gray light outside, was a huge, shaggy shape. A stench emanated from it, filling the cave and making it hard for Frank to breathe without gagging. It stood there motionless, as if puzzled to find that it had a visitor in its home.

Because that's what this cave was, Frank realized now.

He had found the lair of the Terror.

Chapter 22

Before Frank could do anything, Dog attacked the Terror from behind, leaping high on the creature's back and hitting it with such force that even the Terror's massive bulk was jolted forward a step. Dog's fangs flashed as he tore at his enemy.

Frank would have commanded the big cur to stay back if he'd had the chance. Dog was no match for the Terror. The thing reached back, dug clawlike fingers into Dog's pelt, and plucked the big cur off him like a bug. He flung Dog away like a bug, too, sending him crashing into the wall of the cave.

By this time, Frank's Colt was in his hand, and as he heard Dog's pained yelp and saw the way he went rolling limply across the ground, it was all Frank could do not to empty the revolver into the Terror.

But he had given his word to Nancy Chamberlain, for one thing, and for another, he wasn't sure bullets would stop the Terror, or even slow it down. Instead, he shouted as loudly as he could, "Ben! Ben Chamberlain!"

The Terror was in the middle of taking a shuffling step toward him when Frank called out. For some reason, the creature wasn't moving with the blinding speed that he had demonstrated earlier. He stopped short, let out an incoherent roar of rage. Massive arms like the trunks of small trees lifted and shook.

But the Terror had reacted to Ben Chamberlain's name. Frank was sure of it. That wasn't proof that the creature actually *was* Ben, but it increased the likelihood.

Frank raised his left hand, extended it toward the Terror. "Listen to me," he said, keeping his voice as calm and steady as possible. "I'm not going to hurt you. I'm a friend. If you really are Ben Chamberlain, your father sent me —"

Frank realized instantly that he'd made a mistake by mentioning Rutherford Chamberlain. The Terror bellowed again and lurched toward him, swinging those massive arms. Sickened by the smell that washed over him, Frank ducked under the grab and whirled away from the Terror. He lunged toward the cave mouth in an effort to get past the creature.

But one of the Terror's hands snagged his shirt and jerked him back. Frank flew across the cave and smashed into the wall. Pain exploded through his body. He bounced off and fell to the hard-packed dirt floor. The Terror loomed over him, blotting out most of the fading light, and swung clubbed fists at Frank's face. Frank rolled aside just in time.

The Terror was definitely slower now than it had been earlier. Was the creature tired? Or hurt? Frank didn't know, and at the moment, he didn't care. He just wanted to stay out of its reach. He came to a stop against the wall and pushed himself to his feet, ignoring the throbbing ache that filled his body.

"Ben!" he shouted again. "Ben, I know it's you! Nancy sent me! Your sister Nancy! Remember her?"

The Terror hesitated. Frank was getting through to him. He was convinced of it. And now he thought of something else.

His hand went in his pocket, found the necklace and locket he had carried there since his meeting with Nancy Chamberlain at her father's bizarre mansion the day before. Was there enough light left in this cave for the Terror to see the locket and recognize it? Frank didn't know, but he was going to give it a try. That seemed to be the best chance he had.

He fumbled with the locket, searching for the catch. A second later, his fingers found it, but it didn't want to open at first. Finally, as the Terror came slowly toward him, its foul breath rasping in its throat, Frank succeeded in opening the locket. He thrust his left hand forward, the necklace and locket dangling from his fingers.

"Look at it, Ben!" he urged. "It's Nancy's! It belongs to your sister! And that's a picture of you in it, Ben! You!"

The Terror stopped in its tracks, made a little whimpering sound like a hurt animal. It would have been heartbreaking, if not for the very real danger that still filled the cave.

"Take it and look at it, Ben," Frank said. "It won't hurt you."

Slowly, the Terror raised a hand and reached for the necklace. The powerful fingers ended in long, razor-sharp, clawlike nails. Frank suppressed the impulse to jerk his hand away as the Terror's filthy, hairy hand brushed his. The creature took the necklace from him and brought it close to its face. Frank knew the Terror was studying the tiny photographs inside the locket. On one side was a picture of Nancy; on the other, a pale, intense-looking young man with bushy side whiskers peered out from the sepia-toned photograph.

"That's you, Ben," Frank said softly. "Remember? Remember what you used to look like? Remember Nancy?"

The sound that came from the Terror's throat was so rusty and garbled that for a second Frank didn't recognize it as a word. Then the Terror uttered it again, and Frank knew he was trying to say *Nancy*.

The creature closed its huge fist around the locket and held it close against its breast. "Nan . . . cy," it rasped again, clearer this time. "Nan . . . cy . . . and . . . Ben."

"That's right," Frank said. "That's right."

He was having a hard time standing up now. His head spun dizzily, crazily. He still hurt all over, and his pulse pounded in his head like the tremulous beat of distant drums. He shuddered from the chill that had him in its grip, and fought to keep his teeth from chattering together.

The Terror fell to its knees and said again, "Nan . . . cy."

Then it pitched forward on its face, either dead or out cold, and didn't move again. For a second, Frank stared at the huge, motionless body on the cave floor, and then he felt his eyes rolling up in their sockets.

He had reached the end of his rope. Even though the last thing he wanted to do was to pass out right here beside this huge, shaggy, murderous creature, there was nothing he could do about it.

He lost consciousness as he was falling, and never felt himself strike the hard-packed dirt.

Passing out was one thing; passing out next to a monster was something else entirely. If there was one time in his life when Frank Morgan truly didn't expect to wake up again, this was it.

But he had to be alive, Frank thought as he bit back a groan. Not even Hell could smell this bad.

Funny thing, though . . . He saw a flickering red glow against his closed eyelids and felt the heat of flames. Maybe he *was* dead, after all.

The smell got worse. Something slid under Frank's head and lifted it. He felt water splash against his parched lips and sucked at it greedily. Gradually, he was able to pry his eyes open.

He was looking up into the face of the Terror as the creature leaned curiously over him.

Or rather, it was the face of Ben Chamberlain, because Frank saw something human in the eyes now, some flicker of intelligence that hadn't been there before. The sight of the locket, with his own picture and that of his sister inside it, must have somehow shocked Ben back to his senses, part of the way at least.

Ben had made a cup out of some sort of large, fernlike leaf, and it was from this that he dribbled water into Frank's mouth. Why Ben was trying to help him, instead of tearing him apart like all the other men he'd encountered in the forest recently, Frank didn't know, but he was grateful anyway. He was in no shape to fight right now. Anyway, he wanted to get through to Ben, not kill him. He had promised Nancy.

"Thank . . . you," Frank croaked. "Thank you . . . for your help."

Ben leaned closer and said, "Nan . . . cy?"

"She's . . . at home." Frank was careful not to mention Rutherford Chamberlain or the timber baron's redwood mansion. Just the word *home* might be enough to set Ben off again in another rage.

It didn't, though. Ben said, "Hoooome."

Frank glanced around. He saw that Ben had started a fire somehow, only a small blaze, but it filled the cave with welcome light and heat. He didn't see Dog, though.

The big cur had been lying near the wall, evidently unconscious, the last glimpse Frank had gotten of him. Maybe Dog had woken up while Frank and Ben were both unconscious and had left the cave . . .

Ben reached over, out of Frank's line of sight, and brought back a blood-dripping haunch of raw meat that looked like it had been torn directly off a carcass. "Eeeeeat," he urged.

Frank saw the coarse gray hair clinging to the flesh, and his stomach revolted. "Dog!" he yelled as he fought his way into a sitting position. Filled with rage of his own, not caring how Ben reacted, he slapped the giant's hand aside. "You son of a —"

A whine from the cave mouth brought him up short. Frank's head jerked toward the opening. He saw Dog standing there, a quizzical look on his face.

"Dog," Frank breathed in relief. He still didn't want any of the bloody meat Ben had offered him, but at least it hadn't come from his old friend.

Dog came tentatively into the cave, all the way to Frank's side. He started licking Frank's face. Ben leaned back against the rocky wall and watched the reunion. Frank couldn't be sure because of the thick beard, but he thought Ben was smiling.

Frank put his arms around Dog's neck and hugged the big cur for a long moment. Dog must have been watching from outside, and had seen that Ben wasn't hurting Frank. He still cast wary looks toward the massive, shaggy man, but he seemed willing to tolerate being around Ben, at least for the moment.

Frank was still chilled, but the warmth from the fire helped. So did having Dog pressed against him. The trembling inside him eased. As it did, he became aware of how thirsty he still was. He pointed to the leaf in Ben's hand and said, "Water?"

Ben seemed to understand. He got to his feet and shuffled to the cave mouth. Stretching out his arm, he held the cupped leaf in the drizzle until it was mostly full of water. Then he carried it back carefully to Frank and offered it to him. Frank took it, being equally careful not to spill the liquid, and drank deeply from it.

It was hard to believe that Ben Chamberlain, who was being so gentle and considerate in caring for him, was the same wild, frenzied creature that had brutally killed almost two dozen men. Yet Frank had no doubt of it. He had seen the Terror with his own eyes earlier that day, carrying off the man whose corpse Frank had found later in that redwood. He had heard descriptions from other eyewitnesses who had survived encounters with the monster.

Because that's what the Terror was, Frank mused . . . man and monster in one body.

What would happen if he was able to take Ben Chamberlain back to Eureka? Would he be put on trial for his crimes? Frank believed that justice should be blind and impartial, especially where murder was concerned. A killer was a killer, and ought to be punished accordingly. But he couldn't see hanging Ben. The spectacle that such an event would become bothered him.

It would never come to a trial, Frank realized. A mob would take care of matters before things ever went that far. Given the level of fear and hysteria in these parts, as many as several hundred men might descend on any place where Ben was being held, take him out, and rip him apart just as he had ripped apart so many others. In a way, that would be a fitting end for him, Frank supposed, but the idea still sickened him.

No, the most merciful thing to do, all the way around, might be to wait until Ben went to sleep, put a Colt to his head, and blow his brains out. That would mean breaking Frank's promise to Nancy, he reminded himself, but he wasn't sure she had thought out exactly what she was asking him to do. Bringing her brother back to civilization was just going to wind up tormenting him that much more.

Whatever Frank decided, he told himself, he didn't have to make up his mind tonight. Soon enough, yes, but not tonight. He would rest instead, and try to get his strength back.

He had to have something to eat, too. Ben had laid that haunch on the cave floor. Frank didn't know what sort of animal it was from, and wasn't about to ask. He picked it up, brushed the dirt off it, and drew his knife. He used the blade to carve off a hunk of meat with no hide attached, then speared it on the knife and leaned forward to hold it over the flames. Ben watched him, apparently fascinated. The smell of roasting meat soon filled the cave.

When it was cooked enough, Frank took it out of the fire and blew on it, waiting for it to cool. After a few minutes, he tore off a piece and held it out toward Ben. The giant hesitated, then reached out and started to take it. He pulled his fingers back when he felt that the meat was still warm. Clearly, he wasn't used to that anymore. Frank said, "It's all right. Go ahead and take it."

To demonstrate, he bit a piece off the meat still stuck on the knife and started to chew. It was pretty gamy, but the juices gave him a jolt of strength anyway. He ate the whole piece while Ben worked up the courage to take the morsel Frank was offering him and sample it. When he finally did, though, he seemed to like it.

Frank roasted more of the meat, which he thought might be wolf. This time, Ben was eager to share. As they were gnawing on the meat, Frank tried something.

"You remember Jules Verne, Ben?" he asked.

Ben glanced up. "Juuuules . . . Verne?" He looked confused — at least Frank thought so, although it was difficult to be sure with all that hair obscuring his face — but after a moment, he said, "Neeeeemo."

"That's right, Captain Nemo from *Twenty Thousand Leagues Under the Sea*. I saw that book. It belonged to you, didn't it?"

Ben took a deep breath. "My . . . boooook."

"I like to read, too. I've read that one, and *Five Weeks in a—*"

Before Frank could finish saying the title of the novel he had found in the primitive cabin, Ben jerked back, cowering against the wall. He put his huge hands over his

318

face and said, "No, no, no, no . . ."

"Take it easy, Ben," Frank said quickly. "We won't talk about it anymore. Just settle down —"

Ben didn't settle down. He lunged to his feet and ran out into the night before Frank could stop him. Frank climbed painfully to his feet, limped over to the cave mouth, and looked out into the thick, wet darkness. He would never find Ben out there. He'd had the Terror, but now the creature was gone.

And he'd never really had him at all, Frank reflected. He and Ben had just been in the same place for a short period of time.

At least now he had food, water, and a fire. All he could do was rest and wait for morning. Then maybe Dog could track Ben again.

And he was certain now that the Terror was really Ben Chamberlain, he reminded himself. That was more than he had known earlier. It didn't make his chore any easier, but it cleared up a mystery.

There were still mysteries to be solved, though, such as what had happened to make Ben like he was now. Sure, according to Nancy he had always been a little eccentric, preferring to live in a world of his own rather than take part in what was actually going on around him. He had gone off to

319

live by himself in the woods, too, and that sort of isolation sometimes wasn't good for a man. It did things to his mind after a while.

But Ben had had his books, and he had visited with Nancy from time to time. He shouldn't have gone mad. *Something* had happened. Something had driven him over the edge of sanity into madness.

Or some*body* had driven him over deliberately. That thought made Frank frown. If that turned out to be the case, then whoever was responsible for turning Ben into a rampaging killer was also to blame for those murders.

Yes, there was still plenty of truth to uncover, and Frank was bound and determined to uncover it. For now, though, he sat down and leaned back against the wall with Dog close beside him to wait for morning. After a while, his eyes closed and he slept.

CHAPTER 23

The drizzle had become an actual rain by the time Jack Grimshaw and his companions rode back into Eureka that evening. They had spent hours looking for Frank Morgan with no success. They were wet and cold and miserable, and about the only thing they had to be thankful for, Grimshaw reflected, was that they hadn't run into that damned Terror again and gotten any more men killed.

They split up just outside of the settlement as usual. Grimshaw said they would meet in the back room of the Bull o' the Woods later. He headed for the Eureka House. He knew that Emmett Bosworth would want a report.

Grimshaw also knew that Bosworth was going to be mighty damned unhappy with what he had to tell him.

He paused on the hotel porch to shake as much of the moisture as he could from his hat and his slicker, which he hadn't gotten around to donning until his clothes were already wet. He went inside, his boots making a squishing sound that drew a frown of disapproval from the desk clerk. The man glanced away hurriedly, though, when Grimshaw returned the look with a cold stare.

It was late enough that Bosworth would be finished with supper. Grimshaw hoped the timber baron hadn't brought a woman back to his room with him. He didn't want to have to stand around waiting while Bosworth got rid of some soiled dove.

Of course, Grimshaw reminded himself, Bosworth was too good for a common prostitute. He would've found some lonely married woman and seduced her, or maybe some spinster who was pretty good-looking when she took off her spectacles and let down her hair. Grimshaw had been with a few gals like that himself, and he knew how wild they could be once they finally let themselves go.

He shook his head, forcing those thoughts out of his brain. Emmett Bosworth's love life was the least of his worries. He still had Frank Morgan to kill — and he thought it was possible that Frank might have heard him yelling out there today during that fight with the Terror. If Frank had recognized his voice and knew he was gunning for him . . .

A chill that had nothing to do with being soaked went down Grimshaw's back as he paused in front of the door to Bosworth's suite and rapped sharply on the panel.

Bosworth jerked open the door a couple of seconds later. He wore a dressing gown and had one of those big cigars in his mouth. One hand clutched a squat glass with a couple of fingers of whiskey in it. He didn't waste any time on preliminaries, instead asking curtly, "Did you find Morgan?"

Grimshaw nodded toward the room and said, "I don't cotton to standing in the hall."

"Fine, fine," Bosworth muttered impatiently as he moved back. Grimshaw stepped into the sitting room. Bosworth closed the door and went on, "Well?"

"We found him, but he's not dead."

Bosworth's teeth clenched angrily on the cigar. "Why the hell not?"

"Because we found something else at the same time. We ran into the Terror."

Bosworth's eyebrows went up in surprise. He took the cigar out of his mouth and said, "Really? The damned thing actually exists?"

"I've got three more dead men to prove it."

"But did you actually see —"

"The thing was standing as close to me as you are now. Big as life, twice as ugly, and smelled ten times as bad."

"Given its history then, I'd say you're very lucky to be alive, Grimshaw."

The gunman nodded. "Yeah. Damned lucky."

"I wish you'd been able to kill Morgan, though. Tell me what happened."

Grimshaw spent the next five minutes doing that. Bosworth puffed on the cigar as he listened. When Grimshaw was finished, he said, "You'll be going back out in the morning to resume the search for Morgan, I take it?"

"We don't know that he's still out there."

"He was on foot and possibly wounded. Do you really think he got away?"

"I wouldn't put anything past Frank Morgan," Grimshaw said flatly. "He's done things you wouldn't think any man could do, and he's got more lives than a cat."

Bosworth waved the cigar. "He's human like anyone else. Put enough bullets in him and he'll die."

"Yeah, but how many of us will he kill first?"

"That's not my worry," Bosworth replied with a smug look on his face. "I'm paying

324

you to take care of that. You keep losing men anyway," he added scathingly.

Grimshaw reined in his temper. Bosworth didn't understand. But he was rich, so he didn't have to.

"Do you need to recruit more men?" the timber baron continued.

Grimshaw shook his head. "There are still eleven of us. Eleven good men. That's enough."

"I would hope so. But fifteen doesn't seem to have been enough, at least so far."

"Morgan'll be dead before the end of the day tomorrow!"

The heated exclamation came out of Grimshaw's mouth before he could stop it. Bosworth just nodded, though, and grinned. "That's what I want to hear." His rugged face grew serious again. "Just be sure you make good on it this time, Grimshaw. Otherwise, I'm going to start thinking that you can't handle what I need you to handle."

"Don't worry," Grimshaw snapped. "Morgan's as good as dead."

The look that Bosworth gave him as he replaced the cigar in his mouth spoke volumes. *Prove it*, Bosworth was saying. Results were all that mattered.

Grimshaw nodded. He left the room and

turned toward the landing. He wanted some dry clothes, some hot food, and a drink. Maybe three or four drinks.

It might take that many to make him forget, even for a little while, that Frank Morgan might be gunning for *him* now.

Erickson stared into the shot glass sitting on the table in front of him. It had about an inch of whiskey in it, and floating in that amber liquid was Sutherland's face.

Not really, of course, but Erickson saw it there anyway. It looked just like it did the last time Erickson had seen it. Sutherland's mouth was wide open in a scream, and his eyes were bugged out so far, it looked like they were going to jump right out of his head. Sutherland was pleading for the others to help him, but there wasn't a damned thing they could do. The Terror was too fast. It was gone, carrying Sutherland with it.

Erickson lifted the glass, threw back the drink. Thumped the empty on the table.

Sutherland still screamed up at him from the glass. Erickson reached for the bottle and poured more whiskey. He'd drown the son of a bitch and make him go away, he thought, no matter how much booze it took.

The other four men sat around the table in the Bull o' the Woods, each of them as sullen and somber as Erickson was. They were putting away the whiskey, too. Nobody had said anything for a while. What was there to say? They had seen their friend and partner carried off by a monster. They had spent a long time looking for Sutherland, but hadn't found hide nor hair of him. Not a single one of them, though, doubted that he was dead.

"I'm done," Jenkins abruptly said into the silence.

Erickson lifted his head to glare at the dour logger. "What do you mean you're done?" he demanded.

"Just what I said. Done. Finished. I'm not goin' back out there, Erickson. Not to fell timber, not to look for Sutherland, and damn sure not to hunt monsters or gunfighters. If you want to go after Frank Morgan and the Terror, that's your business, but count me out."

The whiskey made Erickson angry. So, too, did the fear he had felt that afternoon when the Terror came out of nowhere and snatched Sutherland, but he didn't want to admit that, even to himself.

"You're throwin' away a big payoff," Erickson said. "When Chamberlain ups that bounty to twenty grand tomorrow, that'll be four thousand apiece when we bring in the

Terror's head."

Jenkins grunted. "Yeah, or else I'll wind up with my bones scattered over some god-forsaken hillside like Sutherland."

"We don't know the Terror killed him," Erickson insisted. "He might've gotten away."

That was such a ludicrous idea that none of them could believe it, even Erickson. The grim certainty of Sutherland's death was etched on each man's face.

Roylston poured himself another drink, tossed it back, and said, "I'm with Jenkins. I'm through monster-huntin'."

"Now, damn it, you can't both back out on me," Erickson protested.

"Looks like we just have," Jenkins said.

Erickson turned his head to glare at Dawson and Treadwell. "What about you two? Are you gonna turn tail and run, too?"

Dawson said, "I'll stick. You know that."

"Yeah," Treadwell agreed. "We been ridin' together for a while, Erickson. We're still with you."

Erickson snorted and leaned back in his chair. "Good. I was afraid you two might've turned yellow, too."

Jenkins gave a hollow laugh and shook his head. "Forget it, Erickson. It won't work. Roylston and me, we're loggers, not gunmen. Not hard-cases like the three of you. Neither was Sutherland. We just let greed blind us, that's all. We thought we could throw in with you and be something we're not. We know better now."

"Good riddance then," Erickson muttered. "I don't ride with anybody I can't trust."

Jenkins shoved back his chair and got to his feet. "So long then."

Roylston stood up as well and gave the other three men a curt nod. He followed Jenkins out of the saloon.

"Well, we're back to a three-way split," Dawson said, "and we didn't have to kill those bastards to get there."

"Yeah, we're better off without 'em," Erickson said. He was peering into his glass again, not liking what he saw there.

"We're still going after Morgan?" Treadwell asked.

Erickson frowned. "I don't know. I haven't seen him around town tonight. He may still be out there somewhere in the woods. Hell, maybe the Terror even got him."

"That'd make things simpler for us, wouldn't it?"

"It sure would."

Dawson said, "We can't do anything about any of it tonight, so I'm gonna go find me a gal and not even think about monsters and gunfighters for a while." He downed the last of his whiskey and then settled his hat on his head. "I'd advise you boys to do the same."

"Sounds good to me," Treadwell agreed. "I've had enough hooch to deaden the pain in this wounded arm of mine. Maybe I'll go deaden something else."

Dawson laughed. "That don't even make sense. But I must really be drunk, 'cause it's funny anyway."

The two of them stood up and wandered off, leaving Erickson sitting by himself at the table.

But not completely by himself. He still had company. He picked up the bottle and muttered, "Have some more whiskey, you bastard," as he poured the booze down Sutherland's shrieking throat.

Grimshaw went through the usual charade with Harry the bartender, got the key to the back room, and sat at the table nursing a drink as the other ten men filtered into the room by ones and twos. They passed the bottle around, and when everyone was there, Grimshaw said, "We're goin' out again in the morning to look for Morgan."

"Bosworth still wants him dead?" Radburn asked.

"Why wouldn't he? What's changed since this afternoon?"

"Well, we lost Hargan, Flynn, and Dupree," Radburn said, naming the three men who had died at the hands of the Terror.

Grimshaw shook his head. "Why in the hell would Bosworth care about that? We're just tools to him." He tilted his glass to his lips and drank. "Just like an ax or a saw to a logger."

Hooley said, "Well, by God, I think he needs to pay us more. This is turnin' into a dangerous job."

Grimshaw stared at the man for a couple of seconds, then began to laugh. He couldn't help it.

"Yeah, imagine that. Bein' a hired gun is dangerous work."

Hooley flushed. "You know what I mean. It ain't enough we got to go after Morgan. We have to worry about that damn monster, too. What if it's on the lookout for us now? We don't know how smart the blasted critter really is. People seem to think that it's only attacked folks who happened to run into it. But what if it's really out there *lookin'* for unlucky hombres to rip apart?"

"I can't believe none of us hit it, the way we were throwin' lead around out there,"

Radburn mused. "Hell, it looked to me like we put half a dozen bullet holes in it, at least. But the thing never slowed down, never acted like it was hurt."

"Maybe somethin' was watchin' over it," Grimshaw suggested.

"Like a guardian angel?"

Grimshaw chuckled. "More like a guardian devil, since it looked to me like it crawled up right outta hell."

"That's right," Hooley said. "You got the best look at it of anybody who's still alive, Grimshaw. What did it look like?"

"Like nothin' you ever saw before. Like nothin' *anybody* ever saw before."

Except him, Grimshaw thought. He had seen the Terror close up all right.

But today wasn't the first time.

Because Jack Grimshaw was maybe the only man alive who knew for sure who the Terror really was. He knew because he had been there the day the Terror was born, so to speak.

He wasn't going to think about that, though. Wasn't going to think about all the blood that was on his hands because of what had happened in that cabin . . . He had enough blood on his hands because of his own killings over the years. He didn't need any more.

Radburn grinned and said, "It sounds to me like you're sayin' the Terror is even uglier than ol' Hooley here, Jack."

"Hey!" Hooley protested. "How'd you like it if I went around comparin' you to a monster?"

"Forget it," Grimshaw snapped. "Everybody have a drink, then go get a whore. Better yet, get a good night's sleep. You're liable to need it come mornin'."

"How are we gonna find Morgan?" one of the men asked.

Grimshaw leaned back in his chair and tipped more whiskey into his glass. "I'm not sure we'll have to worry about that," he said. "Chances are, Morgan's going to find us."

Bosworth was pacing, smoking, and drinking when he heard the soft knock on the sitting room door. While things were going fairly well, there had been too many complications to suit him. Once that damned gunfighter Morgan was out of the way, things would be simpler again. And if Grimshaw couldn't do the job and get rid of Morgan, Bosworth would find somebody who could.

He put those thoughts out of his mind, though, and smiled as he went to the door to answer the knock. The lamps in the hallway had been turned down low, so the light was dim. It was enough, though, to show him the slender figure who stood there, wearing a hooded cape to keep the rain off her hair.

"I thought you told me you couldn't come back tonight," he said.

"If you're disappointed, I can leave."

"Not at all." Bosworth stepped back. "Come in, please."

She did so, and as he closed the door behind her, she lowered the hood so that the lamplight in the room reflected off her thick, shiny, auburn hair. "He's asleep," she said as Bosworth turned toward her. "He won't wake up until morning."

"You're sure of that?"

"I've seen what the opium does to him."

She shrugged out of the cape. Bosworth took it from her, hung it on a brass hook near the door. The rain had beaded on it. The droplets rolled slowly down the oilcloth fabric, then began to form a wet spot on the rug.

"Rather irresponsible of him, isn't it?" Bosworth asked as he ran his hands up her arms to her shoulders. She wore a plain dress tonight, not the sort of gaudy thing she sometimes slipped into when she was visiting him. "What if his services are needed? He swore an oath after all."

"What does an oath mean when a man craves what he wants?"

"What indeed?" Bosworth murmured. He pulled her toward him, brought his mouth down hard on hers. She wrapped her arms around his neck and pressed her body to his.

When he drew back, his eyes burned with desire. For a while now, he wouldn't think about monsters, or his rivalry with Rutherford Chamberlain, or all the money he would make when that lease was his and all those beautiful logs were flowing into his sawmills. He wouldn't even think about that gunfighter, Frank Morgan, and the threat Morgan represented to his plans. All he would think about was the woman in his arms.

And, well, maybe . . . just a little . . . about all that money.

CHAPTER 24

By morning, Frank's fever had broken. The rugged life he'd led, plus his own naturally hardy constitution, gave him the ability to throw off illness fairly quickly. His left arm was mighty stiff and sore, though.

Ben Chamberlain hadn't come back to the cave during the night, at least not that Frank was aware of. When Frank walked out into the morning sun, he saw Stormy and Goldy not far away, cropping at the grass. A whistle brought them both trotting toward him.

He had jerky and coffee in his saddlebags, both of which he craved this morning. He carried a small silver flask of whiskey in there, too, which he also wanted, but for a different reason.

As soon as he had rekindled the fire in the cave and started the coffee brewing, he tore the sleeve of his shirt back, washed away the dried blood with water from his canteen, uncapped the flask, and dribbled whiskey into the bullet wound on his arm. The pain caused by the fiery liquor made him grunt and grit his teeth, but he kept it up until he was confident that the whiskey had run all through the wound. Then he got a spare shirt from his saddlebags, tore a strip of fabric from it, and used that as a bandage, wrapping it around his arm and tying it tightly with the help of his teeth.

The efficiency with which he carried this out was a grim testament to how many times he'd been shot over the years. He'd had plenty of experience at patching up bullet wounds, including his own. Too much experience.

By then the coffee was ready. He drank from the tin cup he always carried with him and ate a couple of strips of jerky. The simple breakfast made him feel almost human again.

He switched the saddle from Stormy to Goldy, and was trying to figure out the best place to start searching for Ben again when Dog growled. Frank saw the big cur staring into the woods as the hair ruffled up on his neck, and when Frank looked in the same direction, after a moment he spotted Ben standing there. With the long, shaggy hair and the crude coat of pelts he wore, Ben blended into the shadows so that it was hard to see him. But he was there, and Frank put a smile on his face as he said, "Come on out, Ben. We need to talk."

Ben took a tentative step toward Frank and said, "Nan . . . cy?"

"You want me to take you to Nancy?"

"My . . . siiiiister."

Frank kept smiling as he nodded. "That's right. Nancy is your sister, and she loves you, Ben. She wants to see you. I'll take you to her."

If he could get Ben back to the Chamberlain mansion, then maybe Rockwell, Cobb, and those other hardcases who worked for Rutherford Chamberlain could keep any mobs from storming the place and killing him once word got out that he was there, as it was bound to do. That might buy Frank some time, until he could consult with Chamberlain and the law and figure out what needed to be done. Maybe Ben could be locked up somewhere, in a place where he couldn't hurt anybody anymore.

But being locked up like that might be an even worse punishment than death for someone like Ben, Frank reflected. He still wasn't sure that a bullet in the brain wouldn't be the most merciful course.

He was damned if he was going to be judge, jury, and executioner, though, at least not without knowing the full story. He motioned for Ben to come closer and said, "Come on. We'll go see Nancy. I'll take you to her."

Ben stepped out into the sunlight. Frank got his first really good look at the man who was now known as the Terror of the Redwoods.

It was a fitting name. Ben's appearance was enough to strike terror into anyone's heart. With the long, tangled hair that fell around his shoulders and the thick, bushy beard that reached to the center of his chest, plus the bulky coat, he looked more like an animal than a human being. He was so hairy that not much of his face was visible except for the deep-set, burning eyes and a few patches of pink, sick-looking bare flesh. After a moment, Frank realized that those pink patches were scars. From the looks of them, Ben has suffered some severe burns on his face, sometime in the past.

Ben was at least six and a half feet tall, maybe a little more. It was difficult to judge his weight because the coat concealed the shape of his body, but Frank reckoned he weighed at least two hundred pounds, probably more like two-thirty or two-forty. With that size and those razor-sharp talons, Ben Chamberlain was one of the deadliest two-legged weapons Frank had ever encountered. He had seen with his own eyes that Ben was incredibly fast and strong, too.

Frank knew that if he hadn't been able to get through to Ben and awaken the man slumbering inside the monster, he never would have been able to take him alive. With a still-maddened Ben, killing would have been the only option. And it might come to that yet, of course, if Ben lost control of himself again. Frank knew he would have to be mighty careful in the way he handled the young man.

He put a foot in the stirrup and swung up into the saddle. Ben stepped back hurriedly, an upset look on his face.

"It's all right," Frank said. Clearly, Ben didn't like men on horseback. That might mean something. Quickly, Frank went on. "This is a good horse. He won't hurt you." Dealing with Ben was a little like dealing with a young child, he realized. "His name is Goldy."

"Gol . . . dy," Ben repeated.

Frank nodded. "That's right. And the other horse is Stormy."

"Stor . . . my."

"You're getting it." Even that tiny bit of praise brought a sudden smile to Ben's face under the bushy beard. Frank pointed to the big cur and said, "Dog."

"Dog!" Ben could handle that one without any trouble, and he was excited about it.

Frank pointed to himself. "And I'm Frank." He supposed that Ben had never heard his name until now.

"Fraaaank."

"Yeah, close enough," Frank said with a grin. "Come on, walk with me now."

They started through the forest. Ben shuffled along, his long legs easily allowing him to keep up with the horses. As Frank rode, he tried to spot some landmarks and figure out exactly where they were. He wanted to avoid Ben's old cabin, since that place might hold such bad memories for Ben that he could lose the fragile grip he had on his humanity if he saw it again.

However, in a vast expanse of timber like this, finding any landmarks was difficult. Even steering by the sun wasn't easy once you were under the trees, because it wasn't very visible. The branches diffused the sunlight, so that it might have come from any direction, and gave it a greenish tint.

Frank was pretty sure they were headed north, though. If they kept going in that direction, sooner or later they would reach the coastline, and he could follow that all the way to Humboldt Bay and Eureka if he had to. That wasn't what he wanted to do, though. He wasn't sure if he could persuade Ben to enter the town, and if he did, the sight of him would be liable to set off a riot. If Frank could get Ben to the Chamberlain mansion, he was counting on Nancy's presence to keep him calm enough to deal with.

"Beautiful day, isn't it, Ben?" Frank said. He wanted to keep talking to Ben, keep making contact with the man inside the monster.

Ben didn't say anything, but he looked around at the trees for a moment, and Frank would have sworn he saw the giant nod and smile a shy little smile.

Definitely like a child, Frank thought.

They moved on, Frank talking about nothing in particular, and after a while they came to a rough road, one of the logging roads that Rutherford Chamberlain's men had cut through this wilderness. Ben stopped short and acted like he didn't want to venture out onto the road. Frank had to coax him onto it with promises that it would be all right, that nothing would hurt him. Finally, Ben began to trudge along beside Goldy.

They hadn't gone very far, though, when Frank heard axes ringing against trees somewhere not far off. Ben heard it, too, and reacted violently. He drew back, shaking his head from side to side, and rumbled, "Baaaad! Baaaad!"

Frank reined in and quickly dismounted. He stepped toward Ben, holding out a hand in a calming gesture. "Take it easy, Ben," he urged. "They won't hurt you. If you leave those men alone, they won't bother you. I won't let them. I swear it."

"Baaaad!" Ben rasped again. Frank could tell that he was about to bolt, and he knew that if Ben started running through the woods, he would be so caught up in his frenzy that he would attack anyone who crossed his path.

But as Ben took several stumbling steps backward, he suddenly swayed as if he couldn't keep his balance. He tried to turn, but as he did so, he fell to one knee. A deep groan came from him. He tried to struggle up, but couldn't do it, and Frank didn't dare get too close because he might startle Ben and set him off on a rampage. Frank remembered how Ben had collapsed in the cave the night before. He never had found out why that happened.

Ben tilted his head back, groaned again, and then toppled over. He crashed to the ground on his side and didn't move. Frank circled him warily. Dog came up and sniffed at him, equally wary.

"Looks like he's passed out, Dog," Frank said. Ben's eyes were closed. For a second, Frank couldn't even tell if he was still breathing. The bulky coat make it difficult to determine if his chest was rising and falling. As Frank leaned closer, though, he heard the raspy wheeze of air moving through Ben's throat.

What the hell had happened to him? Frank risked reaching for the coat. It was held together with crude fasteners made of gut and bone, probably from the small animals that provided Ben with his food. Frank worked at them until he was able to spread the coat open.

His breath hissed between his teeth at what he saw. Under the coat, Ben wore a shirt that might have been a red-checked flannel at one time. It was so dirty that the original color was hard to determine.

But it wasn't just dirt that stained the fabric. In several places, large black blotches stood out. Frank knew those were dried bloodstains, and as he touched them, he could tell that they weren't too old. Ben had been wounded recently, and more than once. He might have matching wounds on his back where the bullets had gone through, but Frank would have been willing

344

to bet that the giant was carrying around some lead inside him, too.

No wonder Ben wasn't moving as fast now. He was badly injured. He must have been hit during that battle with Bosworth's men the day before. As Frank hunkered there beside him, he knew that he had to get some medical attention for Ben, and soon, if the young man was going to have a chance to pull through.

There had to be a logging camp somewhere close by. He could still hear the axes. The loggers would probably have a wagon, and with their help, Frank could load Ben into the vehicle and take him to the Chamberlain mansion. Chamberlain could send someone to town to fetch Dr. Connelly.

Frank straightened to his feet. He didn't like it, but he was going to have to leave Ben here. He couldn't just ride off and abandon him in the middle of the logging road, though. He fetched his rope from the saddle and went to work getting it looped around Ben's massive chest, under the huge arms. Frank's own injured arm made that difficult, and he was sweating by the time he finished, but he finally managed. Then he tied the other end of the rope to his saddle horn and took up Goldy's reins.

"Come on, boy," he urged. "You can haul

that much weight without any problem."

In a few more minutes, Frank had used Goldy to drag Ben off the road and into the thick undergrowth. He pulled some brush and fallen branches around and used them to conceal the unconscious behemoth as much as possible. Most likely, anybody passing by wouldn't notice Ben, at least as long as he remained passed out.

Frank coiled his rope and then swung back up into the saddle. "I'll be back as soon as I can, Ben," he said, even though he knew Ben couldn't hear him. Then he set out to find those loggers.

They might try to argue with him when they found out they were going to help save the Terror's life. He would persuade them to cooperate, though, Frank thought . . . at gunpoint, if necessary.

At least the rain had stopped, Jack Grimshaw thought as he led the other ten men toward the spot where they had last seen Frank Morgan the day before. It wasn't much of a starting place, but it was all they had.

"If Morgan don't show up back in Eureka with the Terror by three o'clock this afternoon, Chamberlain's bounty is back on," Radburn said as he rode alongside Grimshaw. "Only it doubles to twenty thousand. I heard some fellas talkin' about it."

"I know, I know."

"If that happens, we'll have a hundred men out here pokin' through the woods, lookin' for that monster so they can collect. We won't be able to do anything without somebody noticin', Jack."

Grimshaw nodded. "I reckon in that case, Bosworth will want us to lay low for a while."

"What about Morgan? He'll still be huntin' for the Terror, too."

"Hell, I don't know!" Grimshaw exploded, taking Radburn by surprise. The whole thing had been simple starting out. Bosworth wanted what Chamberlain had, and he was willing to pay tough men, men good with their guns, to take what he wanted. To force Chamberlain out. Then Bosworth had gotten cold feet for a while, because of what had happened early on, and now that he'd finally decided it was time to start moving against Chamberlain again, Frank Morgan had to come along and foul everything up.

It sure wasn't like the old days, when you loaded up your guns and went out to fight, and the ones who lived took what they wanted and everybody else could go to hell. Grimshaw missed those days.

The way he understood it, Chamberlain had some big house in the woods, guarded by gunmen he had hired. If Grimshaw had been running things, he would have taken his men and gone there and shot it out, maybe burned the place to the ground. If Chamberlain survived, he would know better than to stay around here. He'd turn tail and run, and then Bosworth could move in and take over. Simple. No deception, no making things look like something they weren't.

But those days were gone now, Grimshaw reflected with a sigh as he ignored the hurt look Radburn gave him. Businessmen like Bosworth didn't really care whether or not they broke the law, but they wanted everything to *look* like they were upstanding, law-abiding citizens. They didn't want any evidence connecting them to the men they hired to do the dirty work for them. That was why he had to meet with Bosworth in secret, why the rest of the bunch had to get together in the back room of the Bull o' the Woods. You could lie, cheat, steal, even kill, but you couldn't let anybody see you doing it.

"Who put a burr under your saddle, Jack?" Radburn asked.

"Nobody," Grimshaw replied. "Just modern times, that's all."

"Oh." Clearly, Radburn didn't understand. He wasn't going to press the issue, though.

After a few minutes, an idea came to Grimshaw. He didn't like it, but it made sense and it might help them find Morgan. Frank was looking for the Terror after all, and sooner or later he was bound to come across the place where the whole business started. Grimshaw intended to leave some of the men there to set up an ambush while the rest of them continued searching for Morgan.

"Where are we goin' now?" Hooley asked as Grimshaw turned his horse back toward the east. "I thought we were headed over to the coast where we had that dustup yesterday."

"I changed my mind," Grimshaw said. He didn't feel like explaining himself to anyone, least of all Hooley.

"Fine. No need to bite my head off."

"Yeah," one of the other men said to Hooley, "the Terror will do that, one of these days."

"Like hell. I'm gonna blow that damn monster full o' holes."

"Bosworth wants him alive for the time being," Grimshaw said.

"Well, once that twenty-grand bounty goes into effect, Bosworth ain't gonna have much say in the matter, now is he?"

Grimshaw didn't reply, but he had to admit to himself that Hooley was right. After today, everything would be different, and there wouldn't be anything Bosworth could do to change that.

A short time later, they came to the long, narrow clearing next to the bluff where trees had toppled off to form a crazy jumble of logs at the bottom. Grimshaw was the only one who had been here before.

"What's this place?" Radburn asked. "Is that a cabin over there at the base of the bluff?"

"Yeah," Grimshaw said. "A fella used to live there, but it's empty now."

"What are we doin' here?"

"I think maybe the Terror comes here sometimes. If Morgan gets on the thing's trail, then he may show up here, too." They rode up to the cabin and reined to a halt. Grimshaw went on. "Hooley, you and Darrell and Whiteside are gonna stay here. Find some place to hide your horses, then hole up inside that cabin in case Morgan comes along. If he does, he won't be expectin' anybody to be in there. You can ambush him

350

and be done with it. Just be sure you kill him."

Hooley frowned as he looked at the cabin's empty doorway. "I dunno," he said. "Looks sort o' snaky in there to me."

"There aren't any snakes, and even if there are, you can shoot 'em."

"What about the rest of you?"

"We're gonna keep on lookin' for Morgan," Grimshaw explained. He was starting to lose his patience.

"What if the Terror comes along?" Whiteside asked. "Do we kill it?"

"No, blast it, I told you Bosworth wants the damn thing alive for now, so it can take the blame for things like us wipin' out that camp of Chamberlain's yesterday. It's Morgan he wants dead. That's how we're gonna proceed until Mr. Emmett Bosworth his own self gives us different orders." Grimshaw jerked a thumb toward the cabin. "Now get in there."

"All right, all right," Hooley muttered. He swung down from his mount and drew his rifle from its saddle boot. "I'll check the place out while Whiteside and Darrell hide the horses."

Grimshaw nodded. He didn't care how they went about it, just as long as they went ahead and got hidden in there so they could bushwhack Frank Morgan if he came along.

Hooley gave his reins to Darrell, then stalked into the cabin, pausing at the door to look around for a second first. He went out of sight, then a second later exclaimed, "What the hell!"

Grimshaw stiffened in the saddle. "Hooley!" he said. "What's wrong?"

A woman's scream came from inside the cabin. The men outside drew their guns. They didn't have anything to worry about, though, because Hooley reappeared in the doorway a moment later, one arm looped around the neck of a pretty blond woman about twenty years old. She was well dressed and looked scared out of her wits.

"Look what I found!" Hooley crowed with a lecherous grin. "You didn't tell me this ol' cabin was furnished with its own pretty little gal, Grimshaw."

"Son of a . . ." Grimshaw breathed. He recognized the young woman. He had seen her in Eureka the day before in Rutherford Chamberlain's carriage. She was Chamberlain's daughter.

And if she'd been hiding in that cabin for some reason, then she was bound to have heard them talking about how they worked for Emmett Bosworth — and how Bosworth wanted Frank Morgan dead.

As if things hadn't been complicated enough already, Grimshaw thought bitterly. Now he was going to have to kill a woman, too.

CHAPTER 25

Frank followed the sound of axes for several minutes until he came to a clearing where several trees had already been felled. Four men were working on another of the giant redwoods. Frank recognized them as the crew he had met a couple of days earlier, when he first became aware of the Terror. Karl Wilcox was their leader, Frank recalled, and the other three men were named Neville, Peterson, and Trotter.

The loggers heard the hoofbeats and stopped what they were doing, turning toward the road to see who was coming. Each man wore a revolver, Frank noted, and he saw several rifles and shotguns lying nearby on the big stumps. The air of tension about the men eased slightly as they recognized him.

"Mr. Morgan," Wilcox said. "Lots of talk about you in town this morning, since you didn't come back last night. Folks were wonderin' if you'd run into the Terror."

"As a matter of fact, I did," Frank said as he reined Goldy to a stop. "He's less than half a mile from here."

The men stiffened again. "You found the damned thing?" Trotter asked.

"You killed it?" Neville added.

"No, he's hurt, but he's still alive," Frank said. "That's why I need your help."

Wilcox frowned and said, "You keep callin' it *he*. What's that all about, Morgan?"

Frank took a deep breath. People had to know the truth eventually. He might as well start revealing it now.

"The Terror's not a monster. He's a man. A man who's done some awful things, but he's still human."

The four loggers stared at him in disbelief. Finally, Wilcox demanded, "Who is he? Who'd do the sort of things that the Terror's done?"

"He's Ben Chamberlain," Frank said. "Rutherford Chamberlain's son."

That revelation made the men stare even more. Gus Trotter exclaimed, "Hell, that can't be true! Old Man Chamberlain's boy ran off to San Francisco a couple of years ago!"

Frank shook his head. "I know Chamberlain believes that, but it's not true. Ben has

355

been living out here in the woods since he left home. Something happened to him, though. His mind's not right —"

Wilcox snorted. "I'll say it ain't right! The Terror is a mad-dog killer! It's worse'n a rabid skunk!"

The other three men muttered in agreement.

"Listen to me," Frank said. "Like I told you, Ben Chamberlain has been hurt. He's been shot, and he needs a doctor. I want you boys to bring your wagon and come with me. We'll load him up and take him back to his father's mansion."

"Us, help the Terror after it killed our friends?" Wilcox shook his head. "I'm not sure I believe you to start with about that thing bein' the Chamberlain boy, but even if you're right, Morgan, he's still a murderer a dozen times over. Why should we help a thing like that?"

Peterson said, "Yeah, I say we leave him in the woods and let him die. He's got it comin' to him!"

Frank couldn't argue with that. But he'd made a promise to Nancy Chamberlain, and his word still meant something to him.

"I told the boy's sister I'd bring him home." The Colt came out of Frank's holster without him hurrying the draw. The move was so smooth, in fact, that his hand barely seemed to move. The revolver just appeared in it as if by magic. "Get in the wagon. You're going to help me."

Wilcox glared at him. "You'd take us right to that monster?"

"I told you, he's in no shape to hurt you or anybody else. When I left him, he was out cold. He's lost a lot of blood and he may not pull through, no matter what we do. But I said I'd bring him home, and by God, I'm going to do it."

Neville said nervously, "I reckon that gunfighter means business, Karl."

Wilcox sighed. "Yeah, I reckon you're right." To Frank, he said, "All right, Morgan, we'll do what you say. But we don't have to like it."

"Didn't ask you to like it," Frank said. "Just asked you to give me a hand."

The men gathered up the rifles and shotguns and placed them in the back of the wagon, then climbed onto the vehicle. Wilcox handled the reins of the mule team while Trotter sat beside him and Peterson and Neville climbed in the back. Following Frank's orders, Wilcox turned the wagon around and started back along the road toward the spot where Frank had left Ben Chamberlain hidden in the brush.

"Just what do you plan on doin' with the critter once you get it to Chamberlain's house?" Wilcox asked as Frank rode alongside the wagon.

"Somebody will have to hightail it to Eureka and bring back a sawbones. Dr. Connelly, I think. He seems like a good man."

"Then what? You gonna turn it over to the law?" Wilcox shook his head. "I'm not sure anybody could build a gallows big enough to hang that bastard."

"I don't know," Frank said honestly. "Right now, I'm just trying to see to it that he pulls through."

"Why?" asked Trotter. "If you ask me, if he's really Ben Chamberlain, he'd be better off dead, the things he's done."

The others nodded in solemn agreement.

Frank had no answers for them, only his own stubborn determination to keep his promise to Nancy Chamberlain. A minute later, he recognized the spot where Goldy had dragged Ben off the road.

"Hold it right here," he told Wilcox. "Ben's hidden in the brush, just off the road." Frank dismounted. "I'll go check on him first. He's sort of friends with me now, so maybe he won't panic if he sees just me. I'll have to get him used to the idea that you fellas are going to help us."

"I'm still tryin' to get used to that idea myself," Wilcox said bitterly.

Frank ignored the comment and made his way into the undergrowth. He pushed the brush aside that he had used for camouflage, expecting to see Ben still lying there on the ground.

The problem was, Ben was nowhere to be seen. Frank stiffened in alarm as he realized that the young giant was gone. Ben must have come to, not known where he was, and wandered off. Given his mental condition, Ben might not even be aware that he'd been shot. That didn't really matter, Frank realized.

What was important was that the Terror of the Redwoods was on the loose again.

Grimshaw wasn't going to take the responsibility for killing Nancy Chamberlain. The hell with that. He worked for Bosworth, and it was Bosworth's plans that were threatened by what Nancy had overheard.

"The rest of you men stay here," he ordered. "I'm goin' to Eureka."

"What about Morgan?" Radburn asked. "We were supposed to be lookin' for him."

"The hell with Morgan. This is more important." Grimshaw narrowed his eyes.

"I'm makin' you responsible for that girl's safety, Radburn. Keep her here, but see to it that she's not hurt."

Radburn frowned. "I didn't ask to be put in charge of anything, let alone some rich gal."

"Well, I'm puttin' you in charge anyway." Grimshaw looked around at the other men. "You hear that? No harm comes to that girl while I'm gone, understand? If it does, I'll kill the man who's to blame for it. Got that, Hooley?"

"Why're you singlin' me out?" Hooley demanded resentfully. "What'd I do?"

"Just remember what I said," Grimshaw snapped. "Now let go of her. I want to talk to her before I leave."

With obvious reluctance, Hooley released his grip on Nancy Chamberlain. His hand had been straying dangerously close to her breasts as he held her, Grimshaw noted. Despite his orders, the girl might have to put up with a little pawing while he was gone, but really, that was the least of her worries. Grimshaw figured that Bosworth would order him to get rid of her.

He motioned Nancy over and asked her, "What are you doin' out here, gal?"

Even though she was obviously terrified, she managed to jut her chin out in defiance as she answered, "That's none of your business."

Grimshaw lowered his voice so the others couldn't hear. "Lookin' for your brother maybe?"

Nancy gasped in surprise. "How did you know —"

"Never mind about that. Where's your buggy?"

She shook her head. "I didn't bring a buggy. I came out on horseback. My horse is hidden over there in the trees. I . . . I wanted to come up to the cabin on foot."

"Didn't want to spook him if he was here, eh?" Grimshaw nodded. "I understand."

Nancy lifted a hand as if she wanted to reach out and touch his arm, but she drew it back in fear. "What do you know about what happened to him?"

"Like I told you, never mind about that. Anybody know you're here?"

She hesitated, and he knew she was thinking about how she ought to answer that question. When she said, "I told the men who work for my father, Rockwell and Cobb and the others," he knew she was lying. Nobody knew she was here.

"Well, we'll see about that. Go over there and sit down on that log." Grimshaw pointed. "Don't budge until I get back, and then we'll figure out what to do with you."

By that time, he thought, he would have his orders concerning her — and he had a pretty good idea what they would be. She didn't have to know that just yet, though.

Nancy sat down where he told her. Grimshaw said to the men, "Don't forget what I told you," and mounted up again. He rode off toward Eureka.

It took about an hour to reach the settlement, and Grimshaw didn't feel a bit better when he got there than he had when he left the cabin. He went straight to the Eureka House and up the stairs to Bosworth's suite. He pounded hard on the door of the sitting room. Bosworth jerked it open and demanded angrily, "What?" He looked surprised when he saw Grimshaw standing there in the corridor.

"We got to talk," Grimshaw said. He didn't wait for Bosworth to invite him in. He bulled into the room, forcing the timber baron to step back. Bosworth's face flushed even darker.

Grimshaw smelled coffee and glanced around, spotting a breakfast tray sitting on one of the tables. Bosworth was still in his nightclothes. The bastard was just getting up, Grimshaw thought, when he and his men had been out on the trail for hours.

Bosworth closed the door and snapped, "What the hell is this? You're supposed to be out looking for Morgan."

"Forget about that," Grimshaw said. "You've got more to worry about than Frank Morgan. While we were lookin' for him this morning, we came across something else."

"The Terror?"

Grimshaw shook his head. "Nancy Chamberlain."

Bosworth looked confused for a second. "You mean Chamberlain's daughter? What does she have to do with anything?"

"She was at that old cabin her brother used. The one where he was staying when —"

Bosworth lifted a hand to stop him. "I told you before, I don't want to hear about that."

"Well, you'll want to hear about this even less. We didn't know the girl was there when we rode up. She heard us talking about Morgan . . . and about you."

Bosworth's face hardened. "What the hell do you mean?"

"I mean she knows that we're working for you. She knows that you sent us out to kill Frank Morgan. She knows that we're the ones who attacked her pa's logging camp yesterday morning, and that we were followin' your orders. In other words, she knows the whole damn thing, and she can put your neck in a noose right along with ours."

Bosworth just stared at him for a long moment, looking almost as horrified as if the Terror had just waltzed into his hotel room. Finally, he said, "How . . . how could everything go so wrong?"

"That's why they call it bad luck, I reckon," Grimshaw said with a shrug. "Question now is, what are we gonna do about it?"

"There's only one thing we *can* do about it. Kill the girl." Bosworth rubbed his jaw and frowned in thought. "Maybe you could use ropes and horses to pull her body apart. That would look even more like she ran into the Terror and it killed her."

Grimshaw swallowed the bitter, sour taste that welled up under his tongue at the death sentence for Nancy that Bosworth had handed out so casually. He had known the girl would have to die as soon as he saw her, but to hear Bosworth talk about it like that . . .

But then Bosworth said suddenly, "Wait a minute. We don't need to kill her just yet."

"What?"

"That would be wasting an opportunity."

Bosworth began to pace back and forth as he thought. "Fate has dropped Nancy Chamberlain in our laps. We'd be fools not to use her."

Grimshaw shook his head. "I don't get it."

"Get the girl. Meet me at that crazy mansion of Chamberlain's in the woods. He's going to sign his timber lease over to me in exchange for the safe return of his daughter."

"That's loco!" Grimshaw burst out. "Maybe he'll sign, sure, but then he'll run to the law as soon as he's got the girl back safe and sound. The papers won't hold up in court, and we'll all wind up stretchin' rope when the girl gets through tellin' her story."

Bosworth grinned cockily and shook his head. "She won't tell anyone. Because as soon as Chamberlain and I have concluded our business arrangement, the Terror is going to come along and burn down that mansion, with Chamberlain and his daughter and all his hired guns inside it. No one will ever be able to prove that Chamberlain didn't just get tired of dealing with the Terror and sign over his lease to me so he could get out of the business."

Grimshaw frowned. "You reckon people

will really believe that?"

"They won't be able to prove otherwise. That's all that matters."

"No, I reckon they won't . . . Meet you at Chamberlain's with the girl, you say?"

"That's right. How long will it take you to get there?"

"Probably about an hour and a half."

"That'll put it close to the middle of the day . . . Let's call it noon."

"All right," Grimshaw said with a nod. This would mean committing several more murders, but hell, they were already in so deep, a few more deaths wouldn't make any difference, he supposed.

This was the end of it, though. After today, Bosworth would have what he wanted. Grimshaw was going to take his payoff and ride away, and he was done selling his gun. Things had changed too much. It was too much of a business now, too vicious. There was no honor to it anymore.

Hell, there probably never had been, he thought as he left the hotel. But at least, at times, he had been able to fool himself into believing so. Now even those illusions were gone.

And nothing was left but the killing. Just the way it had always been.

■ ■ ■ ■

There was no point in keeping Wilcox and the other loggers from their work. Since Ben Chamberlain was gone, Frank had no need of the wagon.

"What are you going to do now, Morgan?" Wilcox asked as Frank mounted up again.

"Try to find Ben," Frank answered. "Dog's pretty good at tracking, and he's been able to find Ben's trail several times so far. He can do it again."

The wagon rolled back up the road toward the clearing where the four men had been working. Frank told Dog to find Ben's scent, and the big cur soon had his nose to the ground, trotting along with Frank following on Goldy and leading Stormy.

After a few minutes, Frank began to get an inkling of where they were headed. Ben's old, primitive cabin was in this direction, and even though Frank had the impression that Ben had been avoiding the place, maybe being wounded had him even more addled than usual and he was headed back to someplace he knew. That made sense. The farther he followed Dog, the more convinced Frank was that he was right.

They were coming at the place from a different direction, though, and when they got there, Frank found himself on top of the heavily timbered ridge, rather than in the clearing down below. Realizing where he was, he reined in well short of the edge and dismounted to go ahead on foot. If Ben was down there, he didn't want the sound of hoofbeats to spook the giant.

Frank motioned for Dog to be quiet, and moved silently through the timber himself. Even before he reached the edge of the ridge, he knew something was wrong, because he heard men's voices drifting up from below. He bellied down, pushed his rifle in front of him, and crawled forward until he could peer over the sharp drop-off.

Ten horses grazed in front of the tumbled-up logs. Frank saw the men they belonged to scattered around, evidently waiting for something. He didn't recognize any of them, but he had a feeling he was looking at Emmett Bosworth's gang of gunwolves, the same men he'd shot it out with the day before, when the Terror had intervened in the battle.

He saw no sign of Ben Chamberlain now, but an even more shocking sight met his eyes. Ben's sister Nancy was down there, sitting on a log and looking pale and scared. A couple of the hardcases stood next to her, keeping an eye on her, and it was obvious that she was a prisoner. Frank asked himself what in blazes was going on here. Why were Bosworth's men at the cabin, and why was Nancy Chamberlain their prisoner?

Regardless of the answers, he couldn't make a move against the men right now. From up here, he could cut down several of them with the Winchester before they knew what was going on, but there were too many of them to get them all. Anyway, Nancy would be in too much danger if bullets started flying around. Frank knew he was going to have to bide his time and find out a little more about what was happening here.

He didn't see Jack Grimshaw among the men, which came as a bit of a surprise. He'd been convinced that Grimshaw was one of the gunmen working for Bosworth. He knew he had heard Grimshaw's voice the day before. Maybe his old friend had been killed by the Terror. In that case, he'd be sorry . . . but Grimshaw never should have gone to work for a man like Emmett Bosworth.

As Frank listened, Nancy asked in a voice on the verge of trembling, "What are you going to do with me?"

One of the men watching her, an hombre with a square, florid face, said, "Well, little lady, I don't really know. I reckon that'll be up to somebody else."

"Mr. Bosworth," Nancy said. "That's who you mean."

Her captor shrugged. "Man with the money gives the orders. That's how it works in this life."

"I have money, too, you know. My father has a lot of money. He'll pay you to keep me safe."

"Sorry, Miss Chamberlain. It ain't my decision to make."

Nancy looked down at the ground in despair.

If Frank needed any more proof that these hired killers worked for Emmett Bosworth, the conversation he'd just overheard had given it to him. If he could get Nancy away from them, her testimony would put Bosworth behind bars, if not on a gallows.

The man who was talking to Nancy went on. "Anyway, Jack ought to be back soon, I reckon, and then we'll all find out what's gonna happen."

Frank's heart sank. He knew the man had to be talking about Grimshaw, who must be alive after all. Well, the line was definitely drawn in the sand now, Frank thought, and he and Grimshaw were on different sides of it.

As long as the men weren't threatening Nancy, he could afford to wait, so that was what he did. A half hour went by. The sun began to grow warm as it rose higher in the sky. Here on the edge of the timber, Frank could actually feel its rays.

Movement caught his eye, and he lifted his head to see a man riding out of the trees on the far side of the clearing, heading toward the cabin. Right away, Frank recognized the newcomer as Jack Grimshaw. Anger surged up inside him. Jack had always taken the easy way out, and now that tendency had put them on opposite sides, so that Frank might easily wind up having to kill him.

Or maybe Jack would kill *him*, Frank mused. Grimshaw was a tough man, a good man with a gun. He had never been anywhere near as fast on the draw as Frank, but in a gunfight, you never could tell for sure what was going to happen.

The other men saw Grimshaw coming, and gathered around Nancy Chamberlain to wait for him. As Grimshaw rode up and brought his horse to a stop, one of the men asked, "Well, what's it gonna be?"

"The girl said her horse was over in the trees," Grimshaw replied. "Somebody go and find it. She'll need a mount. We're takin' her back to her father's mansion."

The square-faced man said, "Why the hell are we doin' that?"

"Those are the boss's orders," Grimshaw said. "He's gonna meet us there."

The glance he shot at Nancy Chamberlain told Frank that there was more to it than that, however. Bosworth wouldn't be returning Nancy to her father without something else in mind, some sort of double cross. Maybe he intended to hold her hostage until Chamberlain agreed to give up this stretch of prime timber.

But if that were the case, then Bosworth couldn't afford to let any of the witnesses live afterward. Frank's eyes narrowed as he thought about that. This was the showdown, he realized. Bosworth's finishing stroke that would wipe out his competition once and for all.

And it was up to Frank to prevent it.

He slid back away from the edge of the ridge as down below the group of gunmen got ready to ride. He had to get to Chamberlain's mansion to stop whatever Bosworth had planned. It would be easier, though, if he had some help. If he could get Wilcox and the other loggers, maybe some more men from Chamberlain's crews, and reach the bizarre redwood mansion before

Bosworth had time to launch his scheme, he might still be able to save Nancy and ruin Bosworth's plans. When he was well out of sight of Grimshaw and the other killers, he stood up and jogged toward the spot where he had left Stormy and Goldy. Dog was at his side.

The big cur stopped suddenly and growled. Frank tensed and looked around. Ben Chamberlain was still roaming around out here somewhere, he reminded himself, and in Ben's current state, there was no telling what he might do.

But it wasn't Ben who stepped out from behind three of the massive trees and leveled rifles at Frank, though. It was Erickson and his two monster-hunting partners. Erickson said, "Hold it, Morgan! Make a move and we'll fill you full of lead!"

Then he grinned and added, "Of course, it don't really matter — because we're gonna kill you anyway!"

CHAPTER 26

Frank stood absolutely still. They had him boxed in, covered from three angles. The Winchester was in his hands, with a bullet in the chamber. All he had to do was point it and pull the trigger. He knew he could get one of them before they ever got lead in him. He might even be able to drop two of them.

But the third man would tag him. No doubt about that. Frank figured he would live long enough to kill that hombre, too. But he might not live to stop Bosworth from whatever he was planning to do to Nancy and her father.

"Is this about that bounty on the Terror?" Frank asked. It might be a good idea to keep Erickson talking.

"Damn right. With you out of the way, it'll be twenty thousand dollars. That's more money than I've ever seen in my life, Morgan."

Frank shook his head. "You'll never collect a penny of it. Rutherford Chamberlain's not going to pay off on his own son."

"His son?" Erickson repeated with a frown. "What the hell are you talkin' about?"

"The Terror. He's really Ben Chamberlain."

"You're crazy! The Terror's some sort of monster!"

"No, he's not," Frank insisted. "He's just a young man who had something terrible happen to him. I don't know what it was just yet, but I plan to find out."

Erickson shook his head. "You're wastin' your breath. I don't believe a word of it." The barrel of his rifle came up a little. "Say your prayers, Morgan —"

Ben stepped out from behind the same tree where Erickson had been lying in wait for Frank. He reached out and closed his massive hands around Erickson's head. Erickson started to scream, but it was choked off as Ben twisted hard.

Frank was already moving, pivoting toward the man on his left. From the corner of his eye, he saw a fountain of blood and something flying through the air, something with long red hair attached to it, but then he saw only the target in front of his gun.

The Winchester cracked, and the second gunman spun off his feet without getting a shot off as the slug drilled cleanly through his chest.

The third man managed to fire a couple of frenzied shots before Dog flashed across the open space and crashed into him, knocking him over backward. The man had barely started to scream when the big cur's fangs sank into his throat and ripped it open. Arms and legs spasmed as the man died.

The fight had taken only seconds. Frank quickly checked the man he had shot and found that he was dead. There was no doubt about the other two. Ben had twisted Erickson's head right off his body, and Dog had done for the third man.

Ben sagged against a tree trunk. As Frank hurried over to him, the giant smiled and said, "Fraaaank."

"I don't know where you came from, Ben, but I'm glad you got here when you did," Frank said. "Were you hit by either of those shots?"

"Hiiiit?"

Carefully, Frank reached out. "Can I look under your coat?"

Ben didn't make any move to stop him. Frank pulled the crazy quilt of pelts back and saw fresh crimson welling from a black-rimmed hole in Ben's shirt.

"We need to get you some help, Ben," Frank said. "I'm going to take you home."

Ben pulled back and started to shake his head.

"Nancy's there," Frank went on. "I'm going to take you to see Nancy. You want that, don't you?"

"Nan . . . cy," Ben rasped. "See . . . Nan . . . cy."

"Come with me then. Can you make it?"

Ben pushed away from the tree and took a staggering step. "Maaaake . . . it."

There was no time now to find Wilcox and the other loggers, Frank thought. Grimshaw and the rest of Bosworth's gunmen were on their way to the Chamberlain mansion. They had probably heard the shots, and that might speed them up even more. He would have to hope that Chamberlain's men would be able to hold off any attack until he and Ben could get there.

Frank didn't think that Bosworth would order a direct attack, though, at least not at first. The man was too devious for that. He would probably offer to trade Nancy's safety for Chamberlain signing over that timber lease to him. Once that happened, then Bosworth would pull his double cross. With a signed lease in his pocket, no one was safe from Bosworth.

Stormy and Goldy started to shy away from Ben, but Frank stopped them with a word. He hated to ask Ben to run all the way to the mansion, but he didn't have much choice.

As he was swinging up into the saddle, though, he heard a crashing in the brush, and then Wilcox, Peterson, Trotter, and Neville burst out into the open, brandishing guns. They jerked the weapons up when they saw Ben, who let out a furious roar and spread his arms as if he were about to charge them.

"Hold it!" Frank bellowed at the top of his lungs. "Put those guns down! Ben, stop! They won't hurt you!"

For a tense second, the loggers didn't lower their weapons. Then Wilcox motioned for the others to do as Frank said. "My God," he said in a hollow voice. "I remember Old Man Chamberlain's kid. That really is him, isn't it?"

"Yeah," Frank said. "Do you have that wagon with you?"

Wilcox jerked a thumb over his shoulder. "Back there about a hundred yards. We heard the shootin' and came to see what it was about."

"Lead the way," Frank ordered as he lifted the reins. "We have to get to the Chamberlain mansion as fast as we can, because there's about to be a showdown there between him and Emmett Bosworth. And I reckon Bosworth has a trick or two up his sleeve."

"If we help you with this . . . critter . . . we get to fight Bosworth and his bunch?"

"I'd say there's a good chance of it."

Wilcox nodded. "Come on, boys, let's get that wagon. It's about time Bosworth got what's comin' to him."

"What about the Terror?" Neville asked.

Frank said, "Leave him to me." He turned to the huge, foul-smelling giant. "Ben, listen to me. These men are our friends. They won't hurt you, and you don't need to hurt them."

Ben didn't look convinced. He waved a massive paw at the loggers and rumbled, "Cut down . . . treeees."

"I know, and you don't like that." Frank was starting to understand why Ben had attacked the loggers. To Ben's twisted way of thinking, he was just trying to protect the trees from them. All the other men Ben had gone after had attacked him first. "Right now it can't be helped. We have to save Nancy. She's in danger."

"Nan . . . cy? Daaaanger?"

Frank nodded. "That's right. Are you with me, Ben?"

Ben lifted both hands and curled them into fists the size of nail kegs. "Wiiiith . . . you," he said. "Help . . . Nan . . . cy."

"That's right," Frank said.

He just hoped they wouldn't be too late.

Grimshaw had seen the Chamberlain mansion from a distance before, but it was even more impressive up close. Impressive — or downright bizarre, take your pick, he thought. He couldn't imagine living in such a crazy place.

Chamberlain's men must have seen them coming, because half a dozen of them rode out quickly to intercept the riders approaching the mansion. They were tough, hard-looking men, but they wouldn't be any match for his bunch, Grimshaw told himself. For one thing, his men outnumbered Chamberlain's men almost two to one.

Bosworth was already here. Grimshaw recognized the fancy carriage parked in front of the mansion. That meant Chamberlain probably knew already that they had the girl. From the angry looks on the faces of Chamberlain's men as they approached, Grimshaw knew that was true.

He turned in the saddle and motioned for Radburn to bring Nancy up alongside him. Chamberlain's men would be a lot less likely to start throwing lead around if Nancy was front and center where she'd be liable to get in the way of some of it.

As the two groups of gunmen came to a halt facing each other, Grimshaw said, "We're here to see your boss. But I reckon you already know that."

"Let Miss Chamberlain go," one of the men said. "Then we'll talk about what you want."

Grimshaw smiled thinly and shook his head. "It don't work that way, and you know it. We got our orders, the same as you boys do. Move aside now, and let us ride on to the house."

"And if we don't?" the leader of Chamberlain's men challenged.

"Then I'll have to shoot you, Cobb," one of the others said, and Grimshaw felt a surge of surprise when he saw that the man had slipped out his gun and fallen back a little, so that he could cover his companions from behind.

"What the hell!" the man called Cobb exclaimed as he twisted around in his saddle. "Rockwell, you double-crosser! You're workin' for Bosworth?"

Cobb didn't wait for an answer. He clawed at the revolver on his hip. Rockwell fired, his gun spouting smoke and flame, and Cobb rocked to the side in his saddle as the bullet thudded into his barrel chest. Cursing, he pawed at his chest for a second before he toppled off the horse and crashed to the ground to lie motionless.

The rest of Chamberlain's men hadn't moved except to stare in surprise at the one called Rockwell. Grimshaw drew his gun, and so did the rest of his men. "Drop 'em, boys," Grimshaw ordered. "It's over."

Chamberlain's men knew they were in a bind. Carefully, they took their guns out and tossed them on the ground.

"Now, we're goin' in," Grimshaw said.

With half a dozen prisoners now instead of just one, the hired killers moved on toward the mansion, reining in when they reached it. Grimshaw dismounted and said, "The rest of you boys stay out here and keep an eye on Chamberlain's men. Miss Chamberlain, you come with me. You're about to see your father again, I reckon."

Grimshaw wrapped his left hand around Nancy's right arm and led her up the steps to the porch. A pale-faced butler must have been watching from inside. He opened the door before they reached it and said in a shaky voice, "Miss Nancy, are you all right?"

"I'm fine, Dennis," she said, although she didn't sound fine. She sounded scared to death, and with good reason, although she couldn't know that yet.

"Your father and . . . and Mr. Bosworth are waiting in the library," said the butler.

"Take us there," Grimshaw snapped.

The butler escorted them along the hall to the double doors that opened into the library. When they went inside, they stepped into an atmosphere of tension and hatred. Rutherford Chamberlain and Emmett Bosworth stood there, staring at each other, evidently at a standoff.

Chamberlain turned sharply toward the newcomers. "Nancy!" he exclaimed. He started to rush toward her, but Bosworth stepped over so that he blocked the older man's path.

"Not yet, Chamberlain," Bosworth said. "You can see for yourself that your daughter's all right, but you know the deal. You don't get her back until you sign that timber lease over to me."

Chamberlain glared at his rival. "You really think such a document will stand up in court, with a signature coerced on it that way?"

"You let me worry about that." Bosworth

pointed to the desk, where a document was laid out. "You just sign that contract I brought with me."

"You'll never get away with this!" Chamberlain looked at Nancy. "What were you doing out there wandering around alone in the woods anyway?"

"I was looking for Ben," she shot back with a flare of anger of her own. "You never would believe me, and I didn't know if Mr. Morgan would ever find him, so I . . . I thought I'd take another look around, before you put out another of those damned bounties."

Chamberlain stared at her in disbelief. "Are you still clinging to that insane notion about the Terror being your brother —"

"Actually, he is," Grimshaw said. He wasn't quite sure what prompted him to speak up, unless he was just too damned sick and tired of carrying around what he knew. "The Terror is your son, Chamberlain."

"How do you know?" Chamberlain demanded. "You're nothing but one of Bosworth's cheap gunmen!"

"Not so cheap," Grimshaw muttered. He went on. "I rode up to that cabin one day, not long after I'd come to these parts to work for Mr. Bosworth. I had another fella

384

with me, named Macklin."

Bosworth said, "There's no need to go into all this."

Grimshaw tightened his grip on Nancy's arm. "I reckon there is," he said. "I know you pay my wages, Mr. Bosworth, but I think these two deserve to know the truth after all this time."

And it wouldn't matter anyway, Grimshaw thought, because in just a little while, Chamberlain and Nancy would both be dead.

Nancy turned toward him and pleaded, "Tell me. I . . . I was afraid the Terror was Ben, but I could never be sure . . ."

"He's your brother, all right, miss. Macklin and I found him there at that cabin where he'd been stayin'. We were out scoutin' around, lookin' for some way to cause trouble for your pa. When we met your brother and realized who he was, Macklin got the idea we ought to scare him a little. He thought that might convince your pa to sell out to our boss here." Grimshaw shook his head. "But it didn't work out that way. Things got out of hand. Macklin used to do a little rustling, so he had a runnin' iron in his saddlebags. He heated it up and used it to singe some of your brother's beard off and burn his face."

385

Nancy let out a sob as she listened to the story. Chamberlain stood there stony-faced.

"Before that, your brother wouldn't fight no matter what we did to prod him," Grimshaw went on. "Even after Macklin burned him, he just wanted us to leave him alone. But then Macklin got into a trunk your brother had in the cabin and started tearin' up the books he found there . . . and that set your brother off good and proper. He went wild. He jumped Macklin and, well, started tearin' him apart. I took a shot at him and hit him in the head. I thought I'd killed him. I was so shook up, I lit out of there and didn't even try to take Macklin's body with me. I didn't tell anybody what had happened except Mr. Bosworth, and he said we ought to just lie low for a while, see if anybody found out about it. I went back a week later. Macklin's body was still there, what was left of it . . . but Ben Chamberlain was gone. I hadn't killed him after all."

"My God, man," Chamberlain breathed. "A head wound like that can do things to a man's brain . . ."

Grimshaw nodded. "I reckon it did, sure enough. Because after that, there wasn't any Ben Chamberlain anymore. There was just the Terror." He sighed. "I gathered up all of Macklin I could find and took the remains and buried 'em. Hadn't been back to the place until today."

"All right," Bosworth said harshly. "You've told your little story and gotten it all off your chest. Now stay out of it while Chamberlain and I finish our deal." He pointed to the document on the desk again. "Sign it, Chamberlain, and we'll get out of here and leave you and your daughter alone."

"Don't listen to him," Nancy warned. "We know too much. He'll never let us live now."

Chamberlain squared his shoulders. "I'm well aware of that, my dear. I don't intend to let this man win." He faced Bosworth. "Go to hell, Emmett. I won't sign your paper, now or ever."

"Well, that's a damned shame," Bosworth said as he took a pistol from under his coat. "I guess I'll just have to forge your signature and take my chances in court, after you and your daughter have met with an unfortunate accident . . ."

Outside, with no warning, guns blasted. Men began to yell as more and more shots rang out. Grimshaw turned instinctively toward the window.

That was when Nancy twisted in his grasp and lunged at him, clawing his face with both hands, trying to get her fingernails in his eyes. Grimshaw let out a curse and swatted her away. His gun came swiftly and smoothly from its holster, swung toward Nancy.

Behind him, Frank Morgan called, "Jack!"

So this is how it ends, Grimshaw thought as he started to turn. After all these years, and not even a proper test of speed between the two of them. He was already pulling the trigger as he turned, smoke jetting from the barrel of his gun, but the crashes of Morgan's shots blended with his own, and he felt the hammer blows against his body driving him back. He stumbled against something, fell over it as a great, searing heat washed through his body, and as he lay there, he realized that he had collapsed on Rutherford Chamberlain's desk. The timber lease document lay beside him, with crimson splashes of blood on it now. A bitter laugh welled up in Grimshaw's throat. All this for a damned piece of paper. All the death and fear and misery, for a piece of paper that represented trees that men would cut down and use to make more paper that didn't really mean anything . . .

"Frank," Grimshaw croaked, "I wish . . . we could've . . . gone out fightin' . . . side by side . . ."

No one heard the words, or the rattle of

breath as Grimshaw died.

The room was still full of gunfire.

CHAPTER 27

By the time Frank, Ben, and the loggers reached the mansion, their group was even larger because they had run into another half dozen of Chamberlain's men along the way. It was a pretty formidable, well-armed bunch, in fact, even if the loggers weren't professional fighting men. They were plenty tough anyway, and when they found out what Bosworth was up to, they were more than willing to put aside their distrust of Ben, who was on his last legs from the bullet wounds he had suffered over the past couple of days. Frank saw the haggard look on Ben's face, the dimming fire in the giant's eyes, and knew that he wouldn't have to worry about figuring out what to do about Ben.

Fate was going to do that for him.

With Frank leading them like a general, the loggers had spread out, slipped up on the mansion, and launched their attack when Frank gave the signal. As the guns began to roar in front of the mansion, Frank and Ben headed for the back.

They had just gotten inside when Ben groaned and collapsed. Frank managed to prop him up so that he was sitting with his back against a wall and whispered, "Stay here, Ben. I'll go find Nancy and bring her to you."

"Nan . . . cy," Ben said, the name barely audible now because his voice was so weak.

Frank figured Bosworth would be in the library with Chamberlain and Nancy, and maybe Jack Grimshaw. Sure enough, that was the way it had played out. Frank had fired to protect both himself and Nancy, and now Grimshaw was down, lying motionless in death on the big desk.

Bosworth was still alive, though, the pistol in his hand spouting fire as he swept it across the room. Chamberlain grunted as one of the flying slugs winged him, but he managed to grab Nancy and drag her to the floor, out of the line of fire. Frank snapped a shot at Bosworth, but the timber baron was already moving. With a huge crash of glass, he flung himself through the window behind the desk and toppled out of sight.

Frank was about to go after him when another shot blasted and a bullet whipped past his ear. Still in the doorway of the library, he twisted to look down the corridor, and saw a couple of Grimshaw's men charging toward him, guns blazing.

Before he could return their fire, Ben loomed up behind them, roaring defiantly. He grabbed them and jerked them back. The men screamed and twisted around in his grip so that they were able to shove their guns against his body. They fired again and again, the close-range impacts forcing Ben to stumble backward as more slugs ripped through his insides. He found the strength to slam the heads of the two gunmen together, though, again and again until those heads were so broken and misshapen they didn't look human. Their guns were long since emptied. Ben shook the corpses one more time, then let go of them, dropping them to the fancy redwood parquet floor that would never be the same after so much blood had been spilled on it.

"Ben!" Nancy shrieked.

She rushed past Frank as Ben fell to his knees. "Nan . . . cy," he choked out as she reached him and threw her arms around him. She clung to him tightly as sobs wracked her. Frank watched as Ben lifted one huge, trembling hand and gently patted his sister on the back. Then, in a rumbling whisper, he said, "Hoooome . . . Nan . . . cy . . ." and died.

Rutherford Chamberlain stumbled past Frank, saying in a stunned voice, "My boy . . . my boy . . ."

Nancy still stood there, somehow finding the strength in her slender body to hold Ben's massive form upright. Chamberlain joined her, and wrapped his feeble arms around both of them.

With a grimace, Frank turned away from the family tragedy. He still had to deal with the man who had set all this in motion.

When he got outside, the shooting was over. He saw Karl Wilcox limping toward him, blood running down the logger's leg from a deep crease on his thigh.

"We got all of Bosworth's men except for a couple who ran inside, Morgan," Wilcox reported. "The boss's bodyguards got loose, got their hands on their guns, and helped us. That turned the tide. What happened to those other two?"

"They're dead," Frank reported, not bothering to go into detail now. "What about Bosworth?"

A disgusted expression appeared on Wilcox's rugged face. "Do you see his carriage? The bastard managed to get to it and drove off hell-bent-for-leather! We threw some lead after him, but didn't stop him."

"Which way was he headed?"

"Toward Eureka, I'd say."

Frank nodded. Bosworth had to know that there was too much evidence against him. He couldn't hope to bluff his way out of this mess. But he probably had enough money stashed in his hotel room so that he could make a run for it, maybe start over somewhere else, in Canada or Mexico maybe.

Frank didn't intend to let that happen.

He whistled for Goldy. As the horse came up, Wilcox asked, "What happened to the Terror?"

"Ben Chamberlain is inside," Frank said with a hard look. "I know he did a lot of bad things . . . but he died a man, Wilcox, not a monster. You remember that. Everybody damned well better remember that."

"Well . . . sure, Morgan," Wilcox said as Frank swung up into the saddle.

Frank urged Goldy into a gallop, hitting the trail that led to Eureka.

Emmett Bosworth had never been more disgusted in his life. Everything had gone wrong. He had tried to make a bold move and put an end to this, here and now, and instead, the thing had backfired on him, through no fault of his own. It was all Grimshaw, and Morgan, and that damned monster . . .

The law would be after him now. Bosworth knew that. But he had ten thousand dollars in a steamer trunk in his suite at the Eureka House, and if he could get his hands on that money and then get out of town before word reached the settlement of the massacre at the Chamberlain mansion, no one would stop him. He'd have to hide out for a while, and he might have to change his name, but sooner or later he would rebuild his fortune. He always came out on top eventually. It was his destiny.

With dust billowing up from the wheels, he swung the carriage into Patterson's wagon yard and left it there. He'd be taking a saddle horse when he left there, so he could move faster. He stalked up the street to the hotel, ignoring the puzzled looks that people gave him. He supposed he did look a lot more disheveled than usual.

As he went through the hotel lobby, the clerk called to him, "Mr. Bosworth, you've got a —" but Bosworth didn't hear the rest of it. He took the stairs two at a time, and hurried down the hallway to his sitting room.

When he jerked the door open and

stepped inside, he stopped short at the sight of a man standing beside the window. "Who the hell —"

The man turned toward him, tall, thick-bodied, with a shock of graying hair and a close-cropped beard. "We haven't been properly introduced, Mr. Bosworth," he said. "I'm Dr. Patrick Connelly. It's my wife Molly you've been bedding for the past couple of months."

And with that, he lunged at Bosworth, the light from the window glinting on the scalpel in his hand as he swung it at Bosworth's throat.

Bosworth's reflexes barely saved him, jerking him back so that the tip of the razor-sharp scalpel just nicked his throat. He had cut himself worse shaving many times. Connelly stumbled forward, thrown off balance by the missed stroke, and Bosworth slipped his gun from his pocket and jabbed the barrel deep in the doctor's belly. He pulled the trigger, hoping there was still a bullet in the chamber.

There was. Muffled by Connelly's body, the shot was little more than a loud pop that might not have been heard outside in the hallway. Connelly's eyes widened in shock and pain. Bosworth shoved him backward. Connelly collapsed on the divan, and looked down at the blood welling between his fingers as he pressed his hands to his belly. "Where's your wife?" Bosworth grated.

Connelly looked up at him stupidly. "Wha . . . wha . . . You can't . . . can't take her with you . . . I fixed her . . . before I came down here . . . She said . . . she felt poorly . . . so I fixed her a tonic . . ." Connelly managed to laugh. "She didn't know . . . I knew about . . . the two of you . . . never suspected I would . . . do something about it. So you . . . you can't . . . can't have her —"

"I don't want her, you damned fool," Bosworth said. "She complained all the time, and she was barely adequate in bed. I would have left her behind without a second thought, and you could have had her for the rest of your life."

Connelly opened his mouth and tried to say something, but no words came out, only a thin trickle of blood.

Bosworth gave a contemptuous shake of his head and turned away. He got the money from the trunk, reloaded his pistol, and then walked out, carefully closing the door behind him so that no one would walk by and see Connelly's body in there on the divan. The doctor was a pathetic fool who had gotten what he deserved as far as Bosworth was concerned. Ordinary people seemed to think that they had a right to happiness of some sort, but to him, they were just things to be used as needed, and if they came to a bad end . . . well, so did all mortals who tried to meddle in the affairs of gods.

He went downstairs and started across the lobby. The clerk asked him, "Did you talk to Dr. Connelly, Mr. Bosworth?"

"I talked to him," Bosworth said curtly. The law would be after him for killing the doctor, too, but what was one more murder? Just another annoying charge to be squashed when he was rich again. He pushed through the doors, stepped out onto the porch.

Frank Morgan was waiting for him in the street.

Frank was hurrying toward the hotel when he saw Bosworth step outside. He stopped where he was, and so did the timber baron. Slowly, a smile spread over Bosworth's ruggedly handsome face.

"All right," he said. "Fetch the law. I can afford the best attorneys in the country. I'll fight tooth and nail in the courts, Morgan. You know that. I can make this last for years. But the one thing I *won't* do is draw my gun on you. We both know you'd kill me."

"We both know you deserve it," Frank said.

"Well" — still with that smug smile on his face — "people don't always get what they deserve, do they?"

Those words were barely out of Bosworth's mouth when another figure appeared behind him. Someone inside the hotel lobby yelled in alarm. Bosworth didn't have time to turn around, though. The man behind him reached around with one arm, looped it under the timber baron's chin, jerked his head back, and plunged what looked a scalpel into his throat. With a shock of recogition, Frank saw that the second man was Dr. Patrick Connelly. The doctor ripped the scalpel from one side of Bosworth's throat to the other, opening it so that blood cascaded out in sheets. Bosworth made a horrible gurgling noise and thrashed around, but the arm around his neck was like an iron bar holding him there. Connelly didn't let go of him until there was a huge puddle of blood at his feet and Bosworth's body had gone limp.

Then Connelly released Bosworth, letting him fall to the porch. The doctor gasped, "He . . . killed my wife . . . killed me . . ."

Connelly collapsed as well, falling across Bosworth's corpse. Frank took a deep breath, knowing that it was finally all over, and that for once, he hadn't fired the final shot in this bloody, tragic ruckus.

It would be all right with him if he never had to do that again.

But he knew better than to hope for that.

It took a big coffin for Ben Chamberlain, and a bigger grave than usual. But the undertaker managed, and a couple of days later, Ben was laid to rest.

There had been a *lot* of funerals in Eureka the past two days. All too often, that was what happened when he rode into a town, Frank reflected as he stood beside the long mound of dirt that marked the final resting place of the man who had been known for a time as the Terror.

Everyone was gone except Frank, Nancy Chamberlain, and her father, whose left arm was in a black silk sling. Dog, Stormy, and Goldy waited patiently just outside the stone fence that ran around the graveyard.

Nancy had told Frank what Grimshaw said about the events in the primitive cabin that had resulted in her brother becoming the Terror. When he heard the story, Frank was a little less regretful about having to kill

400

his old friend. Jack Grimshaw had stepped way over the line more than once.

Frank had also found out from some of Chamberlain's men about the gunman called Rockwell, who had actually been working for Emmett Bosworth. Frank knew he couldn't prove it, but he was convinced that Rockwell was the man who had shot at him when he first discovered the cabin, probably acting on his own initiative because he knew Bosworth wouldn't want Frank poking around. Frank was satisfied that was the answer.

There were no answers where Dr. Patrick Connelly and his wife were concerned. Nobody in Eureka seemed to know why Bosworth and Connelly had killed each other, and Molly Connelly's death was a complete mystery. Everything in life had an explanation, Frank supposed . . . but that didn't mean folks could expect to know about all of it.

Nancy turned to him now and laid a black-gloved hand on his arm. "Thank you for everything you did, Mr. Morgan," she said.

"I didn't save your brother," Frank said with a shake of his head.

"But you tried to. That was more than anyone else did."

"Not really," Frank told her. "You tried, too. Sometimes, though, you just can't save someone, no matter how much you love them. There are things bigger than us, Nancy, things we can't fight or even explain. They just . . . are."

She smiled sadly. "I suppose you're right." She took a deep breath. "Where will you go now, Mr. Morgan?"

Chamberlain spoke up, saying, "You're welcome to stay with us for a while, if you'd like."

Frank controlled the impulse to shudder. He wouldn't spend any amount of time in that redwood prison Chamberlain had constructed for himself. Anyway, he had some pressing business of his own to take care of.

"I'm heading back down to San Francisco," he said. "A telegram one of my lawyers sent to me just caught up with me this morning. It seems that . . . there's been some trouble in my family, too. A tragedy concerning my son and his wife."

"I'm so sorry," Nancy murmured. "I wish . . . sometimes I wish I was a man, a man like you, Mr. Morgan, so I could just shoot all my troubles!"

"And sometimes," The Drifter said as he settled his hat on his head, "I wish it really worked that way, ma'am."

As Frank rode away, a wind blew in from the sea, over the bay, and stirred the branches of the towering trees that grew to the edge of the graveyard, so that they moved back and forth almost like the arms of giants waving farewell.

The employees of Thorndike Press hope you have enjoyed this Large Print book. All our Thorndike, Wheeler, and Kennebec Large Print titles are designed for easy reading, and all our books are made to last. Other Thorndike Press Large Print books are available at your library, through selected bookstores, or directly from us.

For information about titles, please call:
(800) 223-1244

or visit our Web site at:
http://gale.cengage.com/thorndike

To share your comments, please write:
Publisher
Thorndike Press
10 Water St., Suite 310
Waterville, ME 04901

CPSIA information can be obtained
at www.ICGtesting.com
Printed in the USA
FFOW030905230113
748FF